The Day
She
Vanished

BOOKS BY JEN CRAVEN

The Baby Left Behind
Her Daughter

Best Years of Your Life
All That Shines and Whispers

The Day She Vanished

Jen Craven

bookouture

Published by Bookouture in 2024

An imprint of Storyfire Ltd.
Carmelite House
50 Victoria Embankment
London EC4Y 0DZ

Storyfire Ltd's authorised representative in the EEA is Hachette Ireland
8 Castlecourt Centre
Castleknock Road
Castleknock
Dublin 15 D15 YF6A
Ireland

www.bookouture.com

ISBN: 978-1-83618-009-8
eBook ISBN: 978-1-83618-008-1

For Josephine,

*Watch and pray, dear. Never get tired of trying, and
never think it is impossible to conquer your fault.*

Louisa May Alcott, *Little Women*

ONE

SATURDAY

I'd never considered escaping onto a Ferris wheel until today.

The giant ride has been paused for a solid five minutes. An older woman with a cane tries to get out at the loading deck, struggling to step over the lip. I stare up to the passenger pods stuck at the apex of the wheel and wish for a fleeting moment it was me. It would be like a vacation. *Sorry, Mommy's not available right now, she's trapped three hundred feet in the air.*

These thoughts are fleeting, and I'm not proud of them, yet they come from time to time, a side effect of the enormous weight of motherhood.

Summer pulls on my arm. "Can we ride the carousel? I want to ride the carousel."

"The carousel's *boring*," Merritt says, as if she didn't love it last year. Evidently, turning eleven has made her a full-blown preteen. She crosses her arms. "Gus and I want to do the Wacky Shack."

"Too scary," Summer says, cowering into my leg. "Mommy, please? Please, can we ride the carousel? Pleeeeease?"

My eyes drift up to the Ferris wheel again. It's recommenced its leisurely rotation. Ah, well. I guess vacations can't last forever, but even those few stolen moments would have been nice.

Summer squeezes my hand, popping my daydream. "Mom?"

It's Mommy, I think. *Mom is what your older siblings call me. Not you, Summer, my forever baby.* Her face is my weakness —I'll cave to it ten times out of ten.

"Sure, we can do the carousel," I say brightly. Merritt groans, already annoyed that she's had to suffer through kiddie land because her little sister is too small to ride most anything else. I give a look to Wade, who hasn't chimed in despite being an equal parent in the equation. Merritt rolls her head in theatrical fashion. I steel myself. Merritt—always the tough one.

"We could split up?" Wade whispers to me. "I could take Mer and Gus?" I'm reminded of the soft spot he has for our oldest.

"No," I reply.

This is a family day—a rare one he's able to attend—and I want us all to be together. Summer break will be over in two weeks, and for the first time, all three kids will be in school. It's a milestone I've been waiting for, but finally reaching it feels bittersweet. No more mini-me at home. No more lunch dates with my little redheaded twin. And yet, with Summer starting kindergarten, it's like a whole new world is about to open up for me. Maybe I'll finally go back to work after all. I wonder how marketing has changed in the last ten years.

I face my family. "We'll do the carousel, then head to the Wacky Shack. Deal?"

Summer smiles and Merritt manages a dramatic, *"Fine."* Gus, our generally agreeable middle child, complies. Thank God for Gus.

As we wait in line, I reapply sunscreen to their fair-skinned faces and a little on my own freckled nose. Merritt pulls her phone—a birthday gift—from her pocket. My jaw clenches. I hadn't been thrilled about the phone in the first place, but I relented. Most of her friends have one, and even though I didn't get a cell phone until I went to college, I remind myself that was twenty years ago. Things are different now.

I'm just about to tell her to put it away, that this is family time, when the line moves forward. We scan our wristbands and enter.

On the circular platform, we each saddle onto an animal. I choose a stationary panda because the up-and-down motion paired with the rotation of the ride is a bit too much for my stomach. It hasn't always been this way—I used to love rides. Summer, of course, chooses the white rabbit, her favorite. She says it reminds her of *Alice in Wonderland*. I never much cared for that story—the Cheshire Cat always gave me the spooks. Something about his maniacal grin.

The carousel hums to life. Three minutes and too many spins later, we dismount.

"That was fun!" Summer squeals. "Can we go again? Pleeeeease?"

"Not now, honey," I say. She gives me puppy-dog eyes that are hard to resist. "Maybe later before we leave, okay?" It's enough to appease her, and she smiles and skips out the exit gate. The pure joy coming from such a tiny package makes my heart swell. Oh, the paradox of parenthood. It takes so much of me, and yet I always seem to find more to give. I'd do anything for these kids—including riding around in a never-ending circle to the accompaniment of looped circus music.

"On to the next," Wade says, letting Merritt and Gus take the lead.

Summer's hand is sweaty in mine, the mid-August temperature extra hot by Erie's standards. There's only a slight wind coming off the lake today, making the air thick and stagnant. A film of sweat has made the hairs curl at the base of my neck.

Wonderie Land smells of deep-fried everything, topped off with the sticky sweetness of cotton candy. It's a family-friendly park, a local treasure we're lucky to have not fifteen minutes from home. We get season passes every year. The kids love it.

As we walk, my mind wanders to what to cook for dinner. I check my phone for the time, considering how much longer we'll stay. I smile. Three eighteen. The current time, but also Merritt's birthday. I go to show her—*Look, Mer! March 18!*—but she's too far ahead.

We pass the bumper cars and a drop tower that plummets riders from a sickening height in less than three seconds. Pure thrill spreads across their faces when they hit the bottom, wind-blown hair sticking up at odd angles. Smiles all the way around. Teens hop off, high-fiving. *Kids*, I think. Nothing in the world exists outside their own personal bliss. It's been a long time since I've felt that sort of abandon.

"Whoaaaa," Summer breathes.

Not far from where we stand, a twenty-something couple holds hands as they enter the line for SkyRush, the soaring wooden rollercoaster. The woman giggles, and the man puts his arm around her waist. They disappear around a corner.

Just then, the train of passengers zooms past us, taking a tight turn, wheels clacking against the rails. In an instant, it's gone, speeding along the track. I can feel the riders' exhilaration from yards away.

At once, my body tingles and I'm overcome with an immediate desire. I drop Summer's hand and turn to face my husband. "Let's ride it," I say, voice high and giddy, like a child coming up with a beyond-brilliant idea.

Wade's mouth pulls up into the crooked smile I love—higher on the right than on the left. His crow's feet make his eyes crinkle. "Very funny."

"No, I'm serious. Let's ride it!"

"What are you talking about? Summer's clearly not tall enough. Gus might not be either."

"So?" I say, pawing his chest. "That doesn't mean you and I can't go. C'mon, it'll be fun. We used to love this one!"

Wonderie Land was one of our first dates in college. Having grown up in Erie, I'd been to the park tons of times, but Wade was a Pacific Northwest boy, new to Pennsylvania. I'll never forget taking him on SkyRush and watching his face light up. I don't think we've ridden it since before Merritt was born.

I look around, suddenly frantic for a way to make it possible. "There," I point. "The kids can wait at that table, right by the exit. We'll be able to see them almost the whole time we're in line." My eyes are big and hopeful. *Come on. Why should the kids have all the fun?*

He looks to the table, back to me, then gazes out to where Merritt and Gus have continued their mission toward the Wacky Shack.

"Merritt!" he calls and waves them back.

I can't wipe the stupid grin off my face. This rollercoaster represents everything we were before parenthood—wild and free and fun. I wouldn't trade our life for anything, but in this moment, the need to reclaim a tiny piece of myself screams louder than the whistle of caution in my head.

"What?" Merritt says as they return to us. Her head is cocked, long dark ponytail flung over her shoulder. Hints of fuchsia are visible from the rubber bands on her braces.

"Mom wants to ride SkyRush," Wade says.

Gus makes an X with his wrists. "No way. I'm not going on that."

"You don't have to," I say. "Dad and I are just going to go on it quick. Look, the line's not even that long. You guys can wait right there." I point to the table, shaded by an umbrella. They won't even be in direct sunlight.

Summer looks up at me with her blue eyes. "I don't want you to go."

"Yeah, I thought we were going to the Wacky Shack next," Merritt says.

My chest tightens. *Can't I get a turn for once?* "Guys, listen. It'll be super quick, okay? Just one ride." I look to Wade, but his face reads something completely different than my own. His mouth is set in a line, brows pulled together ever so slightly.

"Greta, I don't know if this is a good idea," he says, taking a cleaver to my enthusiasm.

"Merritt's watched them at home by herself lots of times if I have to run a quick errand."

"But this isn't home."

He's right, this isn't home, but I trust Merritt—I trust all of them. They're good kids.

It's ridiculous how badly I want to go on this ride, if for nothing else but to prove to myself I exist outside of my role as their mom. Doesn't Wade miss being carefree too? We were, after all, a couple before we were parents. I think of the flirty twosome that entered the line moments ago. *That used to be us.*

"It's fine," I assure Wade. "They'll be fine. Merritt, you have your phone. The three of you can just sit there and we'll be right back. Summer, Gus, you guys listen to Merritt, okay? Merritt, keep an eye on them."

"And then we can go to the carousel again, right?" Summer says.

"Right. Sure."

I practically drag Wade toward the ride entrance before he has a chance to protest any further. Before we take our place in line, I look back over my shoulder. The kids have taken a seat at the circular table, each one claiming a bench. They look mopey, but I remind myself it's good for kids not to get everything they want. Builds resilience. They'll survive for a couple minutes, and then the day will be all about them again.

We're out of eyeshot for a second while the line moves forward, and then we turn another bend and can see the kids once more. "See?" I say to Wade. "They're fine."

There are maybe three dozen people ahead of us, and I calculate that we should be able to get on the ride in two more turns. I'm light on my feet, an internal buzz sending vibrations down to my fingertips. "This is gonna be so good," I say, a wide smile stretching across my face. I clasp Wade's hands and press up onto my tiptoes to plant a kiss on his lips. He smiles back, amused by my excitement.

Every few feet we steal a glimpse of the kids. Summer is picking at the blue paint of the table. Gus is leaning over Merritt's shoulder, watching something on her phone. Oh, that damn phone. Merritt gives her brother a little shove. I can hear her voice in my head: *Gus, stoppp it, you're invading my privacy!* In turn, he scowls and presses in further.

The line continues to move, and then we're on the platform, ready to load. I bounce in my white sneakers. I spot a flash of Summer's hair just before we step up to the ride. *They're fine,* I tell myself again. *And besides, the ride can't be more than thirty seconds long.*

Wade and I scoot into the cramped car, and the safety bar lowers. I giggle. "Here we go!" I say as the coaster climbs higher and higher; each click of the track is a second closer to freefall. I can't wait to feel the wind in my hair.

When we reach the tippy-top, Wade takes a final look back. "Can you see them?" I say.

"Uh-uh. Too many trees in the w—"

And we're off, racing down the track. My stomach plummets as we take the first hill. Up and down, around and under, through the wooden maze. "Woohoo!" I shriek, turning to Wade and laughing. This time, he returns the laugh, the ride pulling out his inner child. We raise our hands in the air, and he clasps mine. This is freedom.

What feels like seconds later, we come barreling to a stop. Flyaways have escaped my ponytail, framing my face in what I can only assume must look like a fiery lion's mane. Wade's is just as windswept, and I reach up to smooth his dark strands back behind his ears. He chuckles. "I forgot how bumpy it is!"

We exit the car and my legs wobble. Getting our bearings, we follow the departing passengers down a ramp toward the exit into the park.

"You were right," I say with a laugh, "the kids could never have gone on that one!" I can't wait to tell Gus how fast the coaster went.

Wade is ahead of me, and I follow behind with a skip in my step. That felt amazing. A reset. Just a few minutes, and now I'm ready to return to mommy-land. The kids can ride whatever they want. Maybe I'll even let them play one of those games for a chance to win a stuffed animal that will end up in a future garage sale.

I look ahead. We're a few feet from the table when my heart stops. Merritt and Gus are in the same spot, absorbed with Merritt's phone, but the other side of the table is empty. Summer is gone.

TWO

FIVE MINUTES GONE

I DO A QUICK SCAN LEFT AND RIGHT. SUMMER'S RED HAIR and bright yellow tank top would stick out in a crowd. It's one of the reasons I dressed her in it today.

"Where's Summer?" I say, still spinning in place, thinking she'll pop out from behind the garbage can—*Surprise!*—or that she's wandered a few steps to watch the spinny ride next to SkyRush. There's no panic in my voice. Not yet. But a few seconds pass and I still don't see her, and that's when my pulse quickens.

"Merritt!" Wade's voice booms, catching her attention. She lowers the phone. "Where is your sister?"

Merritt looks to the opposite side of the table, where Summer once sat. Her eyes widen and her mouth drops open. "She was right there." She and Gus stand, copying Wade's and my search.

"Summer!" I call, loud though not frantic. She's probably meandered to a nearby ride. There aren't so many people you can't see through a crowd. This isn't Disneyland. She should be easy to find. Maybe the bright lights of the arcade drew her in. There are so many things that could grab a kid's attention here.

We've talked about this, that you don't just wander off in public places. I swivel to my older two. "You didn't see her leave?"

"No," Merritt says, and Gus shakes his head.

"Maybe she went in to find us," Wade suggests, jogging to SkyRush's entrance and disappearing around the corner.

Yes, I think. *She must have come after us. She said she didn't want me to go. Wade will find her.*

I continue looking around, calling her name, and after what feels like forever, Wade returns. He's empty-handed.

"You haven't found her?" he asks, just as I was about to say the same thing. I sense a subtle edge of blame in his voice, and my gut reaction is to throw it back at him: *Have you found her?*

"No," I say, my breathing picking up speed. My body's tingling all over again, but it's a far different feeling from the tingling I experienced waiting in line for the rollercoaster. This time, it comes with a sharpness that hurts, like a foot fallen asleep for too long.

Wade and I spread out, going in opposite directions, calling her name with more and more urgency. It hits me that I have two other children here, and when I pivot on my heel, I nearly knock Merritt and Gus over. They're following like baby ducks. "Stay with me," I say.

We do a loop around the area. "Have you seen a little girl with red hair?" I ask a woman holding a bag of candied peanuts. "Yellow tank top? About this tall?" Then another woman, and a couple of boys. A skinny teenager with a pockmarked face operating the flying parasol ride. They all shake their heads—no.

Sweat has officially broken out all over my body, and I feel it dripping down my back. Where could she be? I fling open the door to the women's restroom. "Summer!" I holler. "Summer, are you in here?" I catch a glimpse of myself in the mirror. My face has lost all color.

"Are you missing someone, ma'am?"

I spin and there's a heavyset woman wearing a park shirt and name tag.

"My... my daughter. She was with her siblings and... and..." My breath is ragged.

"Would you like me to call security?" The woman pulls out a walkie-talkie.

A light bulb goes off in my head. Suddenly, I know where she is. "The maypole," I announce, rushing from the bathroom, Merritt and Gus in tow. *Dammit, Greta. Why didn't you think of this from the get-go?* We always said if anyone got lost, we'd meet at the large maypole in the center of the park. With its bright colors and flashing light on top, it's impossible to miss. An easy spot for the kids to remember.

"She must be at the maypole," I call to Merritt and Gus over my shoulder. We break into a run, dodging people, nearly taking out a toddler with a basket of French fries.

"Watch it!" someone says, as I hip-check them out of my way. I don't care, I'm a mother on a mission—get to the maypole and find my little girl.

There it is: I can see the top above the roof of a low build-ing. *She has to be there. She's smart. She would have found her way.* Once when Gus was younger, he strayed from me in the middle of Macy's, getting lost among the packed circular racks. I panicked, calling his name, and just as I got to the nearest check-out desk, he appeared.

"I saw the sign up above," he said as I smothered him with kisses.

He'd somehow known to go to the check-out desk for help, and now I pray Summer will remember our designated meeting spot.

I look back to make sure the other two are still following. Their faces are flushed, fear in their eyes. "Stay with me," I say again.

We come around the side of the building that houses Guest

Services and I'm stopped in my tracks as if I've run into a brick wall. Wade is there, one hand to his forehead, the other on his hip. His cheeks are red; he's been running around the park just as I have. He must have had the same idea to meet here.

Only, there's no little redheaded girl with him. No Summer.

Something acidic burns the back of my throat.

"Nothing?" Wade says as we get closer.

I shake my head. Merritt and Gus are panting. Gus's chin quivers. "Is she lost?" he says.

Lost. The word sends a cold shiver down my spine.

"It's okay," I reassure him, though my churning stomach tells me otherwise. Summer must be around here somewhere. This has to be a big false alarm. Things like this don't happen here. The last time I remember Erie being in the national news was the bizarre Pizza Bomber incident my junior year of college. The city has its rough spots, sure, but we're on the good side of town. Wonderie Land is as familiar as the back of my hand. Who comes to an amusement park to take a kid?

I shudder. An amusement park is exactly the place a kidnapper would target.

"We have to keep looking," I say, wasting no time.

I dash off down the midway, past a row of carnival games. A scraggly-looking man operating the dart throw hollers at me. "One dollar per shot! Everyone gets a prize!"

"Have you seen a little girl with red hair?" I blurt, barely waiting for his response before moving down the row. I hurl the same question to the woman at the squirt gun race. She shakes her head. I keep running. My eyes bounce from building to building, ride to ride, park bench to park bench. Up, down, under, through. I feel like I'm in a mad dash to beat an invisible clock. Like those people on the supermarket game show who abandon all sense of refinement and resort to frenzy.

Behind me, Gus breathes hard, trying to keep up. Merritt has gone with Wade in the opposite direction.

"Summer!" I yell over and over.

Back in kiddie land, I check the car ride, the airplane ride, and the mini train. Nothing. We hurry onto the next area, passing a grill that smells like hotdogs that have been on the spinner too long.

"What about the arcade?" Gus says, out of breath.

"Good idea." I nod and we tear off in that direction, entering the darkened room full of neon lights and too many sounds.

"Summer!" I call again, weaving between game machines. I round the corner of one too fast and bang my knee against a hard plastic edge. A bolt of pain shoots down my leg and I wince, but don't stop.

"Mom, are you okay?" Gus says.

I shake it off, hobbling forward. At the photo booth, I whip open the curtain, much to the surprise of the two teen girls inside who jump in fear. No time for apologies. I'm already onto another part of the crowded space.

The arcade proves unsuccessful. Gus and I step back out into the daylight. I squint, the brightness momentarily blinding me. We're running out of places to look. Between Wade going one way, and me going the other, we've scoured just about every foot of this park.

A hollow pit opens up in my chest. Summer really is *gone*.

THREE

TWENTY MINUTES GONE

Gus and I return to the maypole, where Wade and Merritt are already waiting.

"We didn't find her," I say, the words sounding foreign as they leave my mouth.

Wade's face is ashen despite the heat. "Us either."

The four of us are dazed, unsure what to do next. Just then, a man emerges from the Guest Services building. "Is everything alright?" he says, bringing a hand up to block the sun from his eyes. His name tag says Bud.

"We can't find our daughter," Wade blurts, and the reality of it smacks me in the face. We can't find our daughter.

"How old? What does she look like?" Bud asks.

"She's five," I croak, realizing my voice is caught somewhere between my throat and my lips. "She's wearing a yellow tank top."

"She has red hair," Wade adds, "like my wife's."

"Where did you last see her?"

"We were sitting by the big rollercoaster," Gus chimes in through his tears. I pull him close to me and look to Merritt, who hasn't said a word but whose face says all I need to know—she's terrified.

"SkyRush," I say. "One of the blue tables by the exit."

Bud says something into his walkie-talkie, but it's muffled and my ears are ringing so loud I actually look around for some way to turn off the sound. "How long has it been since you saw her?"

Wade and I exchange glances. "Ten, fifteen minutes?" he says. "Maybe more?" Time feels like it's been moving in slow motion. In truth, I have no idea how long it's been, and now I feel guilty for not sounding the alarm from the first second we realized she was gone. I suppose I didn't want to believe it, thought that we'd find her. Informing security would make it real.

"We searched around the area, then split up and crossed the park on our way here," I say. "The maypole is our designated meeting place. We thought maybe she'd—" My voice hitches, and I bite the inside of my cheek to keep it together.

"Okay," Bud says. "I'm going to put out an alert to park staff. We'll make an announcement over the loudspeakers. I'd suggest one of you return to SkyRush in case she goes back there."

We nod along, putting all our faith in this man as if this were something he encountered daily. *Bud must know what to do. Bud will make it all better.*

"I'll go back," Wade says, and as he hurries off, it feels like he's dragging my heart with him. I don't want to be alone. I want to bury my face in his chest and pretend none of this is happening. But his hand trembled when he touched my shoulder a moment ago, and there's a smear of anxiety on his face. Seeing him rattled undoes me.

It feels like an eternity that the kids and I wait there by the rainbow-striped maypole, a far-too-happy-looking symbol for the purpose we'd given it. I hear a man's voice—Bud's?—go out over the loudspeakers. "Missing child alert. Girl, age five, red hair, wearing a yellow tank top."

Summer. Oh, Summer.

"Will they find her?" Gus sniffles beside me.

I can't answer him without wanting to vomit, so I don't. Instead, I give his hand a squeeze and continue my frantic search, eyes darting this way and that as I stand in place. My feet demand to move, to run, to upturn everything in this place, but Bud said to remain here, and so, against all impulses, I do.

Agonizing minutes pass. Ten, twenty. Finally, Wade returns. "I think we need to call the police," he says at the same time Bud steps from the building.

"They're already on their way," he says.

Within another fifteen minutes, two uniformed officers arrive. "Let's step inside," Bud says, gesturing to the door.

"But what if she walks by? What if we miss her?" I say.

The lack of response lands hard in my gut. They don't think Summer's still in the park. Suddenly, the whole of Erie opens up in my mind. Then bigger. Pennsylvania. The tri-state area. The quick skip and hop to Canada.

Somehow, I follow the officers into the building. The space is small, barely big enough for Bud and the police, let alone four additional hot, sweaty people.

"What are your names?" one of the officers asks me.

"Greta Goodman," I say, then point to Wade. "My husband, Wade."

"And your daughter's name?"

"Summer."

"And how old is she?"

I relay all the same information we told Bud. The officers want to know exactly where the kids were sitting, and whether Merritt and Gus saw anything. They ask where I was. Where Wade was.

A lump catches in my throat. "We were on the ride."

The officers look to each other, then back to us. "On the ride? You two? Without the children?"

"Yes," I squeak. "They were waiting for us. My older daughter, she was—"

"We could see them the whole time," Wade cuts in, though I know this isn't true. There were two points in the line where the kids were out of eyeshot, even if it was only for a few seconds.

The officers scribble notes on their pads, and it feels like their pens are scratching a permanent ink tattoo across my forehead: BAD MOM.

"Please," I say, "you have to find her." There's desperation in my voice like I've never heard before. I clasp my hands, as though these men before me are gods and I'm pleading at their feet.

"We intend to."

One of the policemen gets up and leaves, while the other stays and continues to ask us questions. Voices filter in from outside the room.

"... gonna need to see surveillance footage."

"... locking the park down."

"... Amber Alert."

I peer at the clock on the wall. It's four fifteen in the afternoon. *PJ Masks* should be on TV. We should be having cheese sticks and Goldfish for snacks.

I remember the time on my phone right before we stopped at SkyRush. Three eighteen. Merritt's birthday. It couldn't have been more than another handful of minutes by the time we got on the coaster. Which means Summer's been gone for almost an hour.

An hour without my baby.

Summer, where are you?

FOUR

FIVE HOURS, TWELVE MINUTES GONE

WE'RE STILL AT THE PARK AS THE SUN GOES DOWN. IT'S eight thirty, and Summer has been missing for over five hours. My body is numb. The police come and go. Bud offered the kids a plate of chicken fingers, but neither of them has done much more than pick at it. My stomach churns at the thought of food.

Wade and I sit side by side, taking turns putting our heads in our hands. His hairline is greasy from sweat, and I'm sure mine doesn't look much better. Merritt leans into him, their dark hair and eyes making them the contrasting duo compared to the rest of us. It's like they've always shared something that bonds them, something out of reach for me.

The door opens and a man and woman come through. Both are in plain clothes, but it's obvious from the badges around their necks that they're police. The woman's dark, cropped hair is tucked behind her ears. She reminds me of a less polished Halle Berry.

"Mr. and Mrs. Goodman? I'm Georgia Smart," the woman says, "and this is my partner, Victor Ocho. We've been assigned as detectives to your daughter's case."

Our daughter has a case.

We nod.

"We're going to need to hear exactly what happened, starting from the beginning."

My shoulders slump. "We've already told the police and the park officials." *How many more times do we need to relive this nightmare?*

"I understand," Detective Smart says, "but we'll need to hear it first-hand. One more time, I'm afraid."

And so, Wade and I retell everything. Each time, I disassociate a bit more, as if strings to balloons that are holding me up are being cut one by one. Soon, I will fall to the ground completely.

"And you said that the children were at the table near the"— she checks her notes—"SkyRush rollercoaster?"

"Yes."

"By themselves."

"Yes." A queasy sensation floods me.

"You mentioned that you come to Wonderie Land quite often as a family. Did you happen to notice anyone out of the ordinary in the park today? Anyone acting, I don't know, suspicious or lingering around?"

I wrack my brain as though answering in the affirmative will be the key to this whole disturbing riddle. But nothing sparks. "No," I offer meekly, shaking my head.

"Can you remember what you were doing right before splitting up at SkyRush?"

"We'd come from the carousel. It's Summer's favorite." My voice catches. "The kids wanted to go to the Wacky Shack, but we stopped at SkyRush first."

"Okay. That's helpful. We're trying to get a picture of everyone's movements. Officers are doing a sweep through the park as we speak."

"My wife and I searched all over the park," Wade says.

I look to him. "Another loop can't hurt."

"No, I'm just saying we should look outside the park since it seems like she's not here."

Not here.

I feel like I'm going to be sick. Wade doesn't think she's here either.

"Pennsylvania State Police have put out an Amber Alert," Detective Smart says, which I already know because it flashed across my phone hours ago and I wanted to die. "Local police are aware. We're reviewing surveillance footage from a few different angles, as well as interviewing some witnesses."

"There are witnesses?" I say, suddenly upright, a surge of hope rushing through me. "Someone saw Summer? Someone saw who took her?"

Smart pumps a hand like a slow break. "When I say witnesses, I mean people who were in the general vicinity. Park-goers, staff. We don't know yet if anyone saw anything."

"But someone *had* to see *something*. A little girl doesn't just disappear." I look to Wade. Why isn't he backing me up here? His jaw is hard and a five o'clock shadow has already appeared on his face.

"Trust us, Mrs. Goodman. We're doing everything we can to find Summer. Do you have a recent photo of your daughter?"

I shakily scroll through the camera roll on my phone. An endless selection, but I'm looking for a specific one. I can see it in my head—a shot I captured of Summer just a few weeks ago. We'd been outside playing in the driveway, Merritt reading a graphic novel in the shade, Gus zooming around on his scooter, and Summer drawing with fat chalk at my feet.

"Hey, cutie," I said, and at just the moment she looked up, I snapped the picture. In it, she's giving the big, gummy smile that makes her nose scrunch and baby teeth shine. Her blue eyes are sparkling with pure innocence, her cheeks splattered with a constellation of freckles from the mid-year sun. I love that picture so much; I made a mental note to print it and update Summer's frame in the living room.

Now, the picture that embodied such a happy moment will be used for the unthinkable.

I find it on my phone and hand it to Smart.

"May I email this to the station?" she asks, and I nod. She returns the phone to me. "Can you think of anyone who would want to take Summer? A disgruntled family member? Someone with a vendetta?"

"Vendetta?" Wade says. "God no. We're just regular people, a regular family."

"Where do you both work?"

"I'm at Erie Insurance," Wade says. "Software engineer."

When Smart turns to me, I begin, "I worked in marketing for the college, but now I'm home with the kids..." This admission always comes with a feeling of embarrassment, as though being a stay-at-home mom isn't a real job. Only now, I want nothing more than to lock myself in the house with my babies and never leave. I swallow the emotion that's threatening to bubble up. A few quick blinks keep the tears at bay.

Next to me, Gus yawns.

"I think what's best is for you to take your children home," Smart says. "The park is closing, and we'll be continuing our efforts through the night."

"I'm not leaving," I say, surer than anything I've ever felt.

"I understand, but there's really nothing else you can do at this time. Let us do our work. An officer is waiting to escort you home."

I glance at Wade and give him a look that says, *This lady can't be serious.* She expects us to just leave? To go home with only two-thirds of our kids? Impossible.

"Greta," Wade says, and it strikes me how rarely I'm called by my own name. I'm always just Mom. His eyes droop like a sad cartoon and it breaks my heart in two. "There's nothing we can do here."

Is he crazy? I'm not leaving until they find Summer.

He must sense my incredulity because he reaches out a hand and places it on my knee. "We should go," he says. My mouth hangs open. "They'll find her. They'll bring her home to us."

"We've got officers all over the city," Smart says. Her eyes are kind, and I feel like she genuinely cares. Still, what she's asking is unthinkable.

I'm shaking my head. *No, no, no.* But Wade's guiding me up out of my chair. And then we're back outside, the sky a gunmetal blue that I would normally think was pretty, but now seems only grisly. The rides are still, resting for the night. A lone staff member sweeps popcorn from the pavement. Another empties a garbage can and replaces it with a massive black trash bag for the next day. I examine them: *Did you take my daughter?*

I've never been in the park this late. We always come early and leave early, and being here now feels eerie. Amusement parks aren't supposed to be this quiet.

My feet take me to the car, though I don't feel myself walking. Ours is one of the few left in the parking lot. I don't remember opening the door, but now I'm sitting in the passenger seat, Wade behind the wheel, Merritt and Gus in the back. A police car is in front of us, lights off. It pulls ahead and Wade follows.

What is happening? We're leaving? We're just going to go home and wait?

We exit the parking lot, turning onto the main road that will lead us back to the house where a white twin bed with a pink ruffled quilt will lie empty tonight. I catch a glimpse of the

Wonderie Land sign in the car's side mirror getting smaller and smaller, and it's too much to process.

"Pull over," I say, already reaching for the door handle. The car has barely come to a stop before my stomach empties onto the gravel berm.

FIVE

Our neighborhood is quiet, streetlamps lighting up Pleasant Drive and the cookie-cutter houses that line it. A few driveways down, I see the Baker boy shooting hoops. He stops and watches as the police car pulls up, then quickly abandons the ball and runs into his house. I imagine him telling his parents —*There's a cop at the Goodmans!*—and the grapevine effect of our private lives infiltrating suburbia.

Wade pulls the car into the garage, and I'm thankful for the cover it provides. But when I get out, my legs threaten to buckle under my weight. It all feels real; leaving the park solidified it. I'm still shaky from being sick at the side of the road and standing brings with it a lightheadedness I have to fight from winning.

"Come on, guys," I say to Merritt and Gus, leading them into the house. The detectives are right behind and follow us inside. The clock on the stove reads ten p.m. Past Summer's bedtime. I bite back a cry. It feels like I'm walking into an alternate universe. This house isn't our house without Summer. Everything's off, the whole dynamic. Where are her pattering footsteps on the hardwood? Where's the little bird voice asking for a snack? Her Minnie Mouse purse is hanging by the door, but she's not here.

"Is there anything else we can do for you?" Detective Ocho says, and Smart shoots daggers in his direction.

What kind of question is that? Yes, in fact there is something you can do—you can find my daughter.

Detective Smart steps forward, her face reading nothing but empathy. She must have kids of her own. There's no ring on her finger, but that doesn't mean anything. "We'll be sure to call you if there are any updates," she says. "If I were you, I'd stay inside, keep your blinds drawn." My forehead scrunches, making her clarify. "This is likely to hit the local news soon. Don't speak to reporters."

The thought of reporters and cameras on my lawn makes my abdomen clench even harder. There's no way this will come to that. Summer will be home by morning. She has to be.

Smart and Ocho retreat the way they came, and I'm frozen on the spot, one hand braced against the kitchen island for balance. I can't believe they're leaving and we're supposed to sit here and wait. My shorts stick to the backs of my legs. I can barely feel the air conditioning.

"Mom, I'm hungry," Gus says, pulling me back to reality. He hasn't eaten anything—none of us have—since the over-priced hamburgers before noon. "Can you make me a cheese sandwich?"

It takes me a minute to sift through the confusion—*You want a cheese sandwich when your sister is missing?*—but then I blink and see his freckled face staring up at me.

"Sure, bud," I say in a haze. "I can make you a cheese sandwich."

Merritt and Wade are already at the table, eyes fixed into space. When I offer them anything to eat, they both shake their heads. I can't blame them.

We sit around the circular table that usually welcomes five

bodies, only now one of the chairs is empty. It's the one whose lacquer has worn thin from wiping away residue left by sticky fingers. The one that used to hold a booster seat so Summer wouldn't have to sit on her knees.

This has to be a very, very bad dream.

I stare at the chair as though she's there. I can almost see her. If I just reach out—

In a flash, I leap from my chair and am on my feet. My body moves on autopilot, leaving the kitchen behind and traveling through the living room to the stairs at the front of the house.

"Greta?" I hear Wade's voice far behind.

Summer's room. It's like a drug pulling me. I have to get there.

As I bolt to the top of the steps, I can see her door at the end of the hallway. She *must* be inside. I'll fling the door open to find her playing hair salon with her Barbies or making a track on her floor with paperback books. I've been hallucinating this whole thing.

The thought buoys in my chest. I can picture her so clearly, it nearly brings tears to my eyes. I hurry the dozen steps down the hall and push open her door.

"Summer!" I say, the word heavy with hope.

But her room is empty.

No! Please! I'll never fantasize about escaping on the Ferris wheel again, I promise!

I take it in. Her pink, ruffled bedding bunches in spots where I know she tried her best to make the bed this morning. In a bookshelf cubby, three Barbies sit at attention, pin-straight legs sticking out the edge. Their fixed expressions ridicule me. *What did you do?*

Just then, two slammed car doors make me jump.

Summer! It must be the police bringing her home! Oh, thank God!

I fly from her room, back the way I came. Just as I'm reentering the kitchen, the door bursts open and my parents enter. My breath stops, disappointment popping my brief moment of fantasy. I'd forgotten we'd called them just before leaving the park, when it became clear that this was real—Summer was gone and we were leaving without her. Thirty minutes and a lifetime ago.

Mom's thin auburn hair is twisted back into a claw clip, frazzled at the temples like someone who got ready in a hurry. Dad wears his glasses, which he says help him see better when driving at night.

"Oh, Greta," Mom says, coming straight for me and folding over my shoulders. Seeing them floods my chest with warmth and makes my eyes prickle at the corners. When she lets go, it's Dad's turn.

"I can't believe this is happening," I say.

"They'll find her," Dad says. "I know they will."

His words offer the assurance only a father can. I've trusted and admired this man my whole life, and now more than ever, I want to crawl into his lap and let him stroke my hair, tell me everything's going to be okay.

"Wade," Dad says, pulling my husband close and giving him a solid pat on the back.

My parents' faces are plastered with concern, and it makes my nerves stand on end. This is bigger than us. This will impact many people. Our extended families. Friends, neighbors.

"Come with me, my little lovelies," Mom says to Merritt and Gus. "You should get some rest. Let your parents talk." She gestures for the kids to follow her upstairs, where I know she'll make sure they brush their teeth and put their clothes in the laundry basket.

Gus comes to me first, pressing his face into my chest and squeezing his arms tight around my torso. "It's going to be alright," I say, because what's the alternative? Even though everything in me wants to fall apart, I still have a job to do, and that is to protect my other two children from the damage this whole thing could cause. If nothing else, I need them to go to sleep feeling safe.

"Will you wake me up when Summer gets back?" Gus says. I press my lips together to keep the cry in.

"Yes," I manage. Merritt starts to leave, and I call after her, "Goodnight, Mer." She doesn't turn around.

My shoulders relax as I watch them head toward the stairs, my mother in tow. I'm flushed with gratitude. It's as though she knew exactly what I needed in this moment. A mother's instinct.

And yet... where was *my* mother's instinct when I got the idea to leave the kids alone at that park table?

SIX

SUNDAY: FIVE HOURS, TWELVE MINUTES GONE

I can't sleep. Dark visions haunt me every time my eyes drift. Visions so sinister I refuse to speak them into existence.

We've taken up residence in the living room. My parents insisted on staying; they're curled into each other on the couch, Mom's head resting on Dad's shoulder. I'm grateful sleep finds them for a few hours. No one should have to suffer this agony around the clock.

In the bleak hours of the night, I try to talk to Wade, but he's quiet and withdrawn. My mind races, stumbling over scenario after scenario.

"Should we call the station for an update?" I whisper, but he only shrugs, making my teeth grind. We've barely said more than a handful of sentences to each other in the past four hours. Every time I try, it's like he isn't there. He barely looks at me.

Time inches by as though doing everything in its power to prevent the sunrise. Seconds creep along, and I obsessively check the clock, thinking it must have been hours, when in fact it has only been minutes. Each rotation marks another hour Summer has been missing.

Like a fool, I google facts about missing children, binging on data that makes my mouth go sour. Only when I read the statistic that says seventy-three percent of kidnapping victims are killed within the first three hours do I turn my phone over and promise myself not to touch it again.

Instead, my mind wanders. I trace the blue pattern on the porcelain lamp that sits next to the couch. It's an antique, passed down from my great-grandmother. I've always loved it. Summer used to say it reminded her of an ice castle. Even its surface is cool to the touch. I search the pattern for a happy memory, something to lift me out of this blackness, but nothing comes.

The first light of day finally sneaks in through the curtains, making my parents rustle. I see the question on the tips of their tongues, but my solemn face must give them their answer, and so they don't ask.

"I'll make some coffee," Dad says, standing, his seventy-year-old knees creaking.

It's not long before footsteps above alert us to Merritt and Gus making their way down the stairs.

"Good morning," I force myself to say.

"Did they find Summer?" Merritt asks, eyes hopeful.

I manage a slight shake of the head. I wish this couch would swallow me whole.

Mom swoops in, wrapping them in a group hug. "Did you get some sleep?"

"Yeah," Gus says.

Merritt shrugs. "A little." She takes a seat next to Wade on the couch.

My eyes are dry from being awake all night, and I rub them freely, knowing I'm smudging yesterday's leftover mascara. I'm gross and I smell. Neither Wade nor I have even changed out of the clothes we wore the day before. It's as though time has stopped, and all normal routines must remain at a standstill until order is returned. I can't possibly go through life's ordinary moments knowing my daughter is out there somewhere.

As if on cue, Dad returns and offers me a steaming hot mug. The smell stirs my senses, but I shake my head. I can't stomach anything.

"You can't starve yourself," he says, and though I know it comes from a place of love, I want to scream out, *There are no rules!*

We're all sitting like lumps in a living room wrought with awkward pressure when the sound of voices outside grabs my attention.

Wade stands and goes to the window, peering through a slit in the curtain. "Shit," he says.

I stand. "What?"

But then there's a quick knock at the door.

"Don't answer it," he says.

I meet him at the window to see for myself. A news van has parked at the curb, and a man stands beside it setting up a camera. I lean to see the front stoop, and my stomach drops. Two reporters face the door, one holding a microphone, the other a small journalist's notepad. They knock again.

"Shhhhh," I say instinctively, though no one in the room has made a sound.

"Jesus Christ," Wade whispers.

Gus nears the window. "What is it, Dad?"

"Some reporters," I say. "They probably heard about what happened and they want to talk to us."

"Why do we have to be quiet? Why can't we talk to them?"

I pinch the bridge of my nose. The stress of yesterday, in addition to twenty-four hours of no sleep, has brought on the beginnings of a migraine.

"It's... it's hard to explain, honey," Mom steps in. "We need to make sure we follow the police's instructions. Everyone's working very hard to bring Summer home."

From the other side of the door, a woman's voice filters through. "Mr. and Mrs. Goodman? We're from AllNews24. Do you have a statement on your daughter's disappearance? Has the kidnapper tried to contact you at all?"

"How intrusive can these people be?" Dad mutters under his breath.

We all look around, perplexed. This is our property. Can we force them to leave?

"It's all over the news," I hear from behind me.

I turn to see Wade staring at his phone. "Get off that," I snap. "It's not helping."

Another knock. "Mrs. Goodman? Can we speak with you?"

I peek out the window again, and this time there's a second news vehicle parked behind the first. Two additional sets of reporters and cameramen set up in the grass.

"This is turning into a circus!" I say.

"Greta, let us take the kids home with us," Mom says quietly. "They shouldn't be around all this commotion. We can keep them until things settle down."

How long does she think this is going to last?

Last night, I was convinced Summer would be home by now, but she isn't. A new day is here, and she's still missing. How many days and nights of this can we bear?

"I want them here," I reply.

"But—" Mom starts.

"No. I'm not letting my kids out of my sight." *The two kids I have left*, I want to add, but can't say it.

Mom casts her eyes downward. "Okay, hon. Okay."

Suddenly, my phone comes alive with a string of beeps. I look. Text messages are flooding in, and I catch the first few lines of each as they cross my screen on their way to my inbox.

Oh my God, Greta!

What is happening?!?!

Greta, I'm sooooo sorry.

I didn't call any of our friends last night. Not even Lolly, my best friend and Merritt's godmother. In fact, it never crossed my mind. Once again, I'd had it in my head that this nightmare would come to a close before dawn. There'd be no reason to notify anyone. Call me naïve, but I didn't think it would even reach the media.

I was so, so wrong.

As if she heard me thinking about her, Lolly's name flashes on my phone screen, along with a photo of us from a Jimmy Buffett concert. I don't pick up. I don't know how to explain any of this yet.

I lay my phone face down but stop short of turning it to silent in case the detectives call. Come to think of it—why *haven't* they called yet? Shouldn't we be getting hourly updates?

I take a final glance out the window. Several neighbors across the street have emerged in bathrobes and pajama pants, arms crossed and faces screwed up, taking in the scene before them. Pleasant Drive is a quiet place. It's exactly as its name suggests—pleasant. Bad things don't happen here. News crews don't broadcast from our nicely manicured front lawns.

A new voice fills the room, startling me, and I whip around to find Gus with the TV remote in his hand. My face must read one of surprise, because he quickly comes to his own defense. "I... I thought I could turn on a show."

But the TV isn't tuned to Disney or any of the other stations the kids like. It's the local news—and they're talking about us. The oddest sensation floods over me. That's my house on the screen. That's my driveway and the big maple where the kids hung a tire swing. I stare closer. The camera zooms in. A shadow passes behind the curtain blocking the window. But then, wait! Someone is pulling the edge aside. An eye peeks out. A lock of dark hair.

It hits me. I'm watching my life on the screen. The person is my husband.

I back away from the TV as though it were evil. As though it put a curse on me and caused this whole thing.

"Get away from there," I say to Wade.

On the screen, the camera refocuses on the reporter, a pretty woman with short, coiffed hair and a blouse that matches her lipstick. She's talking about yesterday, about the park, about Summer.

Turn it off, my brain commands, but I don't voice it. I want to know what they're saying. Do they have more information than we do? It feels like we know nothing. Maybe this reporter will spill some tidbit we haven't yet heard.

"... age five, disappeared from Wonderie Land between three twenty and three thirty yesterday afternoon..."

The screen splits in half, and on the right, the photo of Summer—the one I gave to Detective Smart—appears along with basic identifying information. My brain spins. It's like I'm watching a movie, only none of this is fiction. I feel cold. My body hasn't seemed to catch up, hasn't processed the gravity, the realness of what's happening.

There's a hand on my back, and I gasp.

"It's just me," Dad says. Then, "Why don't you try to lie down for a bit?"

I ignore him. My limbs are heavy, and I can't remember the last time I was awake for over a whole day. It feels like the kind of exhaustion from when the kids were newborns, only worse. Those stretches of time came with a happy upside—the child, the gift. A bright smile in the morning to make it all worth it.

Now, we're only in hell.

"Honey," Mom says. "Dad's right. You need to rest."

"I'm fine."

She frowns. "We're going to run home real quick to change, okay? Then we'll be right back."

"You don't have to," I say. What good will it do to have them sitting around here doing nothing?

"Of course we will. We want to know what's going on. We're here to support you."

I nod vacantly. Mom gathers her purse, the only thing they arrived with last night, and Dad leads her out through the garage. I can hear the reporters pouncing before the door even shuts.

The clock on the wall chimes eight, and something snaps inside me. The day has long begun and we're still in limbo. Why haven't the police called?

"That's it," I announce. "I'm calling. I need to know what's going on. It doesn't take all night to look through surveillance tapes."

No one stops me. I dial the number on the business card Detective Smart left. The fondness I felt toward her has vanished, replaced instead with an edge that borders on anger. Smart answers on the second ring.

"Mrs. Goodman," she says before I can get a word out, "I was just about to call you."

My heart leaps so high into my throat I nearly choke. *Call me with good news... or with bad?*

"We're actually on our way to you right now. Can we speak when we get there?"

Cotton mouth prevents me from responding. All I can manage is a quiet "okay" before the line goes dead.

SEVEN

It takes everything in my power not to lunge for Smart and Ocho as Wade lets them in through the front door.

Have you found anything? Do you know who took Summer? Why haven't you called us?

My husband beats me to it. "Did you find her?"

It's a stupid question, really, but the one that's impossible not to ask. If they'd found her, they'd have her here. The fact that the detectives showed up alone is all the answer we need.

"We're working on it," Smart says gently. "We're following a few leads."

"What leads?" I blurt. "Who? Did the tapes show something?"

"Mrs. Goodman, we'd like to talk with Merritt if that's okay. Yesterday was quite chaotic, and by the evening, it was clear the children were tired. If it's alright with you, we'd like to ask Merritt some questions about what she might have seen or heard."

Smart's voice is kind, and perhaps that's the only reason I agree.

"Merritt!" I call into the other room where she and Gus

have turned on a movie, though I doubt either of them is paying full attention.

Merritt comes into the living room, still wearing the leggings and oversized T-shirt she slept in. Her hair is down, with a flat spot on one side. A pillow kiss, we call it.

"Merritt, the detectives want to ask you a few questions about yesterday," I say.

"Am I in trouble?" she says, eyes wide.

Wade puts an arm around her shoulder. "No, honey. No one's in trouble."

Merritt sits on the edge of the couch, folding her hands in her lap like she's in the principal's office, and that's enough to rock me to my core. She's our oldest, the tallest of the three, but right now she looks so small.

"Hi, Merritt. I'm Detective Smart, and this is my partner, Detective Ocho."

"I remember you from yesterday," Merritt says.

"Yes. We're working to find your sister. Part of our job is to collect as much information as possible so we can understand exactly what happened. Since your mom and dad weren't there when Summer went missing, we'd like to talk with you too, okay?"

Merritt nods.

"Okay. When your parents got in line for the ride, what did you and your siblings do?"

"We were sitting at the blue table."

"Right. And were you all next to one another? Like in a row?"

"It was a circle." Merritt lifts a hand as though she's drawing a picture. "I was on this side, and Gus was right here, then Summer on the other side."

"Were you talking to one another?"

"I don't remember."

"You don't remember if you three were chitchatting? Or if you all sat there in silence?"

"I got out my phone."

"Your phone. Okay." Smart writes on a small notepad.

Merritt looks down. "I started playing a game. But only after I couldn't see Mom and Dad anymore because I knew Mom would yell."

Smart looks to me and I feel compelled to explain. "The phone is new. It was a birthday present, meant to be a way for her to communicate with us when she's at a friend's house or when she needs to be picked up from sports. But no social media. And we have a rule about limiting things like games. I don't love all the screen time."

Smart returns to Merritt. "So, you were playing a game on your phone."

"Yes, and Gus scooted around to watch over my shoulder. He's nosy like that. I pushed him away and he called me a jerk and said he'd tell Mom, so I eventually let him watch."

"Then what happened?"

Merritt's head shakes, like there's nothing else to the story. "Then my parents were back, and Summer was gone." Her voice cracks on the last word.

"You didn't hear her leave the table?"

"No."

"Didn't feel the table shift?"

"No."

I lean forward, imploring her. "Think, Merritt," I say. "This is important."

Smart continues. "Summer didn't say anything to you like, 'Hey guys, I'm going over here'?"

"No."

Merritt's eyes fill with tears. I look to Wade for guidance. *Is this okay? Should we stop this?*

Smart flashes me a look, as if asking for permission. I don't stop her. "Are you *sure* she didn't say anything?" Smart says. "Or might she have and you didn't hear because of the game?"

Merritt fumbles. "I didn't hear anything. I didn't see her leave. Don't you think I would have said something if I did?" Her chest rises and falls with heavy, fast breaths. I want to reach out and touch her, but something holds me back. I need these answers as much as the investigators. Merritt and Gus were the last people to see Summer. If we have to squeeze her a bit to help the case, that's what has to happen.

Smart crosses her legs and rests her forearms on her knee. "Do you remember if there were other people near the table?"

"No," Merritt says.

"No there weren't other people, or no you don't remember?"

Merritt slaps her hands against her thighs and shoots up off the couch. "I don't know, okay?" she shouts before running from the room, tears streaking her face. Within seconds I hear footfall rushing up the stairs, and I picture her flinging herself onto her bed.

I close my eyes, the last few minutes adding another dollop onto my mental exhaustion. The right thing to do would be to excuse myself and go console my daughter. But I'm too drained, my legs too weak. My priorities—right or wrong—are here in this room. The investigation. I need to know what's happening with the search. I can talk with Merritt the rest of the day, but every hour that passes decreases the likelihood of Summer's return. I know the statistics.

"I'm sorry," Smart says, clicking her pen shut. "I didn't mean to upset her."

But I don't have time for apologies. "Did you review the surveillance footage?"

She exhales. "We did."

"And?" My lungs balloon.

"And it's not a clear picture."

"But you can see the table? You can see the kids?" I hang on the edge of my seat. I reach out for Wade's hand and he takes it.

Tell us what we want to hear.

"Yes, there is a shot of the table and we can see the kids, but it's blurry. It appears to show Merritt on the phone, like she described, and Gus nearby. Summer is on the left, the backside of the table, if you will."

I know all this. It's exactly how we left them. It's just what Merritt said. What I want is *new* information. What happened to Summer?

"About four minutes after you two enter the ride line," Smart continues, "the image changes."

"Changes? What do you mean changes?"

"The video shows Summer leaving the table."

"Leaving? On her own? She wouldn't have done that. She knows not to go off on her own. We told the kids to sit right there and wait for us."

"Well, she did. She appears to have walked over to the ride next to SkyRush."

Despite my confusion, I'm momentarily relieved—Summer wasn't snatched from the table. But then I realize that's irrelevant. Even if she wasn't taken directly from the table, that doesn't mean she wasn't taken. Something must have happened near the other ride.

"Does the video show anything else?" I ask. "What happened after she wandered away?" *Please tell me she didn't go off camera.*

"There was a woman a few feet away from Summer. She appears to be engaging in conversation with her in the video."

A woman? I'm surprised by how much this revelation shocks me. All this time when I thought about who could have taken Summer, I pictured a man. Men are kidnappers. Sick, creepy men. Not women.

"Can you see her face? What did she look like?" Wade asks.

Detective Smart shakes her head. "Unfortunately, the image is at the wrong angle. Even if it weren't, it was at such a distance, I'm afraid it would have been too pixelated. These aren't the highest-quality cameras. Plus, the woman was wearing a hat that partially obscured her face."

"But you see her take Summer, right? She definitely is the kidnapper, right?" A million questions are flying through my head. *Did she snatch her? Put a hand over her mouth and carry her away? Did she lure her with a toy or candy? Did she hold Summer's hand as she walked off with my daughter?*

I've seen those experiments, the ones where a fake abductor tries to bait a kid, all while the parents watch, horrified, off-screen. *My kid would never do that*, I always told myself.

Smart sighs, looks to her partner then back to us. "The cameras aren't stationary. They pan."

"What do you mean they pan?" A sinking feeling comes over me—I know what she's alluding to, even as I ask.

"They swivel. They don't stay focused on one spot."

"Wait a minute," Wade says. "Are you telling us that the footage shows someone approaching Summer, but doesn't show the actual kidnapping?"

"The camera captured the figure getting closer to Summer, then panned away. When it came back, they were both gone," Smart says.

My stomach drops to the floor. I clutch the neck of my shirt in my fist, twisting. *Oh, God.* She's got to be kidding me. This has to be a joke. A cry escapes my lips.

"This person must be an expert," Wade says. "She had to have planned it. How else would she have known when the camera wasn't pointed at her?"

"It's possible," Smart says. "Or it could be a complete coincidence. We don't know."

I bring both hands to cover my nose and mouth. I take a deep inhale, breathing in my own air. It stinks. I haven't brushed my teeth in over twenty-four hours. *Think, Greta.* I will my brain to work. "So, what do we do now?"

Detective Smart crosses her wrists on her lap. "We're talking with park employees and guests from yesterday to try to identify this person of interest. We also sent the footage out for better testing and enhancements in hopes of getting a clearer picture."

"Okay," I say. This is good. These are good steps. We have some sort of progress. Despite the fact that my baby is missing, this is the first time I've felt anything positive. A woman surely wouldn't hurt a child, right? That means that Summer might be safe even though she isn't here with me.

You're ludicrous, my subconscious says. There are plenty of twisted women out there. Look at the woman who was involved with taking that pretty Mormon girl from Utah. Or the one in Florida who didn't report her own daughter missing for a month.

The detectives stand. "We'll keep you updated as much as possible," Smart says.

I'm dying to handcuff myself to her and flush the key down the toilet so she'll have no choice but to let me tag along. The need to know every tiny development eats away at me. It feels absurd that we, as Summer's parents, aren't on the front lines of this investigation. But then I hear Wade's voice in my head—*Let them do their jobs*—and I know he's right.

I hate it. But he's right.

Just as Smart goes for the doorknob, I remember what waits on the other side. "What do we do about all these reporters?" I ask.

"My advice would be not to talk to them. We need to keep the investigation contained for now. Stay inside. If you need to leave, just say, 'No comment.'"

We heed her advice, watching the detectives slip out the door and locking it behind them. I look at my phone again and see a dozen new messages from friends, neighbors, my cousin Melanie who I haven't talked to in ages. One from Lolly in all caps:

I'M COMING OVER.

Everyone's concerned, everyone's sending prayers. I close out of the app without replying to anyone. Not now. Not yet. There's something else I need to do.

EIGHT

I hear her cries before I reach the top of the stairs. Merritt's room is the first on the right. I approach and give the door a soft knock as I open it.

"Mer?" I say.

She's curled in a ball on her bed, the lavender bedspread and floral sheets tangled from a restless night. Her body tucks into itself, all bony limbs, like a fawn shortly after birth. Dark hair fans out on the pillow. I recall being disappointed when she was born and so closely resembled Wade. Shouldn't babies look like their mothers, the ones who did all the work to bring them into the world? That feeling quickly passed, however—as she grew I was able to look at her and see traits of Wade I loved. She was the first person to awaken a new part of myself I hadn't known before. Still, Merritt always favored her dad, and even though she's only eleven, I find myself worrying about the potential hardships that will face us as mother and daughter during her teenage years. Everyone says daughters come back around, but what if we're different? What if Merritt and I drift apart and never find our way back to each other?

Merritt's shoulders shake as she cries. A child's pain is like nothing I've ever experienced, and yet I stand there without taking another step. I don't rush to her side, don't gather her in my arms and whisper words of comfort. In fact, part of me wants to turn around and walk out. What is wrong with me? Heat swirls in my chest, making it uncomfortable to even be here in this room.

Talk to her, my brain says. I take conscious steps forward and sit on the edge of the bed.

"They're gone," I say. "The detectives, they left."

"Why were they being so mean?" She sniffles, rolling onto her back. Her face is wet with tears, and a few strands of hair get caught in the stream, plastering themselves to her cheeks.

"They weren't being mean, honey. They were just trying to understand what happened."

"But I didn't see anything."

The knot in my belly tightens. I feel the fire crawling up my neck. There are things I want to say, want to scream. Nasty things. Things that will appall me later when the rage subsides.

That's because you were more concerned with your phone!

Why weren't you paying attention?

How could you let this happen?

I close my eyes and breathe.

"Are you mad at me?" her tiny voice says, and I open them again.

"No."

Yes.

"Is it my fault Summer is missing?"

I dig my fingernails into my palms. "No."

Yes. Partly. Why do I feel this way?

These thoughts disgust me, and yet I can't stop them.

Merritt stares at the ceiling. A stray tear drops and circles the line of her ear. The room is quiet, but a high-pitched whistle lives in my head, piercing and incessant, like a steam engine sounding alarm.

I know the right things to say in this moment—*You're not to blame. You didn't do anything wrong*—but saying them feels like a lie. Because the truth is that a bead of resentment has been growing in my gut ever since Wade and I got to the table and saw Summer gone and Merritt on her phone. One simple ask— *Please be responsible for five minutes*—and she couldn't even do it. It's like the times she leaves her clothes on the floor instead of dropping them in the basket one foot away. Or when she refuses to eat the smallest serving of vegetables at dinner. The times that make me want to yell, *Why do you have to be such a challenge?* I know it's unfair, and still the feeling is so big, so loud, I can't think anything else.

Her bedroom is like a pressure cooker. I can't sit here any longer or I might explode. Merritt's not meeting my eye either, so that makes two of us. I stand, and with a final look to the little girl on the bed, I cross the room and leave.

I'm a terrible mother.

Wade finds me outside on the back steps. The reporters haven't trespassed far enough to come around the sides of the house, so for now, this small deck is a safe haven.

I take a drag of a Newport cigarette, lift my chin, and blow it out. Fuck twelve years of healthy lungs. I open the Notes app on my phone to draft a Facebook post no mother dreams she'll have to make.

"You're smoking?" Wade says by way of a greeting.

My fingers type. "I don't need a lecture."

It's a dirty habit and one I'd kicked when I got pregnant with Merritt. Haven't touched a cigarette since. Until today. Turns out keeping a pack tucked away for emergencies was a good idea after all. I don't tell him I'm already on my third one. It is nine a.m., after all.

Wade stands behind me instead of joining me on the step.

"I just got off the phone with Rob," he says. "The company's giving me unlimited personal leave for the time being."

I stop typing. I hadn't even considered the fact that tomorrow is Monday. A new work week—at least for Wade. Sometimes I remember what it was like to get up, shower, put on actual clothes, and head to the college downtown where I'd create everything from admissions pamphlets to direct mailers and online ad campaigns. For eight years I worked in the marketing department. The job gave me the perfect blend of a creative outlet in a professional setting, and I managed to make it work when Merritt was born. But after Gus, it no longer made sense. My salary went straight to childcare, and the stress was simply too much. Still, I have fond memories of being part of that team, having coworkers who were also friends. Feeling intellectually fulfilled. In many ways, it's like a past life. I've been a full-time mom for nearly a decade.

And yet, when these wistful moments come, they're quickly negated by a single truth—if I'd stayed working, we probably wouldn't have had Summer. I can't fathom this possibility, and so I try to lean on more of the sweet than the bitter.

Wade folds his arms. "Rob said not to worry about my accounts. They can handle everything."

"I'd hope so. Our daughter is missing." I take another puff.

Wade grimaces. "Greta, I really think you should try to get some sleep."

I spin, giving him an accusatory look. "What's that supposed to mean? You were up all night too. There are things to do."

"We have to keep a clear head."

"My head is clear, Wade. I'm not thinking about anything but finding Summer."

"Hey, don't snap at me. We're on the same team."

Are we? I can't help but feel the tension between us. It's bringing out insecurities I don't like, the ones where I question if I'm good enough. A good enough mother, good enough wife. I thought I'd left those self-doubts in the past, but now they're coming up again.

I drop my head. My phone dangles at the end of my extended arm. I take a breath, give my head a little shake. Wade's right, we are on the same team. We chose each other in life for a reason. Right now, everything's just heightened, everyone's on edge. But when I look up to apologize, he's gone back into the house.

I light another cigarette. Lift my phone. *What's on your mind?* Facebook prompts me. I type with shaky fingers.

> Yesterday, August 12, our daughter, Summer, was

I stop. I can't believe what I'm writing. The cigarette burns down to an inch. I take a final, long drag.

> kidnapped from Wonderie Land around 3:30 p.m. If anyone knows anything, please, PLEASE, contact the police. We're absolutely devastated and want nothing more than to bring Summer home. Volunteers who want to help the search party can join us at Frontier Park.

I hit Post, then lean forward and cry into my knees.

NINE

NINETEEN HOURS, THIRTY MINUTES GONE

It's impossible, but somehow the minutes pass. Lolly got here not long after the news hit the TV.

"Why didn't you tell me?" she blubbered, bursting through the door without knocking and catching me as I fell into her arms. Her familiar scent was comforting. We've been each other's support through so many ups and downs. But nothing like this. Nothing this horrific.

In the past two hours, she's done a load of laundry and picked up the basement littered with kids' toys. Aside from filling in as housekeeper, she's barely left my side as we drift through the day.

After Wade caught me smoking on the porch, he left to join the search party. We'd agreed to take turns so that one of us was always home with the kids. My skin itches waiting for him to come back so it can be my turn. If anyone can find a missing child, surely it would be their mother. My heart will lead me to her, I just know it.

I get another late-morning update from Detective Smart—they're still pursuing the person of interest—and I call for the second time an hour later but the desk attendant says Smart can't come to the phone. How can the parents of a missing five-year-old possibly be turned away?

"I'm sure they're wrapped up in the search," Lolly offers, but it does little to quell my irritation.

I huff and pull out a notebook. The word BLESSED is printed in all caps across the front, a sick contradiction. I flip to a clean page. If we're not going to be included in the investigation, I'll start my own. My hand moves furiously across the page, making a list of possibilities for the kidnapper's identity. Anything that comes to mind, I write down. Sometimes, I'll be staring off into space when a new idea hits me, and I hurriedly scratch it onto the page in messy scrawl.

A woman strung out on drugs.

A female psychopath.

Someone who's going to ask us for ransom.

Then I get to the hard stuff:

Pedophiles.

Sex trafficking.

I gag. Lolly pulls the notebook away.

When my parents call to say they're on their way back to our house, I turn them around. I appreciate their drop-everything intentions, but the house already feels like it's shrinking with just the four of us plus Lolly. I'm terrified of being alone, but also cringe at the thought of being around any more people asking questions and wiping sad eyes. Mom sounds unsure, but I insist. We'll see them tomorrow. I'm headed shortly to the park not far from Wonderie Land, where the search party has set up.

.   .   .

Around one, Wade returns.

"How was it? Did anyone find anything?" I blurt the second he walks through the door.

He shakes his head without a word, then wanders aimlessly into the other room. Where is his emotion?

With me switching places with Wade, Lolly leaves to go home to her own family—all members present. I walk out with her, calling goodbye to Wade over my shoulder. It's sprinkling, and tiny beads of water settle on my eyelashes.

"I'll be there in a couple hours, okay?" Lolly says, giving me a hug.

"Thanks, Lol."

She pulls out of the driveway and I follow. We split at the end of the street—Lolly heading further into the subdivision, and me making a beeline for the big, grassy park near the bay. With every passing block, my heart feels heavier, burdened by the weight of uncertainty and fear. The sky grows darker with an incoming storm cloud. I can't help but notice the similarity within my own body. Anxiety swirls like a relentless squall, each thundering crack another jab to the chest. I have to remind myself to breathe—in through the nose, out through the mouth. It's the only way I can keep myself from falling apart. I can't afford to lose it right now. A mighty determination keeps me focused. We're going to find her.

When I turn into the lot at Frontier Park, a small gasp escapes my lips. There must be a hundred people here. Tents have been erected. Dozens of cars fill the lot. A man in an orange vest with reflective trim waves me forward, indicating where I should park. I follow his lead, come to a stop, and get out. It's fully raining now. In my haste to leave, I neglected to grab a hat or jacket.

I walk toward what appears to be the main tent, looking for

Detective Smart or Ocho or someone I know. As I get closer, the crowd parts, people stepping back like the parting of the Red Sea to let me through. Either they think I'm a person of importance, or they consider me cursed, a leper they don't want to be near. I keep my eyes focused straight ahead.

At the tent, I approach a man in a windbreaker and ball cap holding a clipboard and talking as though giving orders.

"I'm Greta," I say.

He stares at me for a beat, then extends his hand. "Greta, I'm Dan Shaer, the search coordinator. It's nice to meet you. We've got groups of about five or six people out in a few different areas." He shows me a map fixed to the clipboard. On it, a zoomed-in view of Erie is divided into grids. "I'm just about to send this group east along the shoreline." He gestures to a handful of people standing together a few feet away. "Want to jump in with them?"

"Yes. Absolutely."

"Perfect. Here's a poncho. It's really starting to come down."

To anyone else, the comment might be flippant—just a walk out in the rain—but my mind goes instantly to my daughter who is out there somewhere. Is she being poured on? Is her skin becoming waterlogged?

Stop it, Greta. You will find her.

I slip the poncho on, pull the hood up over my head, and approach the group of three men and two women. I become the sixth.

"I'm Greta," I say again.

One woman turns and shoots me a sharp look that takes me aback. "We know who you are." I freeze, stunned by the coldness in her voice. She turns away from me again and addresses one of the men. "We better get going."

What the hell was that?

We start out on foot heading north through the park and a

bit of housing to the shoreline, where we'll turn east. We walk in a line like a human chain the way I've seen in movies, and I can't believe this is really happening. With each step, it feels more and more like a dream. There's not a whole lot of talking. Every once in a while, the lead man's walkie-talkie will crackle with static or a message from headquarters. Each time, my heart stops for a beat, thinking it will be someone saying they've found her.

Lake Erie comes into view, and our group turns to head up the shore. It's dense with trees and shrubbery in this part, and so our chain breaks. The unfriendly woman takes the lead with the man. I fall back, less concerned about her than finding my daughter. The ground has turned to mud. Our sneakers slosh and creak against sticks and twigs. A squirrel scurries up a tree and disappears into a hole. Everything around us is alive. I feel the beating pulse of nature, and just pray Summer's heart is still beating too.

My eyes burn with strain. I'm not just looking, I'm *looking*. Hard, intense, and with a longing that no one else can possibly understand. More than once, I get choked up, and am grateful for the drum of rain to camouflage my whimpers.

"I'm Terry, by the way," says one of the men who's been walking nearest me. He's older, his hair salty-gray, age lines on his eyes and forehead.

"Thanks for being here," I reply. "I can't believe all the people who came out."

"We all want to help find your little girl."

I swallow hard. "Thank you."

"I can't imagine what this must be like for you. A parent's worst nightmare. Lots of support here for you guys."

I remember the mean woman's earlier comment, the disdain with which she gave me a once-over. My eyes instinctually flick in her direction.

Terry catches me looking and flaps his hand dismissively. "Don't pay that any attention. Of course you should be here."

I'm resigned to silence. If I continue speaking, I'll crumble, and right now I need to be strong despite the immense helplessness that threatens to overtake everything.

"You know," Terry says a moment later as we continue walking, "I remember a time when I was hiking in the mountains with my kids. They're grown now, this was ages ago. We got caught in a sudden thunderstorm, and visibility dropped to almost nothing. I was scared, Greta. Scared that we wouldn't make it back to safety. But then, I realized that even in the midst of the storm, there was a moment of clarity. A break in the clouds, a sense of direction. It reminded me that even in our darkest moments, there's always a glimmer of hope to guide us forward."

I choke on a sob and look away. All our faces are wet with rain, but mine is mixed with tears. Terry's message gives me the flash of hope I need. We push forward.

I have no gauge for how much distance we've covered. Miles? Feet? It could be either and both at the same time. The sky continues to darken in incremental shades of ash.

We've been out for nearly three hours when the lead man's walkie-talkie comes to life. I can't quite hear the speaker's words, but the man suddenly stops and turns back to me.

"Greta!" he yells, and my stomach falls to my feet. I stumble forward in a clumsy run, sneakers heavy, to meet him.

"What? What is it? Did they find something?"

"A hair bow. Pink."

A hair bow.

"Was Summer wearing a pink bow?" the man asks me, radio hovering next to his mouth, ready to respond.

My head whirls, thinking back to yesterday. She had on a

yellow tank top, that I'm sure. Little jean shorts. Slip-on sneakers. But her hair—how was her hair? My brain is a foggy mess. I'm going on two days without sleep. *Think*. Summer loves to wear bows. I often pull one side back and clip in a bow to keep the strands from her eyes. But is that what I did yesterday?

The man stares at me with big eyes, waiting for my response. This could be a major clue. I close my eyes and picture Summer on the carousel, walking with me hand in hand, the last glimpse of her at the table.

My body slumps. "No," I say. "She wasn't wearing a bow." The image is clear now. Summer's hair was in a ponytail. I'd pulled it back to be off her neck in the heat. But there was no bow. I'm certain.

The rest of my search group looks to one another, clear disappointment in the air. I almost want to apologize for letting them down, as though it were my fault for not putting a pink bow in Summer's hair yesterday.

Our leader speaks into his walkie-talkie. "Negative. The bow's not hers."

This non-clue feels like a massive blow. A surge of possibility, followed by a crash. I don't know how my feet will keep moving, but the group starts off again.

"Onward," Terry says, putting a gentle hand on my back.

We traipse up the shoreline for the next hour until another message comes through the radio.

"They're turning us back," the lead man says.

"Back? Why?" I say.

"The storm. Everyone was to report back by nine, but with the rain, visibility is less than usual. The police don't want anyone getting stuck out here."

But what if my daughter is stuck out here?

"I'm going to keep going," I say.

"I don't think that's a good idea. We left as a group, we're supposed to return as a group."

"No offense, but I don't think the rules apply here. I'm not going to stop searching just because of a little rain. Let me take your radio." I extend my hand, but he doesn't give it to me.

"Greta, we need to go back."

Rain comes in sideways. "You can. I'm staying. I'm going to find her."

We're standing in a circle, wet and tired, as the raindrops pummel the water, the sky and lake merging into one.

"Go," I say. "It's fine. I appreciate all your help, but—"

"We wouldn't even need to be out here if you'd kept an eye on your daughter," the nasty woman sneers. She glares at me with scorching eyes.

"That's enough, Beth," the man scolds.

I stare back, horrified and embarrassed by her cruelty. How could she say something like that to my face? If I wasn't so shocked, I'd pop her in the nose. *You know nothing.*

"Listen," our leader says, pumping his hands. "There are a lot of emotions flying around. But we all need to head back to the park. Dan called us in."

Terry steps toward me. "Greta, let's take a breather, okay? We can regroup with the rest of the search party and get some updates, hmm? We're not giving up."

But that's exactly what it feels like. I'm giving up.

He puts an arm over my shoulder and turns me around to return the way we came. By the time we get back to the makeshift headquarters, the sky is grim, starless. Just an ominous and unforgiving gray. Lolly is there. So is Officer Smart. She hands me a coffee in a paper cup, but I don't drink. Volunteers watch me, then quickly look away before our eyes meet. So many people, so many stares. And after what Beth said to me back there, I can't be sure what they're all thinking.

A woman with spiral curls piled on top of her head and blue enamel glasses perched on her nose approaches me. "Greta?"

she says. "My name's Nadine. I was wondering if I could talk to you for a min—"

I stop her. I'm far too tired for this. Too exposed. "Thank you so much for being here," I say, "but I can't really talk right now. I—"

"I'm a psychic, and—"

"I'm sorry. Now's not a good time." My mental capacity has hit zero. I wander away, searching for someone who can tell me something real. Psychics are no better than the hypnotist who performed during my freshman year of college and got the quarterback of the football team to quack like a duck onstage. A joke. It was all an act.

The crowd has dwindled, with only two dozen or so people remaining.

I text Wade:

Nothing.

The police officially call off the search for the night and I die a little more inside.

TEN

MONDAY: TWO DAYS GONE

I'VE LEARNED MORE DISTURBING INFORMATION OVER THE last two days than I've ever cared to know. For one, there are four hundred and fifty-two registered sex offenders living in Erie. The map on my computer screen is dotted with red location markers that overlap like clusters of mini balloons. I gawk at the screen. This can't be possible—four hundred and fifty-two registered sex offenders? I zoom in on the west side of the city, closer to where our neighborhood sits. There are far fewer, about ten red dots, but it makes me feel only mildly better. I'm stuck with that first three-digit number. Any one of those four hundred-plus people could have targeted Summer.

From there, I start digging. The surveillance footage showed Summer talking to a woman. Still a surprise to me. I narrow my search to females. The list trims by ninety percent. Forty-three women remain. Just as I'm about to comb through, I'm momentarily halted by a perplexing thought. What if the woman who took Summer was simply a ruse? What if she was a middleman meant to snatch Summer more easily, only to pass her off to someone worse?

I shake my head. I can't fall down a rabbit hole of what-ifs. I have to start somewhere, and forty-three women is a far easier undertaking than the original list.

I scroll through the page, looking at faces, reading their identifying information, a one-sentence summary of their crimes. My lips curl as I read, and soon I'm snarling at the screen, disgusted by these criminals. Anger boils under my skin. How can anyone do such terrible things?

After seeing the surveillance footage for myself, I know what I'm looking for: the woman on the tape was average height and weight, maybe even on the smaller side. Despite the grainy image, the hair that stuck out from under her hat appeared light, so unless she wore a wig, I know I'm not looking for a brunette.

I keep scrolling, carefully studying the information and passing by suspects who don't fit. And then I stop on a listing for a woman named Nicole Pella. It's such a pretty name, it seems odd to see it in such a disturbing place. In her mug shot, Nicole's light hair frames her sunken eyes. She's plain-looking, but I think she could be attractive with hair and makeup. I fleetingly imagine what her life was like before it turned wrong. She could have been a schoolteacher, or a nurse, or worked behind the desk of an office I frequented.

Something about Nicole Pella's image prevents me from scrolling on. The page lists her address as Forrest Drive. My heart stops. Forrest Drive is no more than a stone's throw from Wonderie Land. My whole body tingles in the way it does when it's trying to tell me something. The more I stare at the screen, the more convinced I become that Nicole Pella was the woman on the surveillance footage. It has to be her. Petite. Blonde hair. Criminal history. Living within a mile of Wonderie Land. It makes perfect sense.

This woman took my daughter.

I scribble her information into my notebook, along with a million other possibilities just in case. Within an hour, I have three pages of ideas hastily scratched onto the lined paper. I call the station and ask for Detective Smart. This time, she gets on.

"Hello, Mrs. Goodman. What can I do for you?"

I blink. *What can you do for me?* It's the most absurd question, the formality smacking me in the face.

"I've been thinking," I say fast, as if there's a time limit for me to get this all out, "about who the woman might be, why she would want to take Summer." I decide to start with my alternative possibilities, afraid of what Smart will say if she knew I was digging through the sex offender registry.

"Did you interview all of the employees?" I continue. "What if she works at the park but just changed out of her uniform? We should look into all of them, you know. I don't care if they have clean records, you never really know. If it wasn't any of the park staff, then that means it was a guest. Did you pull transactions? An adult coming to an amusement park by themselves is pretty strange, right? Like, hello—red flag. And who would take a child if they already had kids with them? So we should see if anyone saw a single person walking around. Oh! Or, what if they have a season pass? Then there would be a photo on file. I was also thinking that maybe—"

"Mrs. Goodman," Smart stops me.

I'm out of breath. "Yes?"

"Thank you so much for all of this. We will certainly consider all these lines of investigation. And yes, our team has already looked into many of the points you brought up. We put out a BOLO to all agencies in a three-hundred-mile radius."

"A BOLO?"

"Be on the lookout."

My armor cracks. My voice elevates. "Then why haven't you found her? Why is she still missing?"

"We're working around the clock. We're doing everything in our pow—"

"Put the woman's picture out to the public! Someone has to know her."

"It's not a good picture, Mrs. Goodman. It would be very difficult to identify someone from the footage we have. And on top of that, it's risky."

"Risky?"

"Releasing suspect images can spook perpetrators. We want to make sure Summer is as safe as possible."

Now I feel like I have to pull out my trump card. "Have you searched the sex offender registry? Because I was on it this morning and there are four hundred and fifty-two registered sex offenders in Erie. I filtered out the men since we're looking for a woman, right? And there were still forty-something, but one in particular caught my eye. Her name's—"

"Mrs. Goodman, let me stop you for a second. I understand it's difficult to feel like you're not doing anything, but trust me, it's not a good idea to start your own investigation. Yes, we always take the registry into account in cases like this."

"Her name's Nicole Pella and—"

"We'll be sure to look into it."

Every time she cuts me off, my irritation grows. It's like she's placating me. Like I'm a child she has to deal with. I won't be brushed off, not when the stakes are this high.

"Well, I just think that if you—"

"I promise we—"

This time I cut her off. "Why won't you let me help?" I say, voice elevated on the verge of yelling. "You say you're doing everything to make sure Summer is as safe as possible, but she isn't safe as long as she's not ho—"

Wade appears out of nowhere, grabs the phone from my hand, and puts it to his ear.

"Detective Smart? This is Wade. Yes. Yes, thank you. We understand. Mmhmm, okay. Goodbye." He hangs up.

"Why did you do that?" I hurl, mouth agape.

"Berating the people who are trying to help isn't going to make this any better."

"I wasn't berating! I was offering my ideas. Any little bit helps, Wade! They could have hopped a boat and crossed the lake to Canada for all we know. This woman—this Nicole Pella —she fits the description."

"Who the hell is Nicole Pella?"

"She's a registered sex offender who happens to live half a mile from Wonderie Land, and who *also* happens to look exactly like the woman in the video."

"And you know this how?"

"Because I searched the registry and found her."

"Greta," he breathes. "Don't torture yourself like this." He walks away with a sigh. I watch him go, my face twisted in a question mark. It's like he doesn't even realize his child is *missing*. He's constantly wandering from room to room in seemingly pointless fashion. Each time he passes by me, my blood grows a degree hotter. *Would you stop pacing and help me?*

I return to the table with my computer and a one-track focus. There has to be something I can do, something I can find. If not, powerlessness will destroy me.

ELEVEN

FIVE HOURS AND FOURTEEN OPEN BROWSER TABS LATER, the doorbell rings. Panic shoots to my toes, and I slam the lid closed. Not the damn reporters again. They finally left, and now they're back. I can't handle this. They have no right to waltz up to our house and interrogate us like we're some sort of criminals. Can't they imagine the agony we're in? And they want to capitalize on it?

Not today. My already-thin patience just snapped.

I stomp to the door and whip it open. "What do you WANT?"

But it's not the reporters. There are no cameras in my face. Instead, a woman named Brynn from Wade's office stands holding a tray covered in aluminum foil.

"It's lasagna," she says, face flushed from my verbal attack.

"Oh, Brynn. I'm sorry. I thought you were—"

"It's okay. I wasn't going to stay. Just wanted to drop this off." Her heart-shaped face is accented by her Cupid's bow lips that shine in pale pink gloss. I've always thought she was the prettiest woman in Wade's office.

I rake a hand through my hair, scratching my scalp. It

desperately needs washing. Brynn extends the tray, and I take it. "Thank you."

"How are the kids? Wade?"

"We're... we're hanging in there."

I'm dying.

Brynn sways awkwardly. "I can't imagine what you're going through." There are tears in her eyes, and I have the sudden instinct to reach out and embrace her, as though it were her daughter missing and not mine. She sniffles. "Summer is... I mean, you know we all love the kids."

"I know."

"If there's anything we can do... The office staff is putting together a meal train."

"That's thoughtful. Thank you." Food is essential, but there's nothing more anyone can do. It's like the sentiment of *thoughts and prayers* after a school shooting—they do very little.

Brynn steps forward and pulls me into a one-arm hug, the lasagna wedged between us. It surprises me—I don't know this woman more than from company picnics and the occasional visit to Wade's office.

"Please keep me updated," she says, and I nod. "Anything you need, okay? Just call. And please tell Wade we're thinking of him."

She backtracks down the steps toward her car. I close the door and carry the lasagna to the kitchen, where Wade is drinking his fourth coffee of the day.

"That was Brynn," I say, pulling back the foil to take a look at the meal. Steam floats out.

"Brynn?"

"She brought lasagna." The smell of garlic and tomato sauce hits my nose and my stomach talks back. Suddenly, I'm ravenous. Two days of not eating has caught up to me. I look to Wade. "Still warm."

"I'll get plates," he replies.

Merritt and Gus join us at the table, the four of us a sad sight. I shovel lasagna into my mouth, taste buds exploding, stomach thanking me. Yet with every bite, I barely hold it down. Enjoying a meal feels like the ultimate betrayal of Summer. Is she eating, wherever she is? I can't possibly satisfy my own bodily needs if I'm unsure hers are being met.

Around the table is much of the same. Wade takes a few bites, then brings a knuckle to his mouth and looks away. Merritt and Gus are quiet, eating but only out of necessity. I keep my eyes low. This food is a business transaction, a source of vital energy I need to keep up the search for Summer.

At some point, the kids leave the table. I never even hear them go. Their empty plates are on the counter by the sink. Merritt probably returned to her room, and Gus—to be honest, I don't even know what he's been doing the last twenty-four hours. It's easy for him to disappear into the background.

Wade pushes away from the table and starts toward the living room.

"Don't worry, I'll clean up," I say, sarcasm dripping with each word. He doesn't turn around, and that makes my blood boil even more. I cover the remaining lasagna and put it in the fridge, then move to the sink to tackle the dishes. Fury travels through my hands as I scrub, dropping plates into the dishwasher with little care how they land.

I'm a walking time bomb as I enter the living room and find Wade staring out the window. I plant my feet and cross my arms tight across my chest.

"What is wrong with you?" I hurl.

Wade turns, and the look on his face knocks a peg from my pillar of rage. His face is stern, all hard lines and flared nostrils. "What do you think's wrong with me?"

"I don't know, you've barely said two words since the park. You're a zombie. It's like you aren't even concerned that our daughter is missing."

He steps forward with a finger pointed like a dagger. "Don't you dare."

"What?" I ask, my tone accusing. "I'm the one trying to come up with ideas. I'm the one calling the station for updates."

"I'm trying to let the police do their jobs. They said so themselves—us getting involved could actually hurt the investigation, not help it."

"So you're just going to sit around doing nothing? Sorry, buddy, but that's not happening with me." My arms flail. "I'll search all goddamn night. I'll traipse through every street, every chunk of woods in this town. That's what a mother does."

"Do not call me a bad father," he snarls.

"I didn't say you were."

"You insinuated it." Wade paces, chest heaving. "Just because I'm not barging down to the police station demanding answers doesn't mean I'm not fucking destroyed inside, okay? My little girl is gone, and I've spent the last two days wishing I could go back and change it. None of this had to happen. If you hadn't—"

He stops. So does my heart. The room is dead quiet, save for his ragged breaths.

"If I hadn't what?" I say, voice low and steady.

"Nothing."

"No, say it." A thousand needles prick my body.

Wade turns to me, eyes as black as a shark's. Our gazes are locked. I know what's going to come out before his lips even part.

"Say it," I repeat. A challenge. *Do it, I know you want to. It's what you've been thinking since the beginning.*

His hands clench into fists at his sides. "If you hadn't made us go on that ride, Summer would still be here."

The air doesn't move, and yet I feel like I've been blown off my feet. Wade's eyes don't leave mine. There's a bitterness, a loathing there that I've never seen before and have certainly never been on the receiving end of. My legs feel weak.

"You're not a child, Wade. I didn't force you onto that ride."

"It was your idea."

"And you came willingly."

"I didn't want to! I'm the one who said it wasn't a good idea. But you said it would be fine, and now look what's happened."

Heat burns in my face. "How dare you put this on me. Sorry I wanted to have five minutes of something for myself. God, you have no fucking idea what it's like. You get to go to work, come home, have dinner, and go to bed. When was the last time you took a sick kid to the doctor? Do you know what it's like not to speak to someone over the age of five all day long, every day?"

Wade rolls his head. "Oh, here we go with the bad dad stuff again."

"That's not the point. The point is that you don't understand. It wasn't about the stupid rollercoaster, Wade. It was about reclaiming myself. Reclaiming *us*. I didn't think it would end up like this. Never in a million years. Merritt's always been attentive when we've asked. Only this time..."

Wade's face goes even redder. "Merritt's just a kid, for Christ's sake." His words hiss like a snake spitting venom. "It wasn't her responsibility to parent her siblings."

"But it was!" I say, voice elevating. "I asked her to watch them, and she didn't." Even as I say it, I hear how absurd it sounds.

"This is not her fault."

"Of course I know it's not *entirely* her fault."

"Do you? Because you've barely been able to look at her since it happened."

I avert my eyes. "That's bullshit."

It's not bullshit.

A tiny cry pierces the room, making both of us spin. Merritt sits halfway down the steps, hands clutching the banister rungs. Tears pour down her pale face.

Shit.

"Merritt," I say, taking a step and extending an arm out toward her. But she crawls back up the stairs in a flash.

"Nice work," Wade says, and I meet his face with my own look of horror. A tidal wave of guilt crashes over me.

What have I done?

TWELVE

"I'M GOING TO GO SHOWER," WADE SAYS. WE'VE BEEN standing here in the living room for several tense seconds since Merritt overheard our argument and fled to her room. The exchange ceased in that moment, though resentment hangs heavy in the air, and I sense both of us have more to say.

This isn't us, I want to shout at him. We don't argue. This whole thing—the park, the disappearance, this confrontation—is a major crack in our mostly happy marriage. Sure, I find motherhood overwhelming from time to time, and yes, I sometimes dream of going back to work and regaining balance in my life. What mom doesn't? But it's never boiled over like this, and I'm struck with wondering whether the kidnapping is a catalyst for feelings that were already there.

I peer at Wade from the corner of my eye. Who is this couple that speaks with such spite? Certainly not the Wade and Greta I thought we were. When we met in college, it was his openness I was drawn to first—his shy smile lending warmth to his earnest features. I showed him all of Erie's popular spots, from the beaches at Presque Isle to 8 Great Tuesdays street fairs in the summertime, to wine tours in the vineyards of North

East. It didn't take long for us to become exclusive as a couple, and I spent more time in his dorm room than I did in my own. My parents instantly loved him. One week before graduation, he asked my dad's permission to marry me, and we got hitched a year later. He was my forever, the easiest choice I'd ever made. Unlike some of our friends' marriages which have already ended, ours has held strong for the last seventeen years. Until now.

As Wade climbs the stairs, I picture him going to Merritt. Holding her in his lap. All things that I should be doing. A mother's job. But I just can't.

I let him take the win.

My eyes drift to a collage of framed photos on the wall. Among them is a family shot from a few years back. We'd splurged for a professional photographer—our family was complete, and I'd wanted to capture it in time. It wasn't long before then that Wade and I had found ourselves in a rough patch. Life with little ones was hard; we barely had enough energy for a peck on the lips before crashing into bed. I'd even had thoughts that surely he'd leave me for a better version— someone skinnier, more fun. Someone who didn't smell like baby spit-up. But we'd come through, and cementing ourselves in full color through the lens of a camera surely meant every-thing was going to be okay.

I stare at the photo. Toddler Summer perches on my hip, a sprout of hair coming from the top of her head, her little hand grasping the collar of my shirt. Wade is at my side, tall and proud, while Merritt and Gus fill in the center front. We were the picture-perfect family, so much so that the photographer used our photo in her advertising. "Celebrating life's beautiful moments," the social media ads said. "#Goals," someone had commented.

I'd felt so proud.

I study my own face in the picture. I'd tried to cover the

dark circles under my eyes with makeup that day. Summer had been the earliest riser, our days starting hours before anyone else. I never felt rested. I remember thinking the months and years would only get easier as the kids grew. *You're in the thick of it now. Hold on. It gets better.*

The woman in the picture was so naïve. She thought she was immune to tragedy.

Upstairs, I hear the water turn on. I peer out the front window, as if I'll see Summer walking across the lawn. For a second, I think I do, and then realize it's nothing more than a mirage. I'm so tired. My mind is playing tricks.

The sky changes color. The sun is going to bed, closing the book on another day. My chest aches. Another day without Summer.

I stand there for who knows how long, lost in thought, until I realize the shower's no longer running. The house is quiet, but my brain is in the middle of an orchestra pit. I climb the stairs with heavy feet. Past the kids' bathroom, where the sink is perpetually streaked in blue toothpaste stains. Our room is in the middle, and I thank God that I don't have to pass Summer's to get there.

But first, I come to Merritt's. The door is closed. I pause and place my palm on it, as though it's my daughter's chest and I'm feeling for her heartbeat to connect us again. I press the door open.

"Mer?"

She's buried in her covers. I hear a sniffle from underneath.

"I don't want to talk," she says, voice muffled.

Guilt nips at my ribcage. I back from the room, knowing full well forcing her into a conversation she doesn't want to have will end up pushing us further apart.

"I'm sorry," I whisper, unsure whether she hears me. It's all I can give in this moment.

When I make it to my room, Wade is climbing into bed, his

hair damp. It smells clean in here, like the scent of mint shampoo mixed with fresh laundry. I go into the bathroom, come to my sink, and really stare at my reflection for the first time since Summer has been gone. I'm startled by the woman I see in the mirror—harsh lines, bloodshot eyes. My face is haggard.

Without a word, I close the bathroom door and strip out of my clothes. As I do, it's as if I'm peeling the amusement park from my body. I step into the shower and crank it all the way hot. The water burns my skin, but I let it. *Char me*. I lean my head under the flow. Streams hug the curves of my face, traveling around my nose, across my lips. If I open my mouth and let it fill up my lungs, will I drown?

I turn so the water hits my back, and slowly—so slowly—inch my way down until I'm sitting on the tile floor. I pull my knees into my chest and hug them, pretending it's Summer I'm hugging. And there, in that moment of private abandon, I sob for the first time.

THIRTEEN

TUESDAY: THREE DAYS GONE

MY EYES FLY OPEN AND I JUMP OUT OF BED AS THOUGH there's a fire. Daylight brightens our room even though the overhead light is still off. What time is it? How long did I sleep? I check the clock on my nightstand. Nine. I blink. I slept for twelve hours.

I check my phone, praying I've missed a call from Detective Smart. There has to have been an update. The screen is filled with messages, but nothing from her. My shoulders wilt.

The other side of the bed is empty, the covers replaced from where Wade must have slipped out before I woke. I hear the sound of china clinking in the kitchen downstairs. The rich aroma of coffee has wafted its way up and tickles my nose. It would be a lovely gesture—Wade making me coffee—if it weren't for the fact that our lives have been upended. Any other Tuesday, he'd already be at work and I'd be whisking pancake mix for three hungry mouths before shuffling them off to end-of-summer camp. There's no rhyme or reason to today—we're so off-kilter.

I slide my feet into shearling slippers and tread down the stairs. Merritt and Gus are on their tablets, something I'd normally scoff at so early in the morning, but today I can't muster the energy.

"Mom," Gus says, looking up from his game, "you didn't tuck me in last night."

My mind travels in reverse through time. Last night—the argument, Merritt, me crumbling in the shower. I'd gone straight to bed afterward, my eyelids unable to hold themselves up another second.

"Sorry, bud," I say without stopping. *Why couldn't Dad tuck you in?*

I go into the kitchen, where Wade is emptying the dishwasher.

"Hey," he says.

"Hey."

"Coffee's fresh." He hands me a mug straight from the dishwasher. I take it.

It's not an apology, but it's all we can manage. Things are not forgiven. What he said last night, the blame he threw in my face, stung pretty bad. He can't even look at me for more than a second. Resentment lurks under the surface of his now-calm demeanor. I wonder if it will ever fade, or if this is a nail in our coffin.

"Have you heard from Detective Smart?" I ask, feeling out his interest in talking. Maybe Smart called him instead of me. Maybe he's heard something I haven't.

"No."

I groan and press the sides of my head like a vice. "I can't stay in this house another day. I'm going out."

"And do what?"

"I don't know." I smack a hand on the counter. "Join the search party again, form my own... something! Aren't you going crazy here?"

Wade rubs the back of his neck with his hand. "I think one of us should stay here with the other two."

I nod. "That's fine. We can switch."

It's a temporary truce. Something tells me last night's conversation isn't finished, but for now, it's a new day and that means refocusing on Summer. I don't have time for marriage problems. I have to find my daughter.

I take my coffee back upstairs where I toss on joggers and a T-shirt, and pull my wavy ponytail through a baseball cap. Summer always used to tell me I looked pretty in a hat, at which I'd laugh—hats were for days I *didn't* feel pretty. I wonder if this was part of what drew Summer to the woman at the park. She'd worn a hat too. Maybe Summer felt a sense of comfort in that. Something familiar.

On the way out the door, I say goodbye to Gus and Merritt. "Dad's staying with you guys. I'll be back soon."

There's a sadness in Merritt's eyes, but I don't stay long enough to let it more than linger in my conscience. Ours is another conversation that has been left unresolved, saved for another time.

I look left and right before I back into the street. Next door, Alice Campbell waters the flowers on her front porch. She does a double take when our eyes meet, then quickly looks away. A pang hits my chest. Not even a wave?

My eyes dance frantically as I drive, so much so that I'm probably a hazard on the road. My attention is everywhere but ahead of me. Erie is in its busy morning bustle, and traffic is slow on 26th Street. A small jet flies overhead, nearing the airport a few blocks north. All around me, people go about their days, and I can't help but wonder how. *Don't you know there's a child missing?*

The light turns red and I slam on the brake at the last second, nearly rear-ending the car in front of me. It's like I haven't driven in years. Like I can't perform the most fundamental tasks.

To my right is a large plaza with a supermarket and string of shops. We got the kids' backpacks from a boutique here, had their monograms embroidered on the front pockets. Summer's hangs in her bedroom, brand-new and ready to start the school year. I avert my eyes, trying to focus on something else.

A man on the corner waits for the light to change. He presses the crosswalk button with impatience. *Relax*, I want to say. *Your life can't be that bad.* A sign on the street pole next to him catches my eye. I look closer, and a chill sweeps over me. It's a missing person poster with Summer's picture centered on the page. The photo I gave the police.

My child. On a missing person poster. I wonder who hung it. Detective Smart? One of the volunteers from the search party?

A loud honk zaps me back. Traffic is moving. I let off the brake, watching the sign pass by my window like a surreal dream.

I continue on, still unsure exactly where I'm going or what I'm doing. Half of my brain focuses on the road while the other pings back and forth, searching yards, cross streets, parking lots for a flash of red hair I'd know in a heartbeat.

After heading east toward town for several streetlights, it hits me. Of course. Subconsciously, I knew where I was going before I even left the house. Now I'm sure. Forrest Drive. Nicole Pella. I can't get her out of my head, and if Detective Smart isn't going to pursue her as a lead, then I will.

I make a U-turn at an auto body shop and reverse course before turning north toward the neighborhoods near Wonderie Land. It only takes five or so minutes and I'm there. I've never driven through this particular area. The street is narrow with no markings, a tight sidewalk cutting through yards and the thin strip of grass that edges the road.

I slow my pace, eyeing the numbers on the houses until I come to the address that's seared in my brain. It's a small, cottage-style house, nondescript in every way, with white shutters a contrast to the dull gray siding. The concrete driveway is uneven, but there's a colorful garden flag stuck into the dried-out mulch that tells me someone's tried to put forth some effort.

I stop the car in front of the house. My empty stomach turns, and I feel like I could be sick even though there's nothing to throw up. As I reach for the door handle, I hear Detective Smart's voice in my head. *It's not a good idea to start your own investigation.* I look to the house. *But what if Summer is in there?*

I get out on shaky legs but with a purpose that makes me feel as strong as a bull. Nothing will stop me from doing everything in my power to find my daughter.

As I round the front of my car, I look up and down the street. It's quiet. A workday. Does Nicole Pella have a job? Or like so many other sex offenders, is she unable to get hired? I make my way up the drive and across a brick walkway to the front door. My heart thuds in my chest. I pray she's home. I feel like I'll know the minute she opens the door whether she holds the answer, whether Summer is tucked away within these walls.

I ring the doorbell, then shove my hands in my armpits to keep from shaking. I wait, but no one comes. There's a window next to the door, and I lean to look through but the curtain is too thick to see anything. I press the bell again. Five seconds. Ten. *Dammit.* Just as I'm giving myself a morale boost—*Don't worry, Nicole Pella, I'll be back*—the door cracks open. Half of a woman's face is visible through the slit. I pounce.

"Are you Nicole Pella?"

"Who's asking?"

It's in this moment I realize I don't have a plan for getting information out of this woman. Maybe I should have concocted a story. But there's no time for that. I know it's her because I recognize her from the photo on the registry website.

"Have you seen this girl?" I say, unfolding a picture of Summer I've started carrying with me. I hold it up at eye level.

"That's the girl that went missing from the park?"

"Yes. She's my... Have you seen her?" I'm no detective, but I'm convinced I'll be able to spot a lie. I lock eyes with Nicole, refusing to let go.

"No," she says. Then a cloud crosses her face. "Why are you here?"

I steady my voice. "I know about your history."

She flushes. "You have no right coming to my home. Please leave." She starts to shut the door, but my arm shoots out, holding it open.

"Do you have my daughter in there?"

Nicole's face reads pure terror. "I don't know what you're talking about. No, I don't have your daughter."

I press against the door, fighting to keep it open as hard as Nicole fights to shut it in my face. "Summer!" I shout. "Summer!"

"You're crazy! I didn't take your daughter! Get out of here!"

She opens the door far enough to stick an arm out and shove me backward. And then a voice calls from the house next door. I look to see a woman on the front stoop, phone in hand. "You okay, Nicole?" a large woman in a nightgown says. "Want me to call the cops?"

I right myself, looking between Nicole and this woman who's got fifty pounds on me.

"We're good," Nicole replies. Then to me in a low hiss, "Get the hell off my property."

I falter back, feet clumsy, eyes still intently focused on the house I thought held my daughter. She could still be in there. I could barge through and find her.

Nicole shuts the door and I hear it lock. I wait.

"I don't need Nicole's permission to call," the neighbor woman says, threatening me with her phone.

I retreat to my car and land in the front seat with a thump. Adrenaline pumps through me so hard and fast I shake. I'm not convinced Nicole Pella told me the truth. Felons are criminals. They lie, they cheat... they steal.

But I don't need to go to jail today. That wouldn't help the case. And so I pull away from the house, heading toward the police station. I might not be able to get into that house, but I know who can.

FOURTEEN

Fifteen minutes later, I pull into the station. My body tingles as I walk through the doors.

"I'm here to see Detective Smart," I tell the receptionist at the front desk. She's older than me, hair pulled into a low bun. Her eyes narrow, and I swear I see her lips purse.

"Just a minute," she says. I wait, and then she's back. "Come on through." She buzzes me in with an unfriendly expression.

Before I can take three steps, Smart is here. "Mrs. Goodman," she says, and she too wears a look of irritation. Her face is pinched, not soft like that first day. "We need to talk."

Smart leads me toward a small room with a table and four chairs. One side of the room is all glass windows, which looks out to an open area with a bulletin board and a long table covered in papers. On the board is a map of Erie, areas of the city sectioned off in colored tape.

Search areas. It reminds me of the map on the search coordinator's clipboard.

Detective Smart pulls out a chair, but I don't sit. Her arms are folded across her chest. "Did I or did I not say we were pursuing every lead?"

I pause for a beat before answering. "Yes."

"And did I or did I not advise you not to conduct your own investigation?"

Shit.

My chest gets hot. What does she know? "Yes."

"Then why did I just receive a call only minutes before you arrived from a woman who says you trespassed on her property and accused her of kidnapping your daughter?"

My hands flail and I can feel every defense mechanism in my body on high alert. "I told you about that woman I saw on the sex offender registry. Something about her just struck me. I had a feeling and—"

"You had a feeling?"

"Yes! Mother's instinct, whatever you want to call it. I had to go there. I had to see for myself if she had Summer."

Detective Smart drops her head then looks back at me. "Mrs. Goodman, you can't do that."

"But she's a sex offender! And she matches the woman on the tape!"

"That doesn't mean you can go to her house and attack her."

"I didn't lay a hand on her! Is she saying I—"

Smart shakes her head. "No. But verbal attacks can be considered slander. Defamation of character."

"You're worried about me defaming the character of a *registered sex offender*?"

"That's not the point. The law is the law. And I specifically asked you to let us do our jobs. Do you want to cause more trouble for yourself?" Her expression is hard, her frustration toward me apparent. I feel like a student being reprimanded by the teacher. But the scolding isn't enough. Give me detention. Suspend me. I'd do it all again. My arms tighten across my chest, a show of defiance. Doesn't she see my perspective? I'm convinced any mom would have done the same.

And yet, the woman before me is the drawbridge between

me and my daughter. Cross the line, and she could pull it up. Perhaps I need to play by her rules. A wash of defeat swamps me from head to toe. "I... I had to get out of the house. I just want to help. I want to do *something*."

Detective Smart's face softens again to the expression I remember from before. "I get it. Trust me, I do. Would it make you feel any better to know that we've already eliminated the majority of people from that list?"

"You have?"

"Yes. I'm not lying when I say we're working very hard."

"Well, what about Nicole Pella?"

"She has an alibi for Saturday. She was at work."

Something scratches at my insides. It can't be. This was supposed to be our answer. "But what if she's lying? Can't you check the house?"

"Detective Ocho is on his way there now. His primary goal is to convince her not to press harassment charges against you, but in addition to that, he's going to see if she'd be willing to let him look around."

Temporary relief replaces the defeat. "I saw a poster on my way here," I say. "With Summer's picture."

"Yes. Volunteers hung them all over town."

"Can I have some? I can hang them in new places. Or maybe drive further outside of town."

Smart gives me a gentle smile. "Sure. I can get some printed for you."

The stiffness in my body eases ever so slightly. I'm helping. I'm doing something.

"Have you searched Presque Isle?" I ask. "The beaches?"

The sandy peninsula that arches into Lake Erie is a popular local and tourist attraction. In addition to a string of beaches, the state park contains hiking trails and woodland that is dense in certain areas. The kidnapper could have easily escaped into the brush. It might have been a good hiding spot.

However, what I'm really thinking when I mention Presque Isle is the water. I shiver. I can't get myself to say it. *Are you searching the water?*

"Our teams are scouring a ten-mile radius from the park, so yes, that includes the peninsula."

"And what about…" I make a swooping motion with my hand, as though it were diving into the lake.

"The scuba team has been called."

I take a gulp of air, then cough, choking on my own breath. A sob slips out. "Sorry, I…" I blubber.

Detective Smart places a hand on my back. She conjures a cup of water and slides it in front of me. "Here. Take a minute." Her face is soft. Aside from earlier, she's never raised her voice to me, never made me feel like I'm wasting her time. It must be exhausting conducting an investigation *and* dealing with over-whelmed parents.

Her phone rings and she answers it with a clipped, "Yep." I bring my hands to cover my mouth. It must be Ocho. "Okay," she says. "Yep. Got it." She hangs up and looks to me. "The house was empty."

I gape. "But… but… she must have moved her. She must have known the police would come."

Smart shakes her head sadly. "There was no evidence what-soever of Summer being there. I'm sorry, Mrs. Goodman."

I feel like I'm falling through the sky and crashing through a glass ceiling.

Smart gestures to the chair once more. "Please, have a seat."

I lower myself down, fold my hands on the table.

"I can't even begin to put myself in your shoes," she says. "The unknown, the waiting. The helplessness. I've worked several missing persons cases in the past, but it's always hardest when it's a child. I'm so sorry that you're going through this."

A lump forms in my throat at hearing the compassion in her voice. An unexpected wistfulness comes over me. I want to know this person who is in charge of my daughter's fate. "Do you have children, Detective Smart?"

"Two boys. Fourteen and seventeen."

"Older than mine."

"Kids are always your babies no matter how old they are."

I manage a weak smile. Tears are threatening, but I don't want to cry again. I want to show her I'm strong and capable of helping. I look down at my hands. Still, a surge of emotion is taking over. Detective Smart is the exemplar, a figure of good and justice. I don't know why I'm opening up to this woman, but I am. Maybe it's a need to be understood. To prove to her I'm not a bad mother.

"Do you remember what it was like when they were younger?" I say, voice trembling. "When their every need fell on you? How it was both the most beautiful and demanding thing you'd ever experienced?"

This is the gospel of every mother on Earth—my barest, most inner truth. We don't say it enough, don't dare utter it aloud for fear of backlash. Our Pinterest-driven existences revolve around keeping up with the Joneses, dedicating every waking moment to our offspring, sacrificing small pieces of ourselves. It's exhausting.

"Motherhood is the hardest job in the world," Smart replies, and right then, I imagine her packing lunches before buckling her duty belt. She is me. I am her.

Our eyes meet. We both give a slow nod.

"Trust me, Mrs. Goodman. I will find Summer."

"Promise?" I squeak.

"I promise."

FIFTEEN

Wade is out back pulling overgrown weeds from around the shed when I get home a little before noon.

"Seems crazy," he says, holding up a handful of greens, "but I had to get out of the house too."

I know what he means. We can only stay inside so long before our skin starts to crawl. Thankfully, the reporters can't get to us back here.

"Where did you go?" he says, and it feels like summarizing a five-hundred-page novel to bring him up to speed. My insides unfurl with the relief of letting someone else in on my day. I spit it out in one seemingly long breath, not stopping when his eyes grow.

"You went to her *house?*" he blurts. "Greta, are you crazy?"

"Not crazy, just desperate."

He's still looking at me like I'm nuts, and when he goes to say what I know will be another jab at my mental state, I cut him off. "Don't. Just don't."

He backs off, mouth tight like he's biting the words he wants to throw at me. Things are prickly between us, but we're functioning, knowing we have to.

I relay Smart's updates to Wade, which weren't many, but enough for us to hold onto. The ongoing search team progress, the missing person posters, the continuing interviews with possible witnesses. We're putting all our confidence on the enhanced surveillance footage—whenever that will come back. Smart said it could be any minute, and that she'd call us immediately.

Wade and I share another awkward minute, but with nothing else to say, I go into the house. Halfway through the kitchen, a voice startles me.

"Hi, Mom." Gus is at the table with a sloppy-looking peanut butter and jelly sandwich on a paper plate in front of him.

"Oh, hi, honey," I reply. I point to the sandwich, just then realizing it's lunchtime. "Did you... I mean, are you..."

"It's okay, I got it."

"Okay." I keep walking, relieved, as though making a peanut butter and jelly sandwich would unravel me.

Merritt is in the living room, tucked into the corner of the couch, eyes glued to her phone. My teeth immediately clench.

"Don't you think maybe you should take a break from that?" I say, trying to camouflage any annoyance. It's not the first time I've had the thought that if we hadn't got her that phone, none of this would have happened. Then I'm reminded of the truth—it was me who chose to leave them alone, phone or not. These two facts battle in my head.

"They're talking about us," Merritt says, thumb still scrolling.

"Who?"

"People. They're saying mean things about our family."

My patience goes out the window. "Merritt, you know you're not allowed on social media."

"I'm not," she says vehemently. "It's the news. I googled it. I wanted to know what's going on. The first headline was about

Summer, so I clicked on it, and there are all these comments at the end."

A sourness rolls in my stomach at the thought that my kids have been thrust into a new reality, far too dark, too weighty, for them. They should be thinking about the Scholastic book sale, not what people are saying about their missing sister.

"Give me the phone." I swipe it from her and look to the screen filled with comments on the article from AllNews24. The breath sucks from my lungs; the room goes hot.

DonnaB: *What kind of parents leave their young children unsupervised? SMH...*

BillsFan1: *Parents' fault 100%.*

mrrocknroll: *Hope the ride was worth it. Seriously, some people don't deserve to have kids.*

SkySky509: *Maybe if they wouldn't have given their kid a phone in the first place...*

I scroll. The comments go on and on. For every one expressing sympathy for our plight, another ten criticize us. At the very bottom of the page is a link with the sign-off, "For more on this story and all breaking news, head over to the AllNews24 Facebook page."

Unwisely, I click. Maybe there will be more theories I haven't considered.

One of the top posts is coverage of Summer's disappearance. I don't even read the article. Instead, I click directly on the comments and read furiously.

KatiesMom78: *What were these people thinking? Five years old is far too young to be left alone.*

There are thirty-four replies to this initial comment. My eyes can't move fast enough.

RobertaV: *Agree! They should be charged with neglect IMO.*

markmywords: *Completely irresponsible. The worst example of parenting I've ever seen.*

Naturegirlyyy: *My youngest is ten and I STILL wouldn't leave him by himself.*

ItsSusan: *Hello? Did any of you read the actual article? Her older siblings were with her.*

markmywords: *Oh, so now leave* three *kids in danger? Wow, parents of the year.*

4tuneteller: *Unpopular opinion: Eleven is old enough to babysit. My oldest watches her younger brother all the time.*

WeAre582: *Yeah, well, not when the babysitter is absorbed in a phone. If anyone was looking for more reason why kids should not have smartphones, here it is.*

markmywords: *THIS ^^^ Parents who give kids phones should be arrested.*

ItsSusan: *Were you there? Did you see her "absorbed" in her phone? None of us knows, so none of us should judge. Matthew 7:1*

Jessieinreallife: *Lol bringing God into it. The poor girl is prob with him right now.*

The room tilts and I grab onto the back of the recliner to steady myself. A sick feeling swirls in my stomach and I swallow hard to keep it down. The comments are savage. These people are having a dialogue about something they know nothing about.

"Are you okay?" Merritt says. "You're really white."

"Stay off the internet," I reply. "In fact, no more phone." I tuck it into my pocket.

"That's so unfair!"

I whip my head around. "You want to know what's unfair? Your sister is out there somewhere by herself. Someone took her. *That's* unfair. And you're going to sit here and whine about not having your phone?"

Merritt's face scrunches, as the ultra-sensitive preteen emotion floods in. I feel a twinge of sympathy, but it's buried in so much anger it doesn't have the might to reach the surface. Taking the phone from her is the right thing. I should have done it days ago. I'm protecting her from the hurtful words of strangers.

I storm from the room, leaving a shaken Merritt on the couch, and taking with me the continuous swirl of guilt for not being gentler. I hate this version of me. I stomp through the kitchen toward the back door. Wade should know about this. He should read what's being said.

"Hi, Mom."

I about leap out of my shoes. "Jesus, Gus. Quit scaring me like that."

"I haven't even moved," he says. The sandwich on his plate is half eaten. He stares at me. It's like his eyes are searching me for something. *What?* I want to say. *I'm sorry, but I don't have any of me to give to you right now.* "I have to talk to Dad," I say instead. He nods and returns to his lunch.

Outside, I approach Wade, phone extended in my hand. "Have you seen what they're saying about us?"

"Who?" He echoes the same sentiment I had only moments ago.

"Strangers online. They're slamming us for leaving the kids by themselves. Calling us unfit parents."

Wade shifts, and I can see the wheels in his head turning. The argument from last night works its way to the front of my mind.

"We're not bad parents," I say. "We're not." He doesn't speak. *You're supposed to agree here.* My defenses rise further. I put my hands on my hips. "Oh."

"What?"

"You think I'm a bad mom, don't you?"

He doesn't look at me. "I never said that."

"But you blame me. You said so yourself. If I hadn't had the idea to go on the ride..."

"Greta, let's not start this again."

I kick the grass. "Fuck them. They have no idea what it's like to be living this nightmare. The media should be focused on finding Summer, not persecuting us. All the attention is misplaced. Those people are like tiny martyrs behind their computer screens."

"So don't let it bother you."

"How can you be so calm about it? Doesn't it make you want to punch something?"

"Who says I haven't?"

I picture him going to town on his pillow late at night. Wade's sensibility makes me question everything. He's sane where I'm livid. Nothing is in my control—not the investigation, not public opinion, and not these online smear campaigns. I don't know how to fix anything. The uncertainty of it all claws at my brain. I want to pull my hair out. The only thing I feel I can do to stay on top of what's happening is to remain in close contact with the police. So, despite the fact that I was just there, I dial the direct number Smart gave me.

"Mrs. Goodman, hi," she says.

My words come out fast. "Hi. I know I was just at the station, but I figured I'd call to see if the video enhancement came back. You said it could be any time now." If anxiety had a voice, it would be mine. Now that Nicole Pella has been ruled out, I'm clinging once again to this. This image is our golden ticket. We identify the woman in the footage, we find Summer. I can't wait any longer.

"Actually, yes," Smart says, and I'm stunned, having fully expected her to come back with more of the same: *Wait. Be patient.*

"Oh my God," I say. I put my phone on speaker so Wade can hear. He stops what he's doing. His eyes are saucers. "Can you see her face? Can you tell who it is?"

Through the line I hear Smart sigh. "God, I'm sorry to have to deliver another piece of bad news. The resolution is still too low to tell. We were unable to get a clear picture. I'm afraid the enhancement is not much better than the original."

I drop to my knees and the phone falls to the ground. I can't. I just can't.

"Mrs. Goodman? Are you there?" Smart's voice is faint, calling for me.

I'm already gone.

SIXTEEN

WEDNESDAY: FOUR DAYS GONE

Four days without Summer. We've never been apart this long. Lolly's always harping about the importance of romantic getaways—she and her husband, Jake, go on vacation alone every year—but it just hasn't happened for me and Wade. His work schedule is busy, and kids' activities take up a good part of our free time. Once, Wade and I got a hotel at Lake Chautauqua, but it was only for one night because he had to coach Merritt's soccer game the next day. Even then, I'd felt guilty about putting ourselves before the kids.

"Don't read that shit," Lolly says, leaning against the counter in my kitchen after I tell her about the hurtful comment sections. She's brought her girls over to play with Gus and Merritt, and I thank God because my two were starting to get bored of each other. I haven't let them outside. Earlier, I heard Merritt mutter something about me ruining the last days of summer break.

At nine years old, Lolly's twins, Claire and Ivy, are sandwiched between mine. They've all grown up together. Lolly and I were even pregnant at the same time for a few months. When she found out she was having twins, she decided then and there that she was done. Pregnancy wasn't her thing, she explained. She'd fully planned on having an only child. Two kids at once was a bonus.

Me, I couldn't imagine stopping at one, especially not after growing up an only child myself. In the early years of our relationship, Wade and I spent long hours cuddled together planning our future. I definitely wanted at least two kids, mostly so the first would have a sibling—something I never had. I'd hated being an only child, and so once we had two, the thought occurred to me that we better have another just to be safe. So, we decided on three. I said it so frivolously then, without any weight, like ordering lattes at a coffee shop—*We'll take three, please.* Any talk about potential tragedies was meant to be figurative, not literal. No one *actually* thinks they'll lose a child. Those things happen to other people.

The squeal of laughter above our heads is a foreign sound. Having Lolly and her girls in the house brings both comfort and pain. The group's not quite the same without the littlest of the bunch trying to keep up. It's like a piece of the puzzle is missing.

"I just can't believe people can be so nasty," I say, unable to let the online comments go.

"They're trolls," Lolly says.

"Like, how can you say such awful things about a perfect stranger?"

Lolly puts a hand on my shoulder. "That's the point—they don't know you. It's a lot easier to trash-talk from behind a computer screen. Don't listen to it, Greta. No one knows the whole story except you guys."

But what if they're right? What if Wade's right? That all of this really is my fault alone. It was my idea to go on SkyRush. I knew he didn't want to and only relented to make me happy. If I hadn't put my own needs first, Summer would still be here. None of this would have happened.

We share a minute of companionable silence before Lolly changes the subject. "Where's Wade today?"

"He went to the station. They don't tell us much, but checking in gives us something to do. We've been alternating days."

"Did you decide if you're going to go to the vigil?"

I shrug. Attending a vigil for my own child sounds unbearable. At first, I was horrified by the idea alone. *We can't have a vigil! That means Summer is really lost and might not come home!* A few of the teachers at the kids' school have been organizing it. Detective Smart says it's up to us, but that it's often a comforting experience for parents—a show of unity.

"I don't know yet," I say. "I guess I'm hoping she'll be found before then."

Lolly gives a small sound of acknowledgment.

I put a plate of apple slices on the table along with the pizza Lolly picked up on the way here. "Kids! Lunchtime!" Lolly calls, and soon the patter of feet makes its way to the kitchen. The kids fill the table—every seat except one—and my heart does a flip. Lolly catches me staring at the empty chair and rubs my arm.

"You didn't take the skin off," Gus says, holding up an apple slice.

"Just eat it," I snap, a little sharper than intended. I turn and brace myself against the sink, dropping my head so the children don't see the tears that have welled in my eyes.

"Here," Lolly says, "I'll do it."

I hear the graze of the knife peeling off the apple skin. It wasn't such a big deal, I could have peeled them for him, but even Gus's simple request put me on edge. I pinch my eyes closed and count to ten.

"Everyone getting excited for school to start?" Lolly's voice is high and tight, and I know she's trying to cut through the tension in the room with her good intentions. "Who's your teacher this year?"

"Mrs. Rice," Gus says.

Then Merritt. "Mr. Applebaum."

"I had Mrs. Rice last year," one of the twins says—their voices sound just alike. "We have Mrs. Wooster. I hope Summer gets Miss Baker for kindergarten. She's the best."

Everything goes quiet. No apple chomping, no plates sliding on the table, no feet kicking chair legs. They've broached a forbidden topic and they know it.

A scream rumbles in my lungs, and I dash from the kitchen before it comes out. In the living room, I lean my forearms on the back of the couch and bend forward into my hands. Ragged breaths push through my teeth.

Lolly is there within seconds. "God, Greta, I'm so sorry. Claire didn't mean to... They don't really understand."

I wipe a tear with the back of my hand. "Of course she didn't. It's fine." How can I expect a child to grasp the idea of impermanence when I can't either? The idea of Summer being truly gone—maybe forever—is beyond comprehension.

I face my friend, letting the emotion pour out. "Sometimes it's like she's just having a sleepover at my parents, or playing at a friend's house, you know? But then it all comes barreling back. She's actually *missing*, and I don't know if we'll ever find her."

Lolly's crying now too. She wraps her arms around me, and I drop my chin onto her shoulder. She strokes my hair. "Don't give up hope."

I sneak to the back patio while Lolly plays a game of Uno with the kids. My parents are bringing food over later for dinner, and the thought alone of entertaining, of trying to act anything less than broken, is enough to make me want to hide in a dark closet.

A quick smoke will have to do.

I bring the cigarette to my lips and take a long, deep pull. I hate that I'm smoking again. That I'm sneaking outside to do it and hiding the proof in coat pockets and glove compartments. But it's the only thing that dulls the razor-sharp edge of reality. I could drink, I could pour myself a generous glass of Merlot at eight a.m., but somehow that feels more shameful. I've already been branded a bad mother; I don't need to also be a drunk mother.

The glass door slides open, and I quickly tuck the cigarette under my leg out of view. Too late. Lolly sees it. She presses her lips into a line but doesn't say a word, just joins me on the step. It's three in the afternoon and hot as hell. August is winding down, and soon school will start. We haven't even bought the kids' supplies yet. I'd been so excited to stock Summer's backpack with a glittery pencil case, chunky scissors, erasers in the shape of kissy lips or butterflies. My last little one to go to school. Just thinking about her stepping onto the bus had made me weepy.

Yet, at the same time, I'd been so ready for a new chapter to begin. I'd even been looking at marketing jobs on LinkedIn in case the college didn't have an opening for me.

I sniff and look to the sky. "I feel like I've been yanked from my life and dropped into someone else's," I say to Lolly.

"I know."

"What if she's—" My voice cracks, but I'm interrupted by my phone ringing. It's Wade. He should have been home any minute. So why a phone call? My pulse quickens. He'd only be calling if—

"Hello?" I say with eager thirst.

"Greta." There's urgency in his voice, even with just that one word, and I shoot up off the step. "There's been a sighting."

"A sighting? Where?"

Lolly stands too, hand covering her mouth, eyes huge.

"Smart just got a tip. Someone said they saw Summer at a gas station outside Buffalo."

"Buffalo? Oh my God, they're crossing the border!" It's the first thing that pops into my head.

"The police are leaving now."

"I'm on my way!" I shout, already storming into the house, swiping my car keys off the counter. I don't even have to say anything to Lolly about staying with the kids. She mouths, *Go!*

"Wait, wait," Wade says. "They're coordinating with officers in Buffalo. Smart said we should wait here."

I slam the door. "Like hell. I'm going."

SEVENTEEN

I RUN TWO STOP SIGNS LEAVING MY NEIGHBORHOOD BUT manage to abide by traffic laws the rest of the way to the police station. The last thing I need is a car accident. My pulse hammers in my ears, and I grip the steering wheel so tight my fingers go numb.

Summer is alive.

The words play on a loop in my head. I can't believe it. Actually, yes, I can believe it—I've held onto that thin string of hope for the past four days. It's been me who's trusted my gut, me who's held the faith. Now, it's all coming to fruition. Summer is alive.

Nicole Pella has been erased. My mind spins with new scenarios—who the woman is, where they've been, where they were headed. It must be to Canada. They were nearing the border to disappear into another country.

I know none of this for sure, of course, except that someone saw Summer and called it in. All the other stuff is irrelevant. Right now, all I need is to get to her. I imagine her running into my arms, our tears of relief mixing together. The scene plays out in slow motion in my mind.

I'll never let her go again.

I speed into the station and barely put the car in park before jumping out. My feet smack the pavement. Dampness coats my underarms, my body experiencing a sudden onslaught of adrenaline. Just as I reach for the door, it opens, nearly smacking me in the face.

"Mrs. Goodman," Smart says. Her badge hangs around her neck on a chain.

"I'm coming with you," I blurt, falling in step with her as she hurries toward a parked cruiser.

"You need to stay here."

"No."

"Yes. Greta, we don't know what we're going to find there, okay?"

"She's my daughter!" I cry. "She needs me!"

Smart stops in her tracks. Her eyes bore into mine. We've shared intimate moments over the past few days. She knows how desperate I've been, the helplessness of the situation. My gaze pleads.

Smart blows out a sharp breath through her nose. "Fine. But you'll stay in the car."

I nod quickly, happy to agree to her terms, even though there's no way I'll be able to hold up my end of the bargain when we get there. *Try to hold me back from my daughter. Just try.*

"Greta!" Wade's voice makes me turn just as I'm about to get into the cruiser. He dashes across the parking lot. "What are you doing?"

"I'm going with them."

"But—"

"She's probably terrified, Wade. I have to be there. You can't make me stay."

"Okay, then I'm coming too," he says.

I shake my head. "The kids." I need him to be with them. I can't ask Lolly to stay all day.

It's all happening so fast. A whirlwind. *You stay, I'll go, hurry, hurry, hurry.* Wade steps back from the car, hands on his head. I shut the door and Smart speeds away, sirens wailing.

It would normally take an hour and a half to get from Erie to Buffalo, but at the speed Smart is flying up I-90, we'll get there in under an hour. I wring my hands in my lap as we zoom past cars in the right lane.

"I bet they were going to cross the border at Niagara Falls," I say. It would be the perfect place to get lost in a crowd. So many tourists, so many forgettable faces. We'd talked about taking the kids to see the falls once, but never ended up making the trip. Now, the place will be stained for us. A Wonder of the World, but also where Summer's kidnapper dragged her to disappear from us forever.

Smart's radio goes on and off with transmissions. I listen but don't understand all the codes. She periodically replies with our location.

Trees whiz by in a green blur. "I can't believe we found her," I say, getting choked up again.

"Greta," she cautions, "we're waiting for confirmation from local police. All they're going off of is one sighting. We're lucky the witness got the car's plate number, or else we'd be no better off than we were before."

She'd explained it all the moment I got in the car. The Buffalo police are working to track down the vehicle. It shouldn't take too long. By the time we arrive, they should have Summer in their custody.

"This has been a complete nightmare," I say, leaning back against the headrest.

"Hopefully it's almost over." She presses harder on the gas pedal.

The minutes tick by. Ten, twenty, thirty. We're almost to Fredonia, New York, when her phone rings.

"Smart," she answers.

I hold my breath. This is it, this is the call. They have Summer. I analyze Smart's face for clues of what she's being told. But then, her shoulders slump and everything shatters. She utters a single word. "Fuck."

The floor drops out from under me. I'm falling again.

"What? What is it?" I say. Two scenarios flash through my mind. Either this girl wasn't Summer—a devastating thought— or worse, it *was* Summer but something tragic has happened. The woman caught wind of police closing in. She... she... Oh God, I can't go there. My vision starts to pinhole.

"Ten-four," Smart says into the phone, then hangs up.

My mouth hangs open. "What? What?" I say again, more frenzied.

"I'm so sorry, Greta."

No, no, please don't say it.

Smart's mouth turns down. "It wasn't Summer. It was a false ID."

No. No. No.

I stare. My mouth moves, but words don't form. This isn't possible. They saw her. Someone saw her. How can you mistake a child whose face has been all over the internet? "Are you sure? I mean, what if she just looks different? Maybe she... What if it—"

"The girl was eight. She was with her mother."

"Says who? They could be wrong!"

"They've both been identified. I'm sorry, Greta, it wasn't her."

My chest heaves as my breathing becomes wild. Not again. I can't do this again.

"Breathe, Greta," Smart says, reaching her hand out to me.

My vision clouds. I enter a trance-like state, disappearing into a labyrinth of endless twists and turns.

We keep driving north for another few minutes until the car slows. Smart pulls off into a turnaround, then proceeds in the direction of home. Buffalo gets farther and farther away, taking with it a child I'd hoped was mine.

EIGHTEEN
SEVEN DAYS GONE

THREE DAYS AFTER THE FALSE SIGHTING THAT BROKE MY heart all over again, Wade, the kids, and I park the car along Perry Square downtown, where the vigil for Summer is being held. It's exactly one week since That Horrible Day. The air is warm. Dusk descends like a gentle veil, the last remnants of daylight lingering in an ombré canvas.

"Do all these people know Summer?" Gus says as we cross the street into the grassy area.

"Some, maybe," I say. "But even strangers want to help find her."

"Oh! I see my baseball coach!" He waves, like this is a big family reunion rather than a somber assemblage.

We pass the bronze statue of Commodore Oliver Hazard Perry, naval commander in the Battle of Lake Erie and namesake of the square. Ahead, a crowd of several dozen people gathers near the fountain. There's a speaker set up and a woman holds a microphone. I spot Lolly, Jake, and the girls, and we make our way to them.

"Hi," Lolly whispers, giving me a hug. It's still warm, despite the evening hour, and I wonder if I have sweat marks under my arms. Being here makes me uncomfortable. People look our way. Maybe we shouldn't have come.

A teacher I recognize from the school—Merritt's first grade teacher... or was that second?—gets on the microphone. "Thank you all for coming this evening," she says. "As we gather here tonight, our hearts heavy with grief and uncertainty, we stand united in our shared hope. On behalf of the Goodman family, we'd like to use this time to channel our collective energies toward the search for Summer. Whether you're a friend, family member, neighbor, or you don't know Summer at all, we're all here for the same reason. And so, I'd like to first pass it over to Father Mark from St. Paul's, who will lead us in prayer."

I watch as she hands the microphone to the priest, whose stiff white clerical collar is a bright spot against the twilight. I haven't seen Father Mark since I graduated high school and stopped attending church with my parents. They still go most Sundays, and I can only assume they've arranged for his presence here. This whole thing came together without any input from me or Wade—which is fine. We have enough on our minds.

Father Mark brings the microphone to his mouth. "Good evening, everyone. Let us bow our heads." The audience in whole drops chin to chest. All except me—I can't stop taking everything in. From the unlit candles in everyone's hands to the big poster sign that reads, *Bring Summer Home.*

"Heavenly Father," the priest begins, "we turn to you in this darkest hour, seeking solace in the midst of our pain. Guide us through these turbulent waters of grief, and grant us the strength to endure, the courage to face each day with faith and resilience, and the compassion to support one another in our time of need. We lift up to you, dear Lord, the Goodman family as they wade through the anguish of not knowing the fate of their beloved daughter, Summer. Surround them with your love and comfort. We pray for Summer's safe return, that she may be reunited with her family and loved ones. Grant wisdom to those involved in the search efforts, guiding their steps and leading them to her whereabouts. May your divine hand be upon them, O Lord, as they work tirelessly to bring her home. In your holy name we pray, amen."

"Amen," the crowd says, opening their eyes. Several people wipe away tears.

Father Mark hands the microphone back to the teacher. "We'd now like to proceed with a candle-lighting ceremony. Father Mark will light the first candle, then pass the flame along down the rows from neighbor to neighbor."

The priest lights his candle, then touches the tip to the candle of the man next to him, who turns to the next person, creating a string of soft light. I watch the delicate movements, waiting for it to calm me, but the serenity doesn't come. Instead, I zone out, carried back to my First Holy Communion at the age of eight, when I held a white candle not much different than the ones here tonight. I remember staring at the figure of Jesus on the cross in the big church, hearing Father Something's words, but finding it all odd. If God were real, why did he let bad things happen? Like the bald kids on commercials going through chemotherapy, or the Marcuszis' dog who got hit by a car and died.

Now, in a park filled with people lighting candles, I wonder the same.

"Here," Lolly says, handing the four of us each a candle. I snap from my memory and take the small candle. I run my thumb along its smooth, waxy surface. From somewhere near the front comes the sound of music. A violin, I think, and maybe a guitar. I get on my tiptoes to see two men with their instruments, facing the crowd and playing a slow, melodic song. It's so beautiful my eyes mist up.

I'm so mesmerized by the musicians, it takes me a minute to notice the news crew set up next to the fountain. A large camera on a tripod faces directly at the crowd. The red light, which I can see all the way from here, tells me they're filming.

"The news is here," I whisper to Wade.

"That's good," he whispers back. "More coverage. More awareness."

But something about it feels intrusive, as though they're capitalizing on our pain. Their rating will go up after broadcasting this footage, but at what cost? Don't they know this is a private moment?

"It's okay," Wade says, sensing my unease, and I do my best to let it go.

The snaking flame reaches us, Lolly's family first, then Merritt, who lights Gus's, who turns to his dad, and finally me. As Wade presses the wick of his candle to mine, I take a second to store the moment. The last time we touched candles together was at our wedding. Today, we're united in a different way, not only by our candles, but in our joint sorrow and determination to find Summer. We have to stay strong. We can't let these lights go out.

"Wasn't Father Mark's speech just beautiful?" Mom is beside me now. Dad too. I hadn't seen them in the crowd when we arrived.

"Yes," I say, though I don't carry the same faith they do. Still, Father Mark's voice came with a sense of calm, and despite any doubt, I find myself willing to believe just about anything if it means bringing Summer back to me.

Dad pulls me into a hug, and I take comfort in his measured breathing. My parents flank us like pillars of an otherwise crumbling structure. "We're going to get through this, honey," Mom says.

When all the candles are lit, people stand around in hushed murmurs. There's a stack of missing person posters near the front, which some people take. I recognize many familiar faces here, from Wade's coworkers to schoolmates of the kids. But there are plenty I don't know, too, which fills me with a sense of community. We're not alone in this.

Just then, a woman approaches, holding the hand of a little girl who looks about Summer's age. It takes me a second, and then I put it together—they're from Summer's preschool. We didn't know all the families well, but I remember passing this mom on drop-offs and pick-ups enough to know her face.

I smile at the little girl. "This is for you," she says, holding out a single pink rose. "Summer likes pink."

My voice gets caught in my throat. I open my mouth to thank her, but nothing comes out.

"It's okay," the mother says. "We're thinking of you all."

I nod. "Thank you," Wade replies on my behalf. The two walk away, but their gesture has opened the floodgate of people who want to give us their condolences, a hug, words of encouragement. Over and over, we thank them. Each passing minute sucks away a little more of my soul.

"Mrs. Goodman," a voice says behind me now, and I turn, ready to accept the next offering of support. But it's not a well-wisher. The cameraman and newscaster stand no more than two feet from me. The bright light from the camera shines in my eyes, making me squint.

"How are you feeling tonight?" the woman in the blazer and perfect hair says. "It's been seven days—do you have any updates on the search effort to find Summer?"

I take a step backward as she thrusts the microphone with a big AllNews24 on it in my face.

"Not now, please," Dad says, extending a protective arm between me and the camera.

"Are there any memories of Summer you'd like to share?" the woman continues, clearly unbothered by our less-than-warm reaction. "What would you like to tell the community that has come out in support of your family?"

"I said not now," Dad repeats, louder.

The woman doesn't back down. "There are rumblings of parental neglect in this case. Do you have a comment in that regard?"

That's the final straw. I didn't punch the woman at the search party, but this time I'm not feeling quite as restrained. At once, I spring forward, and it's her who backs up. The camera keeps rolling, but I don't care. My chest heaves with rapid-fire breaths. "I would never endanger my children," I hiss. I feel Wade's hand around my wrist, pulling me back. "How dare you come to a vigil with your intrusive questions? Get the hell out of here!"

"Greta," Wade says, giving me a yank and leading me away from the camera. There's a thumping in my ears, but not loud enough that I don't hear my mother smearing the woman with a crisp, "Have you no heart? Shame on you."

Wade leads me back to the car, and I don't even realize Gus and Merritt are following until they're climbing in the back and slamming the doors shut. Gus whimpers.

I rest an elbow on the door and drop my head into my hand. This is the end of the vigil for us. Perhaps they'll carry on with more speeches, more music. Maybe the news crew will be able to interview people who know nothing about the case but are simply thrilled for their fifteen seconds on TV.

For us, it proved too much. And now we drive home in heavy silence, filled with even more grief than before.

NINETEEN

My alarm sounds and I stretch a heavy arm from under the covers to turn it off. *Damn that stupid beeping.* It's two forty-five in the afternoon. The alarm is set for the same time every day—my reminder to pick up the kids from school. I didn't used to be like this, but now things are different. No more riding the bus. They're safest with me.

I roll out of bed and lumber to the bathroom. I don't bother taking in my appearance because I know it's not pretty. My clothes hang off me, and I don't need a scale to tell me I've lost weight. Sallow skin has aged me far more than I should have in the last two months.

I brush my teeth for the first time today. It's gross and sad, but it's not like I've gone anywhere. Some days when Wade leaves for work, I'm manic, hitting the streets and upturning every corner looking for Summer. Other days, after I drop Merritt and Gus at school, I climb back into bed and draw the covers over my head. Seven hours of silence and darkness. An escape.

In the time immediately after Summer's kidnapping, I couldn't sleep at all. Now, it's all I want to do.

These are my favorite days, the ones where I can sleep to pass the hours, to numb the pain. It's not like my hours and hours of searching have done anything. But not every day allows for this luxury. There are doctor's appointments to attend, errands to run, even the periodic meeting with Georgia. She's no longer Detective Smart, she's Georgia. The last two months have put us on a first-name basis. I know how her eye twitches when she's thinking, and she's seen my very worst ugly cries.

On those days—the ones where I must leave the house—I brush my hair and put on deodorant. Once, I tried adding mascara, but I ended up crying it off within a few hours so have since given up on makeup.

I slip out of my pajamas and into jeans. When Wade gets home, he'll think I've had a productive day. Maybe he'll think I spent hours puttering around on Photoshop like I used to. He won't know that I sat in Summer's room for three hours, holding her dolls, smelling her clothes. This was a down day. I'll make sure to clean up the wads of tissues on my nightstand before he comes into our room—that is, if he decides to sleep in our bed at all.

In the kitchen, I pop a pod into the coffee machine. *Time to wake up, Greta. Time to be a functioning human.* It froths and pops as the cup fills, and I watch it absentmindedly. From my purse, I grab the orange pill bottle, and having forgotten to take one this morning, I place a tablet under my tongue. These little white dots are supposed to help, but nothing takes away the agony of living when you have a missing child.

Nine more weeks have passed since That Horrible Day. Sixty-seven days, twenty-three hours, and thirty-eight minutes without Summer. The case has been handed over to the FBI. After the mistaken sighting in Buffalo, there have been few additional leads. One anonymous tip in September briefly got our attention, but quickly proved to be false. Another letdown.

Each time, my heart breaks a little more, and when it tries to mend itself, it simply hardens.

The coffee machine finishes. I click the cup's lid into place and sling my purse over my shoulder. In the garage I pass Summer's bicycle against the wall. Shimmery blue streamers hang from the handlebars, and I run my fingers through them. Little pieces of her are everywhere in this house. They haunt me like ghosts of long ago. I swear I've heard her musical jewelry box more than once, even though no one's in the room.

After a short drive, I pull into the school's pick-up line and turn off the ignition. A row of cars fills in behind me. The helicopter parents. I used to scoff at these people for not letting their kids ride the bus. Sure, kids will learn bad words and a whole host of other inappropriate garbage, but it's practically a rite of passage. I used to feel sad for the kids whose parents sheltered them so much. Children can't live in a bubble.

Now here I am, filing into the pick-up line.

My gaze drifts out toward the street and lands on a telephone pole near the curb. My brow furrows. The missing person poster I'd hung is gone. I look around, confused. Who would have taken it down? Surely it couldn't have fallen off on its own.

My body heats up, and I impatiently rustle through a bag on the passenger seat, pulling out a new copy from the stack I keep in the car. I've got a stapler too—it's come in handy when bulletin boards are out of tacks. I open the door and get out. The fall air is cool, and I wrap my cardigan tight with one hand. I've never been to Chicago, but I'm convinced Erie could rival its wind.

I stomp over to the telephone pole. A corner of the poster remains—no more than an inch—and I wonder why someone would have removed something so important. I rip the piece off before holding a new poster against the wood and stapling all four corners twice. I step back. Summer's sweet face stares at me. The same picture I gave the police on that first day, only now the posters contain something new—the word REWARD in big, bold letters. One hundred thousand dollars we're happily ready to pull from our savings at a moment's notice.

My breath hitches. It's still surreal to see my daughter on a missing person poster. Her physical details are all there, and I can't help but wonder if she still weighs the same forty-seven pounds. Has she gotten taller in the last two months? Maybe she's outgrown her tiny flip-flops. These are the things that keep me going—the idea that she's still growing, still breathing, even if I don't know where she is.

I stare for another minute before tearing myself away. I don't want to embarrass the kids by melting into a puddle in front of the school.

On the way back to my car, a woman's voice comes from the SUV ahead of mine. "Hey, Greta." I look up. It's the mom of a boy in Gus's class. Audrey, maybe? Her blonde hair falls over her shoulder as she leans her head out the window. Her face is perfect, and I wonder how on Earth she looks so good at this hour of the morning. Then I remember it's not morning. It's three in the afternoon. I'm the only one who just got out of bed.

"Do you know who took down Summer's poster?" I say with assertion, pointing over my shoulder to the pole.

Her smile drops. "Oh, no, I'm sorry, I don't."

"I mean, why would someone take that down?" Anger simmers and poor Audrey is in the line of fire. "The more her face stays out there, the more likely we are to find her. If someone is annoyed with the posters, they can take it up with me. But, I'll tell you right now, I'm just going to put up a new one in its place."

Audrey nods and I can tell she wishes she hadn't rolled down her window to say hello.

I let out a sharp breath, press the space between my eyes. "I'm sorry. I didn't mean to attack you."

"Don't apologize," she says. "I would be upset too."

My defenses recede. It's an unfamiliar feeling to receive empathy from a near stranger.

Audrey clears her throat. "Actually, I was planning to reach out to you. We're looking for another parent to volunteer for the third grade Halloween party next week. The kids are having a costume parade around the school, then they'll pass out candy and have a s'mores bar. Messy, I know." She laughs, and I realize I haven't heard the sound for a while. "Are you interested?"

I used to help in the kids' classrooms any time a teacher asked. When Merritt was in preschool, I came in weekly to read to the kids. *Llama Llama* and *Corduroy* and *If You Give a Moose a Muffin*. Merritt's favorite was always *Madeline*. Being in the classroom used to make me smile. Now, I'm not sure I can enter the school without thinking of Summer. How can I walk past the kindergarten rooms, knowing she should be in there tracing letters and practicing sight words?

Audrey stares at me intently, waiting for an answer. I hesitate. Part of me doesn't want to give up my standing appointment with my bed. My escape from reality. But then I remember what Lolly said the other day: *It's not healthy to never leave your house.*

I push away the overwhelming sense of angst. "Sure," I say as brightly as possible.

She perks up. "Great! I'll message you the details."

I get back in my car and let out a breath, conflicting emotions tugging on both sides of my brain.

This will be good for you.

How dare you do something fun?

Before the voices have a chance to intensify, the back door opens and Gus hops in. "Hi, Mom!"

"Hi, sweetheart."

Merritt's not ten seconds behind. She gets in beside her

brother. "Hey, Mer," I say. She gives me a weak smile. I don't dig to find out why.

We head home, where I will go through the motions of another day. Homework help, preparing dinner, attempting conversation. All with the goal of making it to bed, where I can check out again.

The kids disperse when we get to the house. I feel sluggish —probably because I've had no food today. I don't deserve to eat.

The pot of water boils over, sending gurgles hissing onto the stove.

"Shit," I say, twisting the temperature dial and lifting the pot from the burner. Once it tempers, I drop the pasta in and replace the pot onto the heat. Spaghetti is easy and kid-approved. A win-win. These are the meals I make now. Mind-less, low effort.

The smell of sauce draws the kids into the kitchen. Every-thing's ready, we're just missing one thing.

"Where's your dad?" I say, looking to the clock. He used to be so prompt after work, we could almost pinpoint the minute he'd walk through the door. But ever since Summer's been gone, his arrival time is erratic. It seems as though he gets home later and later.

I huff. Eating together was always something we valued. Even with kids' sports and other unpredictable things that would pop up, we tried to have family dinners most nights. Not anymore. Now that I think about it, he's been late for dinner twice this week.

I leave the kitchen and walk to the front window that over-looks the driveway. I remember peering out the same window the day after the kidnapping and seeing reporters on our lawn. The memory makes me shudder.

Wade's car isn't there.

I wander back to the kitchen and plate the spaghetti.

"Aren't we waiting for Dad?" Gus says.

"No."

"Why not?"

"Because it's dinnertime."

"Where is he?"

I slam a plate onto the table. "I don't know, Gus, okay? It's six thirty and we're hungry, so we're eating."

Gus and Merritt exchange an uneasy look. I continue serving the food.

Ten minutes later, Wade comes in.

"Hi everyone," he says. "Sorry I'm late, I got tied up at the office."

I can't look at him without a suspicious eye. The office closes promptly at five. It takes ten minutes to get home, fifteen with traffic. My teeth grind together. I'm annoyed—at him, at the kids, at everything. Where the hell has he been? The days of long embraces and deep kisses when he walked through the door were an ancient memory before Summer's disappearance, but now things are even more detached. We haven't had sex since before That Horrible Day.

Wade drops his bag and joins us at the table. They eat. I try to eat.

"What'd you do in school today?" he says to the kids. The way he shakes the cheese onto his pasta, sending crumbs flying onto the table, makes me want to scream. So nonchalant, so untroubled. Carrying on like we're a family of four and always have been.

"Nothing," Merritt quickly replies.

Gus brightens. "We're learning about the skeletal sys—"

"Nothing?" Wade says to Merritt. "That's not true. Where's your homework? That'll answer my question."

Merritt shrugs. "Didn't have any."

"No homework?" Wade gives me a skeptical look like I should know.

I think for a second. Merritt hasn't brought home any schoolwork for weeks. It's a strange realization—sixth grade is supposed to be a primer for middle school. Has she been finishing it at school? My mind tries to think, but the feeling is fleeting. *Oh well*, I want to say. *She doesn't have homework. So what?*

I swirl the spaghetti onto my fork and take a bite. Meals have become torturous instead of enjoyable, and I'm grateful when it ends and we disband this pretend happy family. I just want the rest of the hours to pass to an acceptable time for me to go to bed again. I hate feeling this way, but don't know how to break the funk.

Finally, eight o'clock arrives—the golden hour when I can tell the kids to get ready for bed and turn off my own brain. I go into Gus's room first, lean down, and drop a kiss on his forehead. He holds onto my neck for an extra second.

"Night, Mom."

"Night, buddy."

"I don't think I want to be a Frankenstein for Halloween anymore."

"Can we talk about it tomorrow?" I'm too exhausted.

"Okay."

Merritt's in her bed. "Goodnight, Mer," I say from the doorway.

"Love you," she replies.

"Love you too." I say it as I'm leaving. My voice sounds like it's been run over, squashed flat to the ground.

There. I've made it through another day.

Back downstairs, Wade flips through the TV channels and lands on a *Mission: Impossible* movie. I'm in no mood to watch

Tom Cruise save the world. Wade's ability to lose himself in fiction for two hours makes me green with envy. If only it were that simple.

His phone lights up with a text, which he promptly responds to. Is that a smirk on his face? I can't see the screen from where I stand. He finishes typing and turns his phone over on the couch.

Noticing me standing to the side, he pats the cushion. "There's room." It's a lackluster invite.

I shake my head. "I'm going to bed."

I climb the stairs once more and retreat to my place of solace. Covers pulled up to my chin, I proceed with my own form of self-torture—what I do several nights per week. I google Summer's name, click on an article, and read the comments that tear me to shreds. This is my penance.

TWENTY

SIXTY-NINE DAYS GONE

An old pop-up card table and a white board propped against the wall serve as my work hub. A large-scale printed map of Erie lays across the table. I mark different areas with red marker: the places I've already been, the alleys and neighborhoods I've searched. The sea of red expands like a drop of blood in water from its origin point—Wonderie Land. Today, my motivation is surging again, and I'm nearly rabid to find her. I'll move further east into some of the rougher parts of Erie, the streets that I hear mentioned on the news with the latest gun violence or robbery. I used to avoid these areas, but not anymore. Fear doesn't stand a chance against will.

I grip the flyers in my hand, the edges crumpled and damp from sweat. The picture of Summer, her bright smile and twinkling eyes, stares up at me, urging me on. My feet ache from hours of walking, but I push forward, driven by a desperation that won't let me rest. I look up at the row of houses in front of me, each one a potential source of information, each one a possibility.

I approach the first house, its paint peeling and windows

clouded with grime. I take a deep breath and knock. My heart pounds in my chest as I wait. Moments later, the door creaks open a crack, and a wary eye peers out.

"Hi," I say, trying to keep my voice steady. "I'm looking for my daughter, Summer. She's been missing for two months." I hold out the flyer, my hand trembling. "Have you seen her?"

The eye looks at the flyer, then back at me. The door opens a little wider, revealing an older woman with deep lines etched into her face. She takes the flyer from me, squinting at Summer's picture.

"No, I haven't seen her," she says, shaking her head. "I'm sorry."

"Thank you," I manage to say, my voice cracking. I turn away, heading to the next house.

House after house, I knock, I ask, I hand out flyers. Some people are kind, taking the time to look at the picture and express their sympathy. Others are indifferent, barely glancing at the flyer before shutting the door. A few are downright hostile, telling me to get lost or that they don't want to get involved. It doesn't matter. I keep going. I'll knock on every door in this city if I have to.

At one house, a man with tattoos snaking up his arms and a cigarette dangling from his lips takes the flyer and studies it for a moment. "I got a niece about her age," he says, flicking ash onto the ground. "Hope you find her."

"Thanks," I say, my voice barely above a whisper. He nods and closes the door, leaving me standing on the cracked sidewalk.

The sun is starting to set, casting long shadows across the street. I move on to the next house, then the next. My legs feel like lead, and my mouth is dry, but I can't stop. Not now. Not ever.

I approach a house with a chain-link fence and a yard over-grown with weeds. Two kids play on the front steps, their laughter ringing out in stark contrast to the grim surroundings. I walk up to them, forcing a smile.

"Hi there," I say, holding out a flyer. "Have you seen this little girl?"

The older of the two, a boy with a dirty face and wide eyes, takes the flyer and looks at it. "No, ma'am," he says, shaking his head. "We ain't seen her."

As I walk away, I hear their laughter again, and it feels like a knife twisting in my heart. Summer should be playing like that, carefree and happy. Not out there somewhere, alone and scared. The thought propels me forward, giving me the strength to keep going.

I come to a small convenience store at the end of the block. The fluorescent lights inside flicker, casting a harsh glow on the dingy interior. I step inside, the bell above the door jingling. The clerk, a tired-looking man with stubble on his chin, looks up as I approach the counter.

"Can I help you?" he asks, his voice flat.

"I'm looking for my daughter," I say, handing him a flyer. "She's been missing for two months."

He takes the flyer and glances at it, then pins it to a bulletin board behind the counter. "I'll keep an eye out," he says, more out of obligation than genuine concern.

"Thank you," I say, feeling a wave of exhaustion wash over me. I leave the store and step back onto the street. The sky is darkening, the first stars beginning to appear. I've been out here for hours, but I'm not ready to give up yet.

I head to the next block, my determination renewed. I'll keep searching, keep knocking on doors, keep asking questions. Someone out there has to know something.

At the next house, a young woman answers the door, a baby on her hip. She looks at me with curiosity, and I recite my plea, my voice hoarse from so many repetitions.

"Please, if you've seen her, or if you hear anything..."

The woman shakes her head, but there's a softness in her eyes. "I'm sorry. I haven't seen her. But I'll keep an eye out."

"Thank you," I say, feeling a small spark of hope. "Thank you so much."

I turn away, moving on. The night is falling, but I won't stop. I can't stop. Summer is out there somewhere, and I'll do whatever it takes to bring her home.

As the city lights begin to flicker on, I realize that this is my life now. A relentless search, a mother's desperate quest. A battle between doing everything in my human power and falling prey to the power of depression. I am driven by love, by fear, by hope. The lack of answers takes its toll, and some days I can't muster the strength. But until I find her, I will keep walking these streets, knocking on doors, and asking the same question over and over again.

Have you seen my daughter?

Suddenly, a car pulls up to the curb, and a man gets out, his face hard and unfriendly. He strides over to me, and I feel a jolt of fear.

"You need to get out of here," he says, his voice low and threatening. "You're making people nervous."

"I'm just looking for my daughter," I say, my voice shaking. "She's been missing for two months."

"This isn't the place for you," he snaps. "People around here don't like strangers asking questions. You're going to get yourself hurt."

"I don't care," I say, my fear turning into defiance. "I have to find her."

"Lady, I'm telling you for your own good," he says. "Go home. Let the police handle it."

"I can't just sit at home and do nothing," I say, my voice breaking. "She's my little girl."

He looks at me for a long moment, then sighs. "Look, I get it. But this neighborhood... it ain't safe."

That's exactly why I'm here. A criminal took my child. If this is where criminals live, then I'm in the right place.

"I'm fine," I say, though my knees are threatening to buckle.

"Suit yourself." He drives off, and I let out a breath. I look down at Summer's picture and it tells me everything I need to know. Threats and impending danger can't stop me.

I approach a dilapidated house with boarded-up windows. The door is ajar, and I can hear loud voices inside. I hesitate for a moment, then gather my courage and knock on the doorframe.

A man with a scruffy beard and bloodshot eyes stumbles to the door. "What do you want?" he slurs, clearly drunk.

"I'm looking for my daughter," I say, holding out a flyer. "Have you seen her?"

He squints at the flyer, then laughs. "You think I know anything about some kid? Get lost."

"Please," I beg, desperate. "She's only five years old. She's been missing for two months."

"I said get lost!" he shouts, slamming the door in my face.

I stand there for a moment, feeling completely defeated. *Go home*, my aching legs say. But then I take a deep breath and turn to the next house. I have to keep going. For Summer.

The next house is slightly better kept, with a small garden in front. I knock on the door, and a middle-aged woman answers. She looks at me with concern as I explain my situation and hand her a flyer.

"Oh, honey," she says softly. "I'm so sorry. I'll keep an eye out and let you know if I hear anything."

"Thank you," I manage to whisper. I turn to leave, but she stops me.

"Wait," she says, her eyes kind. "Do you need a drink of water or anything? You look exhausted."

"I'm fine," I say, though I'm anything but.

She nods, understanding. "I hope you find her."

"Me too," I say, forcing a smile. "Thank you."

As I walk away, I feel a small glimmer of hope. There are good people out here, people who care. I just have to keep going, keep searching, and maybe, just maybe, I'll find my daughter.

The night is fully upon me now, and the streets are mostly empty. I approach another house, but before I can knock, a police car pulls up beside me. The officer gets out and approaches me, his expression stern. I recognize him from all the time I've spent at the station.

"Ma'am?" he says, and when I don't answer straightaway, "Mrs. Goodman?"

"Yes?"

"We've had some complaints. People are worried about you knocking on doors late at night."

"I'm just looking for my daughter," I say, my voice pleading. They know this. The entire city of Erie knows this.

"I understand," he says, his tone softening. "But it's not safe for you to be out here alone, especially in this neighborhood. You need to go home."

"I can't just sit at home and do nothing," I say, tears welling up in my eyes. "Please, I have to find her. I'll call Georgia and let her know that—"

"Detective Smart sent me."

I'm momentarily stunned. Not even Georgia will let me keep searching?

"Let us help you," the officer says gently. "We're still searching."

I want to fight. I want to tell him to arrest me if he has to. I'm not stopping. But my body can't hold up with my mind. At once, my shoulders slump, and I can't see how I'll possibly make it back to my car, which must now be parked over a mile away.

I nod. "I just... I need to find her."

"I know," he says, giving me a sympathetic look. "But you need to be safe too. Get in, I'll take you back to your car."

I fall into the front seat, heart heavy. Another day of searching only to come up empty. All of a sudden, the mania disappears, making room for the bleakness that usually follows it. My bed is calling. Darkness, quiet, my hideaway from this brutal, brutal reality.

TWENTY-ONE
SEVENTY DAYS GONE

THE MAIL COMES LATER ON SATURDAYS THAN DURING THE week. I walk to the mailbox at the end of the driveway. Next door, Alice Campbell gives a terse smile as she brushes leaves off her porch. I don't bother returning the gesture. Part of me thinks she's behind a neighborhood mission to alienate us. I can't think of the last time any of the neighbors have waved when they've passed, and we didn't get an invite to the Labor Day block party this year.

There are a few envelopes in the mailbox, along with junk like store coupon flyers and political postcards. On one, a well-groomed man in suit and tie gives a thumbs up, and it makes me think of the slimy politician from down near Pittsburgh whose life exploded last year when it came out that he'd assaulted staff members and even got his friend's daughter pregnant. Just goes to show you never know a person's true character—they might look trustworthy on the outside, but underneath, there are often dark secrets.

Like a woman in a hat wandering through an amusement park.

I flip through the rest of the mail on the way back to the

house. Two bills, something from the school with the district's logo at the top. I wonder what that is. I'll read it later. I tear a corner of a third envelope away, then slide my finger along the top to open it. I pull out a plain piece of white paper with angry words written in all caps.

IT'S YOUR FAULT YOUR DAUGHTER IS MISSING.
YOU DON'T DESERVE TO KEEP THE OTHER TWO

I crumple the paper into a ball without reading the rest. It's one of several dozen pieces of hate mail we've received in the last two months. The harassment began shortly after the kidnapping, and while it happened more frequently earlier on, even today we get a letter or a prank call at least twice a week. Each one is another knife in my back. Maybe Alice Campbell is one of the senders. I never liked her much anyway.

I look at the next envelope. It's addressed to me again—most of the nasty letters are, despite the fact that Wade and I were both there that day, both rode that ride. I hesitate to open it. Why subject myself to more badgering? I should throw it straight in the trash.

But there's a tiny voice in the back of my mind that says, *What if it's something good? What if it's someone who knows something?*

I open it and pull out a greeting card. On the front is a watercolor landscape showing a narrow road winding through grassy hills, eventually disappearing into the horizon.

A road to nowhere—just like my life.

I read the inside.

Dear Mrs. Goodman,

I'm sure you've received an outpouring of contact, and so I truly hope this letter finds you. My name is Nadine and I am

a psychic specializing in missing persons cases. I would love
the chance to talk with you about your daughter and visions
I have had. Please feel free to contact me at the number
below.

Sincerely,

Nadine Starr

I puff out an exasperated laugh and shake my head. The
things people will say. Starr—it sounds like a made-up name.
Like she's Jiminy Cricket and going to sing about sending
wishes into the sky. Then I stop, a memory tickling my brain.
There was a woman at the search party one night. She intro-
duced herself as a psychic and I blew her off. What did she say
her name was? Was this the same person? I brush away the
thought. It doesn't matter—it's all nonsense.

I carry the mail to the kitchen and pull out the garbage
drawer. Just as I'm about to drop everything in, I pause. Something about those words... I separate the psychic's letter from
the rest and shove it in the junk drawer, dropping the rest in the
trash.

Leaving the kitchen, I dial Georgia's number.

"Got another one," I say when she answers.

"Death threat?"

"Not quite. Just that I'm the world's worst mother." The
death threats are a whole new level. The first had taken me
completely by surprise. It's one thing to berate someone; it's
another to say you're going to kill them.

"Toss it," Georgia says.

"Already did."

Smart's keeping track of the harassment. She says there's
nothing they can do about the hate mail. The police can only
step in when the danger reaches us in person, and so far, we

haven't had any bricks thrown through our window or slurs spray-painted on our garage doors.

"Anything new this week?" I say, as I carry an overflowing basket of dirty clothes to the laundry room. Our check-ins have dwindled to once or twice a week instead of daily. Even now, she doesn't have much to offer.

"We're still looking," Georgia says. It's more of the same. *We're pursuing every lead. We're doing as much as we can.* It's like the woman in the surveillance video vanished into thin air with my child. I can't fathom how no one noticed anything. Someone out there knows what happened.

"I printed more flyers," I say. "Some of the ones around town look pretty faded. I thought I'd branch out a little further. Maybe take a drive to Pittsburgh or Cleveland and hit up some high-traffic areas."

Smart makes a small noise of approval. She doesn't discourage any attempts I have. Additional posters can't hurt. Paper and ink don't cost much, and after all, Wade and I are the ones hanging them.

"Are you still good for coffee on Monday?" I ask. It's a chance for us to put our heads together. I suspect she agrees to these coffee dates out of sympathy. Either way, I'm grateful. "Oh wait," I say, suddenly remembering. "You said your son has a game or something?"

"Right. Can I take a rain check on coffee?"

"Of course. No problem." My posture wilts.

"Take care of yourself. We'll talk soon," Georgia says before we hang up.

I slip the phone into my pocket and proceed to dump the clothes into the washing machine by the handful. Even though it's only one fewer person in the house, it seems like I do much less laundry now. Summer always had a knack for spilling on herself. The girl loved getting dirty outside. I'd do anything to scrub dirt stains from her clothes again.

On the third grab into the basket, my fingers clasp around something fuzzy. I withdraw the item from the jumble of clothes. My chest pangs. It's Summer's favorite stuffed animal—well, not really stuffed, more like one of those mini lovey blankets with a lamb head on top. Lucy the Lamb. She slept with it every night. The two had never been apart.

I instinctively bring it to my nose and inhale, searching for the scent of Summer. Still there. And then my mouth pinches into a firm line. I drop the basket of clothes and storm from the laundry room, looking for one person. I find him in the garage.

"Why did you put Lucy in the laundry?" I spit, holding up the lamb.

Wade's face is a question mark. "I didn't put it in the laundry."

"She was in with the dirty clothes. I almost tossed her in the wash."

"I don't know what you want me to tell you," Wade blubbers, palms up, feigning innocence.

"Are you trying to erase her from our lives?"

At this, Wade's face goes tomato-red. He knows I'm no longer referring to Lucy. "What are you talking about? No, I didn't intentionally put Summer's lovey in the laundry. It must have gotten mixed in with the kids' clothes."

"You want me to forget her."

"Greta, stop. Don't say that."

"You... You..."

"Stop!" Wade yells. "Just stop. No one is trying to erase Summer. It was an accident. And anyways, it's just a toy. You can't keep fixating on all these things."

I bite my lip to keep it from trembling. "It's all I have left."

There's a deafening silence between us. Then Wade steps toward me. "You have us. Me, Merritt, Gus."

I turn and go, clutching Lucy to my chest. He doesn't understand. He'll never understand.

TWENTY-TWO

SEVENTY-SIX DAYS GONE

AISLE TEN IS MY KRYPTONITE. I PUSH THE GROCERY CART forward and stare straight ahead, as though the rainbow of cereal boxes might jump off the shelf and attack me. In my peripheral vision, I see it anyway, what I'd been avoiding—the bright green of the Apple Jacks box. Summer's favorite.

She used to eat them so much we'd joke, *You're going to turn into an apple!* Now, I can't see the box without picturing her with a small plastic bowl in front of her. She'd eat all the orange ones first so that eventually she'd end up with a bowl full of green circles. Somehow the combination made the milk a purple hue, and I'd always gag watching her drink it down.

Look, Mommy, she'd say. *It's like fairy milk.*

If I could bypass this aisle altogether, I would, but there are other things I need—oatmeal for Wade, granola for me. The kids still eat cereal too, so I hastily grab two boxes of something with characters on the front and drop them in the cart before rushing to a safer place. Aisle eleven isn't much better—this one has her favorite snack packs. Remnants of Summer are everywhere I go.

I reach the cold section and load up the cart with frozen meals. My cooking has become lazier and lazier, but so far no one has complained. Maybe they don't dare—or maybe I was never a stellar cook to begin with. Either way, it's a small victory.

Ahead, two women huddle together. They look my way then give each other a furtive glance. I can see words exchanging, even though their mouths barely move. It's the kind of talking that happens in hushed tones, whispers that slither through the air like poisonous snakes. I keep my focus on the shopping list clutched tightly in my hand.

Ignore them.

But forward is the only way. Turning around would look silly, especially since it's obvious I've noticed them. I'm halfway down the aisle. No one turns around halfway. The women are not exactly discreet with their thinly veiled disdain. My chest tightens. Now I'm feet away. They've got to stop. Will they actually say something to my face? Are these the people who send mail to our house that makes me cry?

The overhead lights bring on dizziness. With a trembling hand, I reach into a freezer for a carton of mint chocolate chip. The weight of the women's eyes is like a pile of bricks, heavy and unmoving. I can feel their collective scrutiny dissecting my every move. *Oh, she feeds her kids full-fat ice cream?* The whispers grow louder—or is that just in my head? I can't bring myself to look them in the eye.

I toss the remaining few items from this aisle into my cart and push on past. The women are quiet as I go, but their judgment swirls around me like a suffocating fog. The next aisle is empty, and I breathe a sigh of relief. All I want to do is get through this mundane task in peace. Keep my family fed. Survive another day.

At the cash register, I place everything on the belt. My

hands are clammy, this lightweight turtleneck no longer feeling quite so lightweight. I hate that I let those women get to me. It's like I'm under a microscope whenever I leave the house. Everyone is an expert on me and my life. Only the truth is they know nothing but their own misplaced assumptions.

The cashier is a woman with dark, curly hair and teeth that overlap sorely in the front. She rings up my items without a word. Silent treatment. Great. I prepare myself for yet another unpleasant interaction.

"One fourteen sixty-two," she says, meeting my eyes for the first time. I slide my card into the reader and wait to punch in my pin. The woman leans forward, her voice low. "I'm sorry for what you're going through." She offers a gentle smile.

I gape at her for a second, caught off guard. Tears prickle the corners of my eyes. I nod in gratitude. "Thank you." For the briefest moment, the cashier's kindness pierces through the cloak of scrutiny I've been living under. My shoulders relax, my chin lifts ever so slightly.

I gather my bags and head toward the exit. There are more stares, but they don't hit quite as hard.

Outside, I load the groceries into the car and get in with a long exhale. Things I used to take for granted—a quick trip to the store—now cause more anxiety than my yearly mammogram.

Just as I'm about to back out of the parking spot, my car beeps in warning. I slam on the brake. A man returning an empty cart appears on the back-up camera screen on my dash. He stops suddenly, a deer in headlights.

"C'mon, buddy," I mutter. *Why isn't he moving?* I can see him in my side mirror, and our gazes lock. It only takes a second, but his expression goes cold. He recognizes me. And just like that, he takes his hands off his cart, turns, and retreats to his vehicle, leaving the cart squarely behind my car.

"Are you kidding me?" I say, waiting to discover it's some

sort of bad joke. But it's not. I throw the car in park and get out. I look for the man, but he's gone, disappeared into one of the dozen cars around mine. I want to chew him out, call him an asshole, knowing that even if we did come face to face, I probably wouldn't say anything. Instead, I push the cart back to the return area. My insides are smoldering, but I refuse to let the cruelty of others crush me.

It's a battle I sometimes lose.

Back in the driver's seat, I notice that I've missed a call from a number I don't recognize. I click on the voicemail, which has appeared in the short time it took to return the cart.

"Hey, Greta, this is Audrey Cook. I was checking to see if you're still planning to help out at the kids' Halloween party today. We just finished passing out candy, and they're getting ready to make their s'mores. There's still time if you can make it!"

"Fuck!" I slam the phone down and hightail it from the parking lot. The clock in the car says one fifteen. Sure enough, I was supposed to be at the school half an hour ago. The details are right there in my Facebook Messenger app from when Audrey sent them last week. I never put it in my calendar. Gus didn't say a word this morning, even though I remember him packing his pirate costume into his backpack. The two things misfired in my brain, never making a connection.

Another mom failure.

I speed to the school, the whole time cursing under my breath. If I'd remembered, I would have made myself a bit more presentable. Now, I swipe on lip gloss I find in the bottom of my purse and tuck loose hair behind my ears. This will have to do. I hurry into the school.

"So, so sorry," I say to Audrey and Gus's teacher, Mrs. Rice, when I enter the classroom. The kids have already gone through the assembly line to make their s'mores and are now back at their seats, bowls of sticky, sugary goodness in front of them. I spy Gus in the third row and make my way to him.

"I thought today was Thursday!" I say with a laugh. "Can you believe it?" I'm trying to turn it into a joke—*Mommy's so silly!*—but Gus doesn't smile.

"You missed the parade. That's the best part," he says quietly.

"I'm sorry, bud. I bet you were the coolest pirate here." There's another pirate in the class—a boy with a cheap acrylic wig—and I wonder if Gus wishes he'd stuck with Frankenstein.

He picks at a piece of graham cracker. "Max's mom was on time."

My heart physically aches. I don't know how to respond. Instead, I press his fluffy head into my belly, telling myself I'll make it up to him.

I help Audrey clean up the mess from the s'mores while Mrs. Rice reads a story about a dancing skeleton. The whole time, I keep an eye on Gus. He talks with the boy next to him. He laughs. I feel a small sense of relief. Kids are like springs—they bounce back. He'll be fine.

"I really am sorry," I say to Audrey.

"Don't worry about it. I'm glad you were able to make it."

She seems sincere, but I can't help but feel like a complete flop as a mother. I've let Gus down, Merritt barely talks to me, and my other child is—

I grab a Lysol wipe and go to town on a smear of chocolate. The party wraps up with nineteen kids on a sugar high and a teacher who looks like she's been through the wringer. It seems silly for me to drive home only to come back shortly to pick them up at the end of the day, but I can't stay in this building without dissolving in tears.

I kiss Gus and tell him I'll see him in a bit. The whole drive home, I laud myself for a semi-successful afternoon. I made it through the store, and even though I was late to the Halloween party, Gus seemed to get over it. I even managed to engage in some chitchat with Audrey. Maybe it's a positive sign for the rest of the day.

When I open the trunk to take in the groceries, I see a river of mint chocolate chip ice cream dripping from one of the bags. A reminder: *Don't get too ahead of yourself.*

TWENTY-THREE

"Ouch," Lolly says over the phone later that afternoon when I recount the Halloween party mishap.

"I know. Break my heart, right? I felt awful. But he'll be fine, won't he? I mean, it was just a school party. They're nothing but pure chaos anyway." Even as I say it, my skin becomes itchy.

"I think he just wanted you there."

"I'm with him every day. I don't know if I've spent *this* much time with the kids ever."

There's a pause. "But are you really... present?"

My lips purse; my hand holding the red marker about to mark off another searched neighborhood stops. "Don't give me that, Lol."

She changes the subject. "Hey, why don't you let them come over for a sleepover this weekend? The girls would love it. Might be good for you, too. You and Wade could spend some time alone."

I hesitate. "I don't know."

"Greta, it's me. You know they're safe at my house."

"Of course I do, it's just—"

"You can't be attached to them twenty-four-seven forever. It'll be fun. I'd love to have them. You deserve a break."

A break.

Moms don't get breaks. Look what happened last time I tried to take a break. I should have known better. Becoming a mother means you sacrifice a big part of yourself, give up things you once took for granted. Like breaks. I'm not sure I'll ever get one again—maybe I'm not worthy of one. And yet... Wade can go off to work every day and leave behind the mental load of fatherhood. Then there's me. Being the default parent is a full-time job.

But Lolly says I deserve a break. The idea is tempting, like something you want but you'll feel guilty taking. She's waiting for my response, and I'm too tired to do anything but appease her.

"Let me see what Wade thinks," I say, agreeing to let her know tomorrow. In the meantime, I have a slew of online forums through which I'll search Summer's name. The internet is a scary place, but not too scary for a desperate mother.

Wade, not surprisingly, is fully in favor of Lolly's idea when I bring it up that evening.

"I think it's a great idea," he says. "They always have fun with the twins. Maybe we could make dinner reservations."

"Go out to eat?" I say like it's the wildest idea ever concocted.

"Yes?" he drawls.

Instantly my chest burns, every nerve in my body coming alive. My jaw tightens. Wade must notice, and I'm not surprised. I've always had a terrible poker face.

"What is it?" he says, a little brusque. "What's so wrong with making dinner plans?"

"Because that's something normal people do. We're not normal people, Wade."

"We're not allowed to eat?"

"We shouldn't be out gallivanting like it's a happy date night or something."

"Who said anything about gallivanting?"

I groan. He knows exactly what I'm getting at, so why is he pushing my buttons? "You know what I mean."

"Greta, I know you're going through a lot. So am I! But at some point, we do have to try to get back to normal."

My mouth unhinges. I was already stewing, but now he's blown my top. "How can you say such a thing? Have you forgotten that we still have a missing child?"

"Of course I haven't forgotten! I think about Summer every minute of every day." His face is red now too. We're twin volcanoes, finally erupting.

"Well then how are you able to just go on with life? Return to work? It's like you've given up the search completely. I'm the one who continues to hang flyers. I'm the one who calls into the station every week."

"What do you want me to do, Greta? Sit around all day? Fall into a depression? Only one of us can do that. Someone has to keep the rest of us afloat."

I gawk at him. "Don't you dare judge me."

"It's the truth. You're a walking ghost. And you know what? You might want to cut it with the smoking. I can smell it on you every day."

"Oh, forgive me for having one small pleasure. Every other minute, my energy is spent focusing on the case, which is more than you can say. You think she's dead, don't you? You think we're never going to find her. Well, guess what? I refuse to believe it."

I storm away. I grab my jacket off the hook by the door and

go outside, needing space. A thin, horned moon hangs in the sky, and there's just enough light left for a walk around the block. Pleasant Drive is speckled with porch pumpkins and pots of vibrant mums. Not ours. Our entryway lacks any festivity.

As I walk, I pull the pack of Newports from my pocket and light one. The smoke travels down my esophagus to my lungs. I imagine them turning black and crumbling like ash to the touch, but I don't care. Within another puff, the tension in my body eases. The nicotine does its job. My mind, on the other hand, is a never-ending spiral. Wade says he's simply being realistic, pragmatic. What I can't understand, however, is *how*. How can he so easily give up? He never even cries.

I walk for nearly an hour, taking a long loop until my shoes start to rub on my pinky toe. When I return, the house is still. It's only seven, but it feels like midnight.

I go to the kitchen and preheat the oven for a frozen meal that may or may not taste like garbage.

Summer's room smells like a candy factory. Between the homemade lip balms and the doll with baby powder skin, it's hard not to smile when you come into her bedroom. Everything's fresh and pure and simple. There are no preteen hormones to battle, no chance of walking into a bad mood, unlike Merritt's room—she's become harder and harder to read.

I sit on Summer's bed and finger the ruffled comforter. Lucy the Lamb rests on my thigh, and I stroke it as if I were stroking Summer's hair. I come in here more often than I probably should. It's not good for me, staring at all her things, emptying her drawers and refolding her clothes. But I'm drawn to this space. A few times, I've actually fallen asleep on her bed and spent the night breathing into her pillow.

Tonight, I open Facebook to the page I created a month ago,

titled "Finding Summer Goodman: Tips and Information." The profile picture is the same one from the missing person poster. My favorite photo, forever stained. The page has become a place of refuge, a corner of the internet I can control—a direct contrast to the toxic comments flying around on other pages. There are over thirteen hundred followers here, all with the goal of finding Summer. I won't tolerate hate—the one time someone got even a little judgy, I blocked her.

I draft a new post.

> Hi everyone. It's been eleven weeks. No new information. Thank you to all who keep searching for Summer. Always open to new ideas. If you have any leads, please don't hesitate to contact the police. Don't forget we have an anonymous tip line, and you can always reach us at bringhomesummergoodman@gmail.com.

I then toggle over to the email account to filter through the junk for anything that could be legit. I do this at least twice a day.

While I'm scrolling emails, a Facebook notification pops up and I make my way back there. Several people have commented on my post.

> *Check with local businesses for surveillance footage. Sometimes they don't always hand everything over unless asked multiple times.*

> *Praying daily! Have you checked abandoned buildings? So many old factories along 12th Street.*

I shiver thinking of Summer being dumped in a run-down building among glass shards and waist-high weeds. Nonetheless, I add it to my list of places to search.

A yawn pulls at my jaw, and I leave Summer's room just as the clock is turning eleven. It's been hours since the mediocre frozen dinner, but the heavily seasoned aroma lingers. Merritt and Gus are long asleep. Wade—I don't know. I'm never sure if we'll sleep in the same bed or if the tension is too much for one of us. After our earlier argument, I wouldn't be surprised if Wade spent the night on the couch.

I kiss the lamb and leave it on Summer's pillow, then pad down the hall to my own room. I open the door. To my surprise, Wade's in bed. I stand there for a moment, debating whether or not to return to Summer's room. Wade's earlier words cut deep, and I don't know if I want to sleep next to someone who can hurt me so badly.

My knees are weak, my entire psyche screaming at me to make a damn decision and get some rest. It's been a hell of a day and I'm spent. I proceed into the room, too tired to fight any mental battle.

After I wash my face and brush my teeth, I pull back the covers and slide into bed. My eyelids lower. *Precious sleep, take me away.*

But then there's a hand on my waist. It slips over my belly and up to my breasts. They're droopy and less full than they were before kids, stretch marks rippled across the undersides from where milk once nourished three babies. I don't love this new version of my body, but Wade has never seemed to mind. He pulls me into him, my back cradled against his chest.

"I'm sorry," he whispers. He gently kisses my neck, then my cheek. He turns my face and goes for my mouth.

"Wade."

"I miss you."

I stiffen. It's like my body is in permanent off mode. There's no response. No one home. I push his hands away. "I can't."

This used to be how we made up. Sex and intimacy healed any silly argument, made us whole again. But tonight wasn't a silly argument. We both said things that came from deep, dark parts of ourselves.

"Please, Gret," he says, trying to bring me close again, but I resist, scooting out of bed. I don't turn back before leaving and spending the night in Summer's room.

TWENTY-FOUR

SEVENTY-SEVEN DAYS GONE

THE CURTAINS IN SUMMER'S WINDOWS CAST A PINK LIGHT through the room, as though I'm waking up inside a bubblegum cloud. I sit up. There's a wet spot on the pillow, and I bring a hand to my eyelashes, which are crusted together in clumps. I must have been crying in my sleep. It wouldn't be the first time. Thank goodness I don't remember the dream.

Our bedroom is empty when I pass by, and so are Merritt's and Gus's. Downstairs, I find them at the table eating breakfast.

"Your parents brought donuts," Wade says. "They didn't want to wake you. Said they'll stop back again later." He fills a mug with fresh coffee and hands it to me.

I manage a small smile.

"Can we go to Claire and Ivy's house for a sleepover?" Gus says.

It catches me off guard. "I don't know," I say, wondering how Gus even knew about Lolly's proposal.

"Aw, please, Mom? Dad said we could."

I look to Wade. We hadn't come to a clear conclusion last night about the sleepover, but apparently he's taken it upon himself to not only tell the kids, but to allow it. I cock my head, giving him dagger eyes. *Thanks a lot. Now, I'm bad cop.*

"I'd rather you guys stayed here," I say. "Maybe we could…" I hurry to think of something to suggest. Something fun, even though fun is the last thing I feel like having. "… watch that new Mario Bros movie?"

"I am *not* watching Mario," Merritt says, taking a bite of a jelly-filled donut.

I try again. "Gus, you said you've been dying to see that movie. Now we finally can."

"I'd rather go to Claire and Ivy's house," he says. "They have fruit roll-ups."

"That's a silly reason to want a sleepover."

Wade sighs and stares into his coffee mug. "We still need to let them be kids, Greta," he says so quietly it's nearly a whisper.

"I don't have time for this," I say. Tension is already forming a knot in my neck and I've only been awake for ten minutes. The idea of the kids going here and there without my supervision makes my heart race. I feel untethered in my own body. And so I abruptly end the conversation. "I'm going to call Georgia," I say, taking my coffee mug to the other room. Calling her is futile, but I do it anyway. It's one of the few things in my control. She doesn't have any updates, and I'm running out of ideas. All I know is that I can't let the case go cold.

"Maybe we should hold another press conference," I suggest. "Keep Summer's face in the public eye."

"We can try to arrange that," Georgia says, and I know she's just appeasing me.

"You said you wouldn't give up."

"I'm not."

I drop my head and let out a long exhale.

"Listen," she says. "I know this is hard. But I promised you then and I promise you now, I'm still working every angle."

It's the most helpless feeling in the world. There's so little we can do. We're waiting for a break that might never come.

"How are things at home?" she says.

"Hit and miss. You know, there's good days and there's bad days."

"That's to be expected."

"I just... I just want to find her."

"We all do, Greta. Trust me."

We hang up with assurances to talk again soon. I can't tell whether our calls make me feel better or worse. Like a compulsion I can't control, I keep reaching out, even when I know there will be nothing but more heartbreak on the other end of the line.

When I return to the kitchen, my parents are there. I hadn't heard them return.

"Hi, honey," Mom says as she braids Merritt's hair at the table.

Dad gives me a kiss on the head. "You were still asleep when we stopped earlier. Was that the detective on the phone?"

I nod. "Yeah. Nothing." I don't elaborate in front of the kids. I don't want my agony to rub off on them any more than it already has.

Mom frowns. Her face has inherited a dozen more wrinkles in the last two months. Then again, so has mine.

"I'm going to take the kids out for a bit," Wade says. It's not a question. His mouth is firm, and I think to myself that I haven't seen his crooked smile in a while.

I give him a curious look—their grandparents just got here to visit—then glance to my parents, who are no longer making eye contact with me. Mom picks at her nails. Something's fishy.

"We'll be back in a little while," Wade says. "C'mon, guys. Grab your coats."

I'm too caught up in the weirdness to even say goodbye before they're quickly out the door. Barely a handful of seconds pass before Dad speaks. "We're worried about you, Gretty." His face wears a troubled expression. Mom folds her hands on the table. My eyes dart between them.

Ah, now I get it. This is an intervention. He hasn't called me Gretty since middle school. Wade and the kids purposely left so that my parents could address me alone.

"Wade's worried about you too," Mom says.

"So he asked you over here to talk to me? Why doesn't he say something himself if he's so concerned?" I'm not in the mood for games. I refill my coffee, suddenly needing an extra shot of caffeine.

"He's tried," Dad says. "He says you're... you're..."

"Let me guess, a walking ghost, right? That was his most recent description."

"Greta," Mom says, standing and putting a hand on my arm. "Your husband is grieving too. This has been devastating for all of us. All we're saying is that we want to support you. We..." She looks to Dad then back to me. "We think you should consider seeing someone."

"You mean a shrink?"

"Someone you both can talk to."

I cross my arms. "I'm already on antidepressants if that's what you're getting at. And to be honest, I don't think they're even working."

Mom's hands shake like she's nervous to be having this conversation. Like I'm a ticking time bomb. "Well, dosages can always be increased."

"I don't need more pills, Mom," I snap, and she recoils a bit.

Dad steps in. "Don't take this out on your mother. We know you're angry, but it's not fair to Wade and the kids for you to check out of life."

I stare at my father like I don't recognize him. How can he be so insensitive? His granddaughter is missing. Gone. Taken. And he's faulting me for not being myself?

"There are therapists trained for these types of things," Dad continues. "They specialize in grief. They know how to help couples."

"Couples? You want me to go to *marriage* counseling?"

"Your husband needs you, Gretty. You might not see it, but he's struggling just as much as you."

Is he? I think of all the times he's been late coming home. The hours I've wondered where he was. The times I've wanted to check his phone for messages from another woman but couldn't bring myself to do it.

"We're fine," I say.

"Greta."

"I just don't think now is the time to be seeking marriage therapy when I'm trying to focus on finding my daughter! Besides, I don't think Wade is even interested."

"He is. He told us."

They have no clue.

My parents exchange a look of unease. "Carole," Dad says, "maybe we... maybe this is too much."

"Honey," Mom says, ignoring him, "we're only saying this because we love you and want to help. You and Wade are the ship, and if the ship sinks, then it's not good for anyone. Give it a try, huh? You're not giving up on Summer just because you make Wade a priority too. Merritt and Gus need their parents. You have to try to provide a bit of stability for them."

But what if I can't? What if Wade's already gone too?

My throat is thick. They've hit a nerve that I've been trying to hide. My marriage is on shaky ground. At once, a wash of embarrassment comes over me. They know. They can see the pieces starting to fall. It took my parents cornering me to finally admit it to myself.

I massage my temples, not wanting to meet their eyes. Mom and Dad have been married forty-two years. They're the example I've always hoped to follow. Then again, my parents have never faced a trial such as this. Who's to say their perfect union wouldn't have cracked if they'd been in our place? A small whimper escapes my lips.

"It's okay," Dad says, coming closer and rubbing my back. It's a touch I've needed but have been resisting. Tears fall from my eyes onto his polo shirt. I don't know how there are any more left inside me. "You're going to get through this."

"You're the strongest person I know," Mom adds.

Am I?

They stay with me until Wade and the kids return an hour later. Part of me wants to feel anger toward my husband for this setup, but like so many other situations, I can't muster the strength. I feel stunned. Depleted.

Wade eyes my parents first and something passes between them. *Did it work? Did she agree?* It's like I'm an addict they're convincing to seek treatment.

"We'll see you all soon, okay?" Mom says, standing and giving the kids a hug and kiss. That's it. They fulfilled their mission for visiting. Then they're gone.

Gus and Merritt disappear into another room. Wade shuffles his feet like he's waiting for me to say something first. I don't. Our eyes dance around each other.

"So," he says.

"So."

He goes to speak again, but I'm already internally cringing. "Wade," I say, stopping him, "I know why you had my parents come over. And yeah, do I think things are a little tense around here? Sure. But we don't need *therapy*, do we? We've always been able to work things out."

"This is different, Greta."

He's pushing, and my temperature is rising. "I'm not going to therapy. Besides, there's no time. I'm focused on finding

Summer. That's my job." It's a lie. He and I both know my days are filled with long stretches of sleep. The hour-by-hour investigation dried up weeks ago.

Wade huffs through his nose. Without a word, he turns and leaves. I'm met with relief. But after a long minute, it becomes something else. Shame, shame, shame.

TWENTY-FIVE

EIGHTY DAYS GONE

I'M JUST ABOUT TO NOD OFF AN HOUR OR SO AFTER dropping the kids at school when the wailing sound of a fire truck crescendos through the house. I fling off my eye mask, hop from the bed, and rush to the window. The siren gets louder, and I search up and down the street to see which direction it's coming from. Heart palpitations make my breathing uneven. Any sort of alarm, especially one from an emergency vehicle, is enough to send me reeling. Is it Summer? Could it be Summer?

Finally, the engine goes racing past our house in a red blur. I watch it go, feeling both glad and disappointed. No one wants a fire truck coming to their house. Then again, it could have been what I've been waiting for for months. I shake my head. Summer wouldn't be arriving on the back of a fire engine. This isn't a parade.

As I stand at the window, my gaze drifts from house to house, wondering what lies inside. So many things unseen—secrets, strife. We only see the outward signs of life, the cheerful Facebook posts when a kid wins the championship baseball game, or when a senior gets into her first-choice college, or when someone announces a new job, a new house, a better *something*. It's always the good stuff.

Before Summer's disappearance, I bet everyone thought we had the perfect life too. I'd thought we were pretty close. But now, I could post daily updates of a whole different type—the kind that would make people hold what they have a little tighter. What I'd want to say is that it can be gone in a blink. The grass isn't always greener—sometimes the other side doesn't have grass at all.

My vision goes blurry, and I realize tears have pooled in my eyes. I wipe them away with the back of my hand until I see clearly again. Only now, the window itself is in focus. I drag a finger across the sill. Lift it up and blow, sending a tiny puff of dust into the air. When was the last time I cleaned the house?

I stare back at the bed calling my name. Faint thrums of the siren remain in my ear, and I know that despite all effort, I won't be able to sleep. Not anymore.

I go to the laundry room and grab a spray bottle and cloth. Back in my room, I hit the window with two squirts of blue liquid, then wipe it off. The cloth comes back darker than before. *Put some elbow grease in it*, Mom would always say when she'd give me chores as a kid. I remember running the vacuum and feeling a sense of accomplishment seeing the lines in the carpet. I've never minded cleaning, unlike Lolly who despises it and spends two hundred dollars a month for a housekeeper.

Now that I look around, the neglect is clear. Clean clothes pile up in laundry baskets, waiting to be folded. Downstairs, I know there are crumbs tucked into floor corners, and the mantle surely has a layer of dust much like my windowsill.

There and then, I decide it's time to clean. I tell myself it will feel good, that maybe a clean house will give me some small sense of command. Maybe Wade will notice when he gets home. Maybe it'll be some sort of olive branch. Set the tone for the evening.

I finish our bedroom first. Clothes hung up. Sink and mirror wiped clean. Then, I move on to the downstairs. As expected, the mantle looks like it hasn't seen a dust rag in weeks. If I remember correctly, Lolly spot-cleaned a couple times in those early days, but as for me, I haven't touched a mop or the Swiffer since. Most days, I feel lucky to get all the dishes in the dishwasher, letting the machine do the rest of the work.

For four solid hours, I clean the house. Living room, kitchen, baseboards, toilet seats. Only once do I stop and cry when I find one of Summer's bracelets under the couch, the rubber band kind she looped together on her fingers. I slide it on my wrist, the bright pinks and purples looking silly on me, the band far too tight for an adult wrist. The find feels like a reminder: *Don't put her out of your mind for too long.* A few minutes later, I'm able to compose myself enough to continue. It proves to be a satisfying way to spend the day—or as close to satisfying as I could expect to get.

I clean through lunch, not that I would have eaten anyway. Finally, as the clock nears two, I stand in the middle of the kitchen, hands on my hips. The air turns from stale to sweet, freshened by the lemon-scented floor pads. I light a candle on the counter, and soon it's doubly fragrant, citrus now mixed with warm vanilla. My house feels livable again. I even karate-chopped the couch pillows for full effect.

I stand back and take it all in, including the carpet lines I love so much, but which will disappear the second the kids get home. That familiar feeling trickles in. I achieved something today. It feels... good. I wrestle with the emotion that's become so foreign, then settle on the decision that celebrating a small win like cleaning my house isn't the same as other happiness I haven't let myself feel.

. . .

Wade walks through the door at five fifteen, which is a surprise, seeing as his arrival times have been all over the place.

"Hey," he says, placing his keys and wallet on the counter.

I smile but stop short of floating across the kitchen to give him a kiss. "How was your day?" On the stove, a mixture of butter and whipping cream sizzles. A few white pops land on the smooth black surface, instantly irritating me after today's deep clean. They'll be easy to wipe off if I get to them before the end of the day instead of waiting weeks.

I wait for him to comment on the transformation of the house. The counters are sparse, things put away, surfaces shiny. But instead, his phone beeps and he looks at it before typing something quick in reply and putting the phone in his back pocket.

"Good. Fine," he says. "Hank is out with the flu, so I've taken on some of his projects." He steps out of his shoes, leaving them on the clean floor, before going to the fridge for a drink. He pulls out a craft beer in a colorful can that looks like it belongs in the seventies, something with a name like Fizzy Zebra or Milk Groove.

I breathe. It's his way to unwind. Drinking a beer isn't a crime. But then he says, "What's for dinner?" and my neck muscles tighten.

"Gus has practice at six," I reply.

Wade gives me a sidelong look like I haven't answered his question. "Right... I was just wondering if you'd thought of dinner."

"Why does it have to be me who thinks of all the meals?" I say, a little too snappy.

He raises his hands in innocence. "Whoa, don't bite my head off. What's wrong?"

"Nothing's wrong."

Everything's wrong.

I fling open the pantry cabinet to see what's available.

"I can make dinner if you want," Wade says. "It was just an honest question, I didn't mean anything by it."

"No, it's fine," I say with enough passive-aggression that even a toddler could detect it. I grab a packet of microwaveable rice before moving on to the fridge for some chicken breast.

"Here, let me do that." Wade takes the chicken from my hands.

I step back and watch as he rinses the meat and unhooks a skillet from where they hang above the island. Now he needs a mallet. He looks around like a lost puppy who is trying to pretend he's the big dog in the ring. He turns the burner to high heat and slaps the chicken onto the pan. I bite my tongue. It only takes thirty seconds for the thing to start smoking.

"You might want to put some oil in the pan so it doesn't burn," I say.

Wade snatches the olive oil from the shelf and drizzles a hearty serving on top. It snaps and crackles against the heat. I would have turned the temperature down, but I'm trying not to tell him what to do. He offered to cook.

Wade's busy chopping broccoli from the stalk into a steamer. We're silent, neither one of us making small talk. Maybe he regrets his offer. He probably wishes I would leave the kitchen, but this is my realm and I feel the need to oversee what happens here.

"The chicken needs to be flipped," I say.

"I'll get it," he responds. But instead of flipping it, he continues with the broccoli, meticulously snipping florets as if it were an artistic skill. *The chicken is burning,* I want to scream.

More smoke comes from the skillet and I can smell the char on the underside. That's it. I appreciate Wade's attempt to cook, but I can't just stand here doing nothing when it's going to be ruined. I reach past him for the tongs in a utensil crock on the counter, then quickly flip the chicken, revealing a deep brown crust.

"I was going to get that," Wade says, annoyance in his voice. "I said I would make dinner, and I will. Why don't you go do something else? I got this."

He probably means it in the nicest way—well, maybe—but it comes off with a little too much sass.

"I would if I wasn't worried about the food burning," I say, sprinkling some salt and pepper and a dash of garlic powder onto the chicken. Wade watches with a taut gaze. Intentionally or not, I've made it clear—I know what I'm doing and he doesn't.

"You know," he says, dropping the kitchen shears to the counter. "I was just trying to help."

"I appreciate that, but it's fine. I'm the one who always makes dinner, why change things now?"

"You act like I've never made a meal before. It's fucking insulting."

Now I'm the one whose tone deepens. "Wade, I said it's not a big deal. Don't worry about it."

"No, screw that. I come home and you're all huffy about God knows what, and I try to give you a hand and it ends up getting shoved in my face. Why do you have to undermine everything I do?"

"Undermine? The chicken was *burning*."

Wade snorts and shakes his head. "Whatever." He throws his hands up in the air. "The last thing I need after a long day is micromanaging from you."

There it is. The work jab. He busts his ass while I get to sit around doing nothing. My chest flares. Standing next to the steam coming from the stove is making me extra hot. "Oh, right, right. You're the only one who works. Did you take a second to notice the house when you got home? The fact that I spent all day cleaning? No. But I didn't rub it in your face, did I?"

Wade rolls his eyes. "'Kay," he says sarcastically, "Let's play the whose-job-is-harder game."

"That's not what this is about," I bark. "It doesn't have to be a competition. All I'm asking for is a little bit of appreciation."

"And I don't get to be appreciated?"

I sigh. "Back to the comparisons." I shake my head in disappointment.

Wade points a finger in my face. "You think you're the only one suffering here, but you're wrong."

We're in a face-off, the only sound coming from the sizzle on the stove. Wade's phone breaks the silence. The beep of another incoming text. When he pulls it from his pocket, I catch the briefest glimpse of the screen. I can't see the name, it's too fast, but I think I saw a Y.

Brynn?

He looks at the screen but doesn't reply. Now I'm fully burning.

"Maybe if you spent less time on your phone..." I let the comment trail off.

"What the hell is that supposed to mean?"

"Just means that you're texting a lot for someone who talks about wanting to get back to normal with *our family*."

Wade's eyes narrow, his mouth turning into a scowl. I can see the fury rising in him and it makes my heart rate gallop.

"You know what? Fuck you, Greta." He says it looking straight into my eyes.

I stare back, feeling something scary pass between us. Anger rages within me. "Yeah? Well, fuck you, too," I say, slow and steady.

A beat of stillness hangs heavy in the room. And then, without ever taking his eyes from me, Wade gestures to the stove. "I think your precious chicken is burning," he says before turning and walking out of the kitchen.

TWENTY-SIX

WADE DOESN'T SLEEP IN OUR BED THAT NIGHT, BUT neither do I. It's as though the space holds too much emotion for either of us. The smells, the familiarity. We can't be in such a sacred place after a fight like that.

Wade and I never speak the way we did. We don't hurl insults and we've never name-called. Replaying the whole thing as I lie in Summer's bed sends reverberations through my entire body. I'm nauseous picturing the words leave his mouth. *Fuck you, Greta.* Even more sick that I said it back. It's a nasty feeling, a feeling that you've somehow stooped to the lowest level, one you'd always prided yourself on never sinking to. We're not those people. We're not that couple who screams and fights.

And yet, that's exactly what happened tonight.

A tear drops onto Summer's pillow. I hug Lucy the Lamb to my chest. Sadness is here, but it's still battling residual anger. By the time the clock hits midnight, I finally fall asleep, body curled in a ball, mind an ever-spinning pinwheel.

. . .

The next morning, the corner of my mouth is crusted with dried drool. I must have slept *hard*. I take a minute to orient myself. I'm in Summer's room. Ah, yes, but not for just any reason. The fight. The F-bombs. Nausea crests again. My body tingles with all the emotions of last night flooding back. Only this time, when I replay everything, it's pain I feel most of all. The anger is still there, but less so. Above all, I'm struck with regret at the people Wade and I were twelve hours ago. I don't recognize those two. The argument didn't even make sense. He didn't care if I stepped in to flip the chicken, just as much as I wasn't truly bothered he didn't comment on the cleaning. Those were veneers—stand-ins for the real grounds on which our lives have become so shaky.

I fumble down the hall to wake up Gus and Merritt for school. Merritt coils in her covers, moaning about needing ten more minutes. "Come on," I say gently. We don't need any more tardies.

When I pass my bedroom, I peek in, but the bed is still made from the day before. I catch a whiff of shampoo, which tells me Wade's already showered and left for work. Brynn's face flashes in my mind. Is she consoling him today? Does he confide in her about my deficiencies as a wife and mother?

The kids are quick to get ready, granting us an extra few minutes to swing through Dunkin' for breakfast for them and a large coffee for me. They're quiet, and I'm unsure if it's just the morning, or whether it's something else. Whether they heard our fight last night. I do my best to put on a smile and send them both off with a kiss.

And then I brood. The argument runs on repeat in my head, along with my mother's words: *You're not giving up on Summer just because you make Wade a priority too.*

The way we acted yesterday adds another layer of despair on top of my already-dark world. This is not who we are. These are not the adults I want my children to see.

. . .

Noon rolls around. I'm browsing police reports for the tri-state area when the sound of the garage door opening makes me sit upright. I check the time out of habit. It's midday—who would be here, and how do they have access to my garage?

I get up, and by the time I'm halfway to the door, Wade's already come through. We both stop in our tracks, staring at each other with an awkwardness that feels foreign. It's like we've become strangers, completely unfamiliar to each other.

"Is everything okay?" I ask. He hasn't come home in the middle of the day since the kids were toddlers. Their bedtimes were so early, he felt like he barely had enough time to spend with them after work, so he'd occasionally pop home for lunch and a few extra hugs.

"Yeah," he says, "I just..." His expression is slacked, chest caved in. Nowhere near the strong, confident husband I've known for half my life. He rubs his forehead, then returns his gaze to me. "I couldn't focus at work, and I just wanted to... I'm really sorry about last night. I feel awful and I can't think of anything else."

My chin wobbles. "Me too."

I've been adamant that we don't need therapy, that I can climb out of all this on my own, but now I'm certain I was wrong. This is too much; the grief of it all feels bottomless. And now on top of everything, my marriage is facing decay.

"We need help," I say. The desperation feels like an all-time low point in our relationship. I didn't think it would come to this, and yet here we are. They say most couples don't survive tragedies like ours. I wonder if Wade and I will end up just another statistic.

But I don't want that. I'm willing to try anything at this point. I study his face, the way his eyes light up with the tiniest spark.

"Rob gave me the name of a woman he says is really good," he says, like he's been prepared to offer this suggestion since before my parents came over and first raised the idea.

Maybe our brains are mush, because it's almost comical. It sounds like we're setting up a threesome. In a way, we are—two broken people and a therapist to put us back together. I want to crawl into a hole and never come out. Just thinking about the effort this will take drains me. But his face is so open, so patient. Again, my parents' words fill my head. *Sinking ships. Do it for yourselves. Do it for the kids.*

"Okay," I say, one part of me hopeful for us, and the other part picturing him with someone else, this whole thing a charade for my parents, for the public. Am I sabotaging myself?

He steps toward me, grabs my hands in his. I let him pull me in. Our bodies press against each other for the first time in a long time. I breathe him in, trying to summon old feelings. I'm so confused. There's a new piece to the puzzle—if Wade's having an affair, we have a whole other thing to deal with.

"We're going to get through this," he says, the same sentiment my dad offered.

I wish I had their confidence.

TWENTY-SEVEN

EIGHTY-SEVEN DAYS GONE

A WEEK LATER, WADE AND I ARE SITTING IN A SMALL ROOM with an exposed brick wall and a leather couch that's worn from use. A low bookshelf holds enough self-help and relationship titles to last a decade. Across from us, our therapist—surreal, we have a therapist—balances a notepad on her knee. She's young, maybe even younger than me, and part of me doubts someone her age has enough life experience to impart wisdom. She doesn't wear a ring. Is she even married?

She's told us her name is Calista, but some people call her Callie. I don't know if I can honestly take advice from a girl named Callie. Shouldn't we be talking to someone named Ruth or Helen or Nancy? She'll remain Calista to me, a woman who probably doesn't even have kids yet is going to counsel us on how to grieve our missing child. I'm skeptical to say the least. But she's wearing a blazer and a dainty gold chain, which looks professional enough, so I'm going to give her a chance.

"Before we begin," Calista says, tucking her thick dark ringlets behind her ears, "I want you to know you have my fullest empathy for what you've been dealing with." She places a hand on her heart. "Parent to parent, I can't even begin to imagine."

Oh, so Calista is *a mom.* I bite my cheek, feeling guilty for assuming otherwise. It's then that I realize I've just done the same thing others have been doing to me—presuming to know things I don't.

I tuck any preconceived notions of Calista away and try my hardest to be present. Wade and I are here to work on our relationship. I have to be open.

"Thank you," Wade says, and I echo his sentiment with a nod.

"Times of grief often steer our priorities in different directions," Calista continues. "However, taking time to strengthen your marriage is one of the best things you can do for yourselves and your family, so I really commend you both for being here. I'd also like to remind you that this is a safe place to express your feelings and that my job is to help navigate these emotions in a supportive, non-judgmental environment."

Wade and I nod along. It's all very textbook, and even though I've never been in therapy before, this opening is exactly what I imagined it would be. The lead-in. The fine print.

Wade's thigh brushes against mine as he shifts on the couch. Our hands are so close, but neither of us reaches out for the other. The keenness of the observation weighs me down into the couch. Now I get why it's so worn. It's formed and shaped to the burdens of its tenants.

Calista picks up her pen. "Let's start with how you two have been communicating. Greta, would you say there have been challenges here?"

"Uh, yeah," I say, as though it were a stupid question. "It's been... difficult."

"Difficult how?"

"Well, it's hard to have a normal conversation with the

elephant in the room. Plus, Wade is back to work, so we don't see each other as much."

"We're sort of passing acquaintances, as terrible as that sounds," Wade adds.

Calista jots things down on her notepad. "Mmhmm. Okay. And when you do get a chance to talk, how does that go?"

Wade and I are both quiet, as if neither of us wants to admit the truth. Those heated arguments, the spiteful words. I sense he's as embarrassed as I am.

Finally, he speaks up. "Not great. There's a lot of... tension. We don't always agree on things."

"Things like...?"

"Like me going back to work, what the kids are and aren't allowed to do, things like that."

My defenses immediately flare. "Sorry if I'm a little over-protective these days."

"No need to apologize, Greta," Calista says. "Remember, no judgment."

Yeah? Then why is my heart pounding out of my chest?

"Let's go back a little," Calista says, uncrossing and re-crossing her legs in the opposite direction. "Tell me about the two of you as a couple. What makes you feel most connected? What are the things you used to do together?"

"We've always had a good marriage," Wade says. "We always enjoyed each other's company. Before kids, we'd go out to eat, to the movies, all the typical things. We liked to go hiking."

I jump in. "Once I started staying home full time, it was harder. I mean, three kids... you know. And Wade works a lot."

"So, in recent years," Calista says, "would you still consider your relationship as solid?"

Wade and I look to each other, then answer at the same time. "Yes."

It's true. Aside from his long hours and the mental load of

motherhood, I would still have classified us as a happy couple. Things weren't the same as pre-kids, but that doesn't mean they were bad. It was a different life, but a good life. At least, until recently. Until my impulsive decision at Wonderie Land.

"This is good," Calista says. "In my experience, couples who have a solid foundation before trauma are more likely to make it through the other end."

My belly flutters, and I spend a few seconds trying to interpret the sensation. Relief? Doubt?

Calista continues. "One of the most important steps, however, is open communication. Grief is complicated enough on an individual level. It's even more complex when shared between two people. We'll need to spend some time unpacking this."

I glance to the dried, pressed flowers hung in frames on the wall. They're beautiful but in a morbid sort of way. Why do we try to hold onto things? The past can't be trapped behind glass forever.

I come to and realize Calista is still talking. She looks at me as though waiting for me to respond.

"I'm sorry?" I say, embarrassed for daydreaming.

"Goals," she says. "I'd like to establish some ideas for what you guys would like to get out of therapy."

Goals? I want to find my daughter. I want to make it through the day.

"I'm also going to assign you some homework. If you're going to work through your issues, it's going to start by spending time together. Remember what I said about communication. So, step one is this—go out to dinner. Just the two of you. Take an hour to be alone outside of the house."

I shove my hands between my thighs. Next to me, I can feel Wade's nervous energy. When neither Wade nor I speak up, Calista takes it as a sign. "Let me be blunt," she says. "Do you want your marriage to work?"

"Yes," Wade says without hesitation, and it surprises me. I haven't let myself go all the way to confronting him on an affair, but the suspicion is always with me. His late evenings. The distance.

But if that were true, if he really is cheating, why suggest counseling? Is this all a cover-up?

Calista looks to me.

"Of course," I say. Of course I want our marriage to work. Whether it will—whether there's a third person already involved—is another story.

"You foresee a future together, regardless of what happens with Summer?" she asks.

It's the first time she's said our daughter's name, and the word is a dizzying zap to my system. I don't know why—we're here in therapy as a direct result of Summer's disappearance, after all. It's not as though we won't be discussing her directly at some point. And yet, hearing her name sucks the air from my lungs.

I let my mind drift to a future I've been actively avoiding. One that includes myself, Wade, Merritt, and Gus, but no Summer. Four people, not five. A huge tangle forms in my gut. Is this my future? Only two kids? Then, I picture what it would be like if Wade weren't there either. Me, alone with Gus and Merritt. Is this image better? Is this what I want instead?

The answer comes swiftly.

No.

I don't want to be alone. I chose Wade seventeen years ago and would choose him again today. I want this marriage to work. Only... wanting something to happen and it actually happening are two different things. I don't know if wanting will be enough to save us. He might already be gone.

"Greta?"

I've been daydreaming again. Calista and Wade both stare

at me. It seems that Wade has already answered the question. What did he say?

"Do you foresee a future with Wade?" Calista repeats.

I look to my husband, the eyes I've gotten lost in so many times. The gold band on his ring finger. The hands that cut our children's umbilical cords. Our path forward looks anything but easy. Resentment gurgles under the surface, and I'm afraid of what it will look like when it comes out.

"Yes," I say, despite it all.

I love this man. But love has limits.

TWENTY-EIGHT
EIGHTY-EIGHT DAYS GONE

A stretch of 12th Street was once home to many large industrial companies, but the past thirty years has seen a deterioration of the area, leaving many of the grand warehouses and factories empty or in need of repair. Weeds grow around the buildings, and peeling paint and crumbling bricks make the corridor look like the perfect place for seedy happenings.

Georgia assures me search efforts have canvassed the entire city, but it can't hurt to look again. I click on my mini flashlight. Despite the mid-morning sun, it's dark and dingy inside. Rusted metal and broken windows are obvious signs of neglect, and I wonder what this place looked like in its heyday. My heart pounds in my chest as I step forward, the crunch of gravel under my feet the only sound in the eerie silence.

"Summer?" I call. I can't begin to count the number of times I've said her name in these past three months. Each time, I imagine her little voice responding. So far, I've received only silence.

I pass through a door hanging off its hinges. The deeper into the building I go, the more ominous it feels. There's something unsettling about being in such a big building all alone. I keep looking up, as though I'm expecting bats to drop down on me from the ceiling.

Every noise makes me jump, my nerves on edge. I think I hear a distant drip of water, but it could also be nothing more than my imagination. I know this is a long shot, but I have to check every possible place. I have to do something.

Everywhere I look, it's nothing more than forgotten tables, old machinery collecting dust. But then, as I turn a corner, the beam of my flashlight catches sight of something else. Something that feels very out of place. I step closer, cautious. It appears to be a makeshift camp. Blankets and crates are arranged into a crude living area, and at once my heart knocks against the walls of my chest.

Someone is living here.

I move closer, my flashlight illuminating the area. Then I see it: a small, tattered doll lying on one of the blankets. My breath catches in my throat. It's a child's doll, and in that moment, I am convinced it must be Summer's. I rush forward, grabbing the doll and frantically searching the area.

"Summer? Summer, are you here?" I shout, my voice echoing through the empty factory.

The sight of the doll sends a shockwave of emotions through me. Desperation fuels my movements as I tear through the makeshift camp. Blankets fly into the air, crates overturn, and my hands are trembling so hard I can barely grip anything.

"Summer? Summer!" I scream, my voice breaking.

My mind races with terrifying images. I imagine Summer huddled in a dark corner, scared and alone. I think of her crying out for me, wondering why I haven't come to save her. The thought is unbearable. I have to find her. I have to know if she was here. If she still is here somewhere.

I rip open a cardboard box, sending its contents spilling out onto the dirty floor. Old clothes, a few cans of food, nothing that gives me any clue about Summer's whereabouts. I hurl the box aside, my frustration boiling over. "Please, Summer, please," I mutter under my breath, my eyes scanning every inch of the small camp.

I notice a pile of newspapers stacked neatly in the corner. I kick them over, desperate for any sign, any clue. The papers scatter, revealing nothing but more dirt and grime. I spin around, my flashlight beam darting over the walls, the floor, the shadows that seem to mock my frantic search.

A noise from behind makes me freeze. I whirl around, the flashlight landing on a figure standing in the shadows. It's a man, his clothes ragged and dirty, his hair a matted mess. He looks at me with wide, startled eyes.

"Who are you?" he asks, his voice rough and wary.

"You took her!" I scream, holding the doll up as evidence. "Where is she? Where's my daughter?"

The man raises his hands, stepping back. "I don't know what you're talking about," he says, his voice shaking. "I didn't take anyone."

"Liar!" I shout, advancing on him. "I found this doll here! It belongs to my daughter. Tell me where she is!"

The man shakes his head, his eyes full of fear. "I swear, I don't know anything about your daughter."

I hold up the doll. "Then what is this? Why do you have this?"

"That's... it was... my daughter's. I... I haven't seen her in years."

"Bullshit!" I say. "What did you do to her? Tell me where Summer is!"

He winces as I get in his face. "Please, please. I'm not lying. I didn't hurt your daughter."

"I don't believe you!"

"I've lived here by myself for months. I've never seen a little girl come through. I promise!"

I stare into his eyes, searching for the truth. After a few long seconds, my shoulders relax and I take a step back, putting space between us again.

"Look," the man says, "I'm really sorry. But I'm telling you, I don't know anything about your kid." He puts his hand out. "Can I have that back, please?"

I look at the doll in my hand and am struck with a clarity that makes me nauseous. I don't know this doll at all. I've cleaned up Summer's toys enough times to recognize anything that belongs to her. This one is a stranger.

"This was your daughter's?" I whisper, the anger slowly draining.

The man nods. "Yes. Addiction took everything from me, including my family. I keep that doll to remind me of her."

The doll slips from my grasp into his, and I stagger backward. The man watches me, his expression a mix of sympathy and sorrow. I thought this was it—I thought for sure the minute I saw that doll, this nightmare was about to come to an end. Instead, this place, like so many others, has turned up nothing.

I back away, shock and despair turning me from human to zombie again.

"Are you... Do you need...?" the man is saying, but I can only half hear. Every search that comes up empty is another blow, slowing shattering pieces of me until I'm sure I'll collapse into a pile of dust.

As I leave the building, I picture the man stacking his crates and folding blankets—rebuilding the home I destroyed. *I'm sorry*, I should have said to him. *I'm good at wrecking things*.

TWENTY-NINE
NINETY-ONE DAYS GONE

It's been four days since our therapy session, and we've agreed that our date night will be tonight. I don't even like using that term—date night. It's far too happy, too flirty. It brings up connotations of two people who are out to have a good time. Wade and I, we're simply completing homework.

"So you'll listen to a therapist but you won't take the same advice from me?" Lolly jokes as she grabs a bottle of water from my fridge. "I've been telling you to spend some time with Wade for ages."

"We're paying her," I say dryly.

"I'll gladly accept compensation for my guidance." She winks, and it makes me smile.

Since I put the kibosh on a sleepover a couple weekends ago, Lolly's convinced me to at least take the kids to the park. It's November, but the weather is still bearable with a hat and jacket. For once, I'm looking forward to getting out of the house. Gus is bringing a frisbee to play with the twins and, even though she's eleven, Merritt can still spend hours on a swing humming songs to herself.

I toss another couple of water bottles into my bag, then

follow Lolly's car down the street. We get stuck at a red light. My gaze drifts to the missing person poster. I've made sure there is at least one on every corner across Erie. Thousands. Tens of thousands.

When we get to the park, Gus jumps out while the car is practically still moving.

"Careful!" I yell, but he's gone, running toward Claire and Ivy, who beat us there and are already climbing a cargo net. Merritt trudges across the grass, hands shoved in the front pocket of her hoodie. On the far side, two sets of parents sit at a picnic table while their children play.

Lolly scoots down along the bench where she's sitting and pats the wooden slats. "Have a seat."

I drop down next to her.

"How are you guys doing?" she says, as though we don't talk almost every day.

I exhale, thinking about two days ago when Wade texted that he and his boss, Rob, were going out for a drink after work. A cold sweat had made me fan my shirt for air. Wade doesn't even like bars. But I don't need Lolly to know this. Our family is already so fractured, I don't need more cracks showing.

"Oh, you know," I say. "Wade's on first base, I'm somewhere in the outfield."

"And the kids?"

"In the bleachers maybe?"

Lolly watches the kids play. "You'll find yourselves again."

I don't respond. My mind goes back to last week's therapy session. The tension. The blame that eats at me. My resentment toward Merritt. Just like Wade's after-work outing, I don't tell Lolly all these details. Some things are just too private to share.

I follow her gaze onto the playground.

"Be careful, Gus," I urge as he hangs upside down by the knees.

"Look at me, Mom!" he calls.

"Maybe you shouldn't—"

He lets go and drops to the ground, landing like a cat on all fours.

"Jesus," I say. "A broken bone is just what we need."

Lolly chuckles. Her girls dart past in a blur of pink and giggles.

Gus jumps from one playground landing to the next, slips down the green plastic slides on his belly and behind. The third time, he approaches the slide standing. I jump up from the bench and dash over. "I don't think so," I say to him. "Not on your feet. You're going to fall and break your neck."

He laughs me away, taking the slide on his behind like I asked. I thank him, but now he's got me nervous. I stand on the chipped rubber ground in a wide stance, arms folded.

Lolly waves me back. "Come sit!"

"I better stay out here in case they need me," I say. She doesn't respond but gets up and joins me in the middle of the playground.

"Watch your face," I say to Gus, who's moved on to the frisbee with one of the twins. I can just picture the hard disc smacking him in the forehead followed by a set of stitches.

Lolly tries to restart the conversation. "So, where are you guys going to din—"

"Oh, Merritt, careful!" I interrupt, abandoning Lolly to assist Merritt on the monkey bars. I grab her narrow waist as she swings to the next rung.

"Mom, stop!"

"What? I'm just helping."

She kicks me away with one leg, then drops halfway across. Her lips curl. "I'm not a baby. You don't need to watch every single thing I do."

"I'm not—"

"Yes, you were!" She stomps away.

My face burns with equal parts embarrassment and frustration.

The other parents stare. I was only trying to help. Why does every-thing with Merritt have to be so difficult? I turn to Lolly. "Holy hormones." I try to play it off. "So much for trying to protect them."

Lolly smiles, but it doesn't feel real. She looks away.

"What?" I ask.

Lolly spreads a clump of rubber ground with her shoe. "Maybe she just wants a little space. The kids have played here hundreds of times and never gotten hurt."

I pause. "Are you saying I'm hovering?"

"A little." She studies me as if she's deciding whether I'll bite her head off. "Merritt told me you made her hold the cart at the grocery store the other day."

"Kids get snatched at stores all the time!"

Lolly tilts her head. "Greta."

My teeth grind, but I keep my cool. This is Lolly, my best friend. We've always been able to be honest with each other. She wouldn't say anything unless it were a big deal.

"Fuck," I say, slumping back onto the bench. "I'm a goddamn helicopter, aren't I?" First the school pick-up line and now this.

"Real talk?"

"Hit me."

"Yep, you are. But, hey, I get it. I mean, I probably would be too. You love your kids, and given everything that's happened..."

I stare across the playground to where Merritt is spinning alone on the merry-go-round. Lolly's right. I'm acting like any normal parent would in my situation.

Lolly gives me an elbow to the arm and grins. "I'll have to get you some aviator goggles." I scrunch my nose, trying to follow. "You know," she says, "since you're a helicopter pilot now."

Her grin grows. *Get it? Helicopter mom? Goggles? Ha. Ha. Ha.*

As dumb as the joke is, it lands. A laugh bellows from my abdomen, hearty and full, and leaves my lips. It's a feeling I haven't experienced in what feels like forever. For a moment, any stress melts away. My chin tips up to the sky and I let the laugh release a burst of dopamine in my brain.

Just as quickly, panic seizes. I bring both hands to cover my mouth and look to Lolly, capsized by shock. Her smile drops too.

"Hey," she says, bracing my shoulders. "It's okay to laugh. It's okay to have moments of joy again."

I shake my head, hands still clasped over my mouth.

"Yes," she insists. "Yes."

Water fills my eyes. She pulls me into a hug.

I laughed. How could I let myself laugh?

A car turns into the parking lot. Two young kids—a boy and girl who look to be about two and four—hop out and run toward the playground. A woman in jeans and a Fair Isle sweater follows. She meets them at the top of the slide, arms extended up, and helps the youngest glide down.

See? I think. *Moms watch over their children's safety. That's all I was doing.*

Only this woman's children are far younger than Merritt.

The woman laughs at her daughter, who flies down the slide and lands on her bum. She plops the toddler back on her feet and gives a little pat as the girl runs off to do it again. The three of them are having a good time, sharing laughs, making memories—I'm slightly mesmerized.

Then the woman's gaze pans the perimeter of the playground and lands on me. Her expression quickly changes. It's as though a freeze has swept through, turning her warm smile to a cold stare. She wanders over to the other parents at the picnic table, and it's just like the day in the grocery store. I feel their scorn without hearing a single word.

"Don't pay them any attention," Lolly says, linking her arm through mine.

I try, but it's not easy.

We stay at the park for another hour, letting the kids run and climb and swing. I resist every urge to hang too close. I don't need Merritt snapping at me again, nor do I want to come off as any more of a helicopter mom than I already am.

When it's time to leave, Gus's hairline is sweaty.

"Do we have to go?" he whines.

"Daddy and I are going out to dinner," I say. "Grandma and Grandpa are coming to babysit."

He pumps his arm. "Yes!" I know what he's thinking— grandparents babysitting means an extra scoop of ice cream after dinner. His delight brings a smile to my face, but only for so long. I'm not exactly looking forward to our "date."

We say goodbye to Lolly and the girls and return home. I'm unsure what Wade's been doing, but it clearly hasn't been washing the dishes in the sink. Maybe he's been busy texting a mystery person. The thought of snooping through his phone briefly crosses my mind, but I dismiss it. We've never been that type. *Don't ruin tonight*, I tell myself.

I ease onto the couch, feeling like I need a decompression period after the playground. Gus asks me if I'll play Guess Who? with him, and I say maybe later. A Facebook notification pings on my phone. I open the app and click the little red circle.

You have one new post in Erie Mom's Group, the notification reads.

I click on it, and the breath drains from my lungs. It's a picture of me at the park from only an hour ago. The image was taken from across the playground. It's slightly pixelated, but clear enough to see an open-mouth smile stretching across my face. My head is tilted back, eyes squinting. Anyone who saw it would quickly identify someone in a moment of pure, blithe laughter.

And that's exactly correct. It was the precise moment Lolly made the joke that split through my wall of armor and made me whoop.

Someone had been watching. And someone caught it on camera.

It had to have been one of the parents at the picnic table.

Now, the picture is online with a caption that reads:

How can a mother possibly be smiling when her child is miss-ing?? #FindSummer #NeverForget

There are a dozen comments, but my hands are shaking too much to tap the button. My mouth falls open. I'm utterly flab-bergasted. Whoever took the picture had been waiting for this split second. Waiting for an opportunity to drag me through the mud even more.

Drums pound in my ears. I don't hear Wade come into the room until his voice makes me startle. "What is it?" he says, and I realize I'm gawking at the phone.

"People are horrible," I say, my words cracking as they come out. "Just horrible." I hand him the phone. "That was literally an hour ago. Lolly said something that made me laugh and some woman—some *bitch*—took my picture and posted it."

"Are you kidding me?" His eyes go dark with rage as he reads the caption.

"I seriously can't get a break with these people. Everyone thinks they're so high and mighty. I bet they didn't see me start crying one second after that laugh." A storm brews inside me. I snatch my phone back and my thumbs tap wildly on the screen.

"What are you doing?" Wade says.

"Telling them to fuck off."

"Greta, don't." His anger turns to concern. "It's not worth it."

"Why shouldn't I? Don't I have a right to defend myself?"

"They're only going to go harder. They don't even know you."

"Exactly. They don't know me, and yet they think they have the right to blast my face all over the internet and say things that aren't true."

I'm so mad I could punch the wall. Everything in me wants to write a nasty message on this post, but I know Wade is right. Damn him for being so level-headed. I chuck my phone across the couch. It bounces off and lands on the floor.

"On second thought," he says, whipping out his own phone. "Screw that." He swipes it open, scrolls for a moment, then starts typing with furious fingers.

"What are you doing?" Now I'm the curious one.

"Exactly what you said, telling them to fuck off."

I get a little buzz of energy watching him come to my defense. I've never played the damsel in distress card, but this feels nice. For once, it's not just me against everyone else.

Wade finishes and tucks his phone away. "There."

"What did you say?"

"I said they're a bunch of keyboard warriors who are getting pleasure from someone else's pain... and that they can keep their comments to themselves."

"That's it?" I'm surprised, given the way he'd typed with such fury.

"I also might have called them motherfuckers."

I bring a hand up to my lips. *Wade!*

"Seriously, Gret," Wade says. "Don't spend any energy on them."

I give a one-shoulder shrug. "That's the same thing Lolly said."

"Great minds think alike." He pinches a smile, and I know he's trying to lift my mood. "I'm going to go change. Your parents should be here soon, right?"

My mind turns. He and Lolly had the exact same sentiment. He and Lolly. The Y on the name of the incoming text I saw on his phone. Could it be...?

I give myself an internal slap across the face. *Snap out of it. Are you crazy? Wade is not sleeping with Lolly.*

Wade waits for a response. I sigh. "Can we take a rain check on dinner? This photo bullshit has me all worked up." The truth is that while I am mentally exhausted and probably will be stewing about the picture all evening, it's also a good excuse not to go out. My brain hurts from too much thinking. I can easily cancel my parents and call it a night. The idea of Summer's bed fills me with much more warmth than dinner at a restaurant.

Wade cocks his head. "You know what Calista said. It's our homework." The message is unspoken—if we don't go tonight, we'll probably never reschedule. I'm surprised he's pushing so hard. For someone who might be cheating, he sure is sending mixed signals.

"Okay," I say, trying to hide any distaste. He gives a quick nod. I keep my forced smile in place until he leaves the room.

THIRTY

Oliver's Rooftop has a great view of the lake from the eighth floor of a hotel right on the bayfront, and the first thing I think is whether or not Wade has brought another woman here. The thought quickly dissipates. We're still enough in the public eye that he'd be insane to bring a mistress to a restaurant.

From our table, I can see the *Brig Niagara*, the old flagship docked at port. Last year, we took the kids through the maritime museum. Gus had repeatedly asked if there would be pirates and was disappointed when there weren't.

Wade orders a beer. The server looks to me next, but I say I'm fine with water. People are watching.

"Get a drink," Wade says.

I look around then think, *What the hell.* "Oh, fine, I'll have a Cabernet." The server nods and leaves. When he returns moments later, I all but guzzle the wine, hoping it will go straight to my bloodstream. I'm wound tight, and not even the cigarette I snuck before leaving the house is doing the trick. This dinner—this homework—is supposed to be a step in helping our marriage. It's not going to work if I can't relax.

Wade watches me with caution. He takes a sip of his beer. "I was thinking we could take the kids to the pumpkin farm tomorrow. Might be one of the last decent weekends before it gets too cold."

Tomorrow. Sunday. The day of rest. I mentally grumble about the idea of leaving the house on a Sunday. As if I don't also rest Monday through Friday. The pumpkin farm is an annual tradition, one where I take pictures of the kids in a massive pit of corn kernels, we take a hayride through the field, and each of them gets to choose a gourd for my dining room centerpiece. Summer always chose bumpy ones, saying they looked like witch's warts. I can't imagine going to such a fun place without her.

I hear Calista's words about communication. *Try*, I plead with myself. *Just try.*

"Sure," I say.

Wade smiles, pleased. He's probably telling himself it will be a lovely family day. Doesn't he remember the last lovely family day we had? One of our children was stolen. And here we are out to a nice dinner, drinking wine and beer, pretending to be happy doing something for ourselves. In fact, that's the exact thing that got us into this mess—me wanting something for myself. Trying to hold onto the past, to us as a couple. Now, it's like we don't even know what to talk about. Our eyes dart around any place but each other's faces. This was a massive mistake.

My gaze lands on a table not far from ours. A slice of cheesecake drizzled with chocolate sits on the tablecloth between a couple. One piece, two forks. But the couple isn't looking at the cake. Their faces are pointed in my direction. As soon as I catch them staring, they turn away. At another table, two women are far less subtle. One has a hand blocking her mouth, speaking to her friend, whose eyes go big then look my way. It's as though we're back in high school.

"Good God," I murmur.

Wade follows my line of vision. He does a double take.

"See what I have to deal with?" I hiss.

"Ignore them."

"Everywhere I go, people stare and whisper. I feel like I'm living in the goddamn *Scarlet Letter*."

"Maybe they're talking about me, not you."

What? Why would he say that? Is he guilty of something I don't know about?

"Yeah, right," I say. None of the online criticism has been directed at Wade. They only come after me. The mom.

"I called a few more places today to ask about surveillance footage," Wade says. "The gas station said they checked and didn't see anything. And the tiki bar on the corner—"

"I thought we'd already checked with the tiki bar."

"We did, but I figured I'd ask again. New manager, someone said. Maybe they'll be a little more useful than the last."

I give a grunt of acknowledgement. We're like hamsters on a spinning wheel—even when we come back to the same pieces of information, places we've already checked, we can't help but be hopeful.

"Are you nervous for tomorrow?" he asks.

Our third press conference, the one I suggested to Georgia. The one I requested to keep Summer's face in the public eye.

"A little. It's not exactly something you ever envision having on your bingo card."

"I know." Wade lays his hand out on the table, an invitation. I stare at it, internal confusion pervading my brain like a fast-spreading disease. He's so hot and cold. Is this how someone who's cheating behaves?

He wiggles his fingers. He's always been able to calm me down. I know that palm so well, know every little crease, the scar that runs along the inside of his pointer finger from a home improvement debacle. And yet, his hand seems so unfamiliar now, like something I knew in a former life.

Again, I tell myself what to do. *Hold his hand.*

We're trying so hard. If the circumstances were different, we might even laugh about it. The pressure to connect. The desire to make this dinner successful so we can go back and report to Calista. *Did we get an A+?*

I lay my hand in his and attempt to block out the rest of the room and the imaginary person who lives in my mind. It's just us. He wouldn't be here otherwise. We have to make this work.

The server returns to take our orders, and our hands part. We don't touch again for the rest of the evening.

THIRTY-ONE

NINETY-TWO DAYS GONE

THE AIR IS THICK WITH ANTICIPATION AS I WALK INTO THE police station, my heart pounding in my chest. I stand beside Georgia at the podium, facing a sea of reporters and cameras. The flashbulbs momentarily blind me, and I feel a rush of nausea. I can't believe this is my life.

Georgia steps forward, her face set with determination. She's a good woman, dedicated, and I trust her—yet there's still a part of me that faces constant frustration that we haven't found my daughter.

Georgia clears her throat and begins to speak into the microphone, her voice steady and clear. "Thank you all for coming. We're here today to provide an update on the ongoing investigation into Summer Goodman's disappearance," she says, her eyes scanning the room. "First and foremost, I want to reassure the public that we are doing everything in our power to find Summer. This case remains our top priority."

The room is silent, every ear straining to catch her words. I take a deep breath, trying to steady my nerves. This is another chance to reach out to the public, to plead for their help. The thought of speaking in front of all these people is terrifying, but not as terrifying as doing nothing.

"We've followed up on over a thousand tips and leads, and we continue to pursue every possible avenue," Georgia continues. "We've expanded our search to include areas outside of Erie, and we're working closely with state and federal agencies."

I glance at Wade, standing next to me, his face a mask of stoic support. We're in this together, but sometimes it feels like we're worlds apart. I turn back to the crowd as Georgia gestures for us to step forward. Did she introduce us? Everything is a blur. My hands tremble, and I clutch the edge of the podium to steady myself.

"We want to thank the police for their tireless efforts and the community for their unwavering support," Wade begins. "We haven't given up hope, and we're asking for your continued help. If anyone has any information, please come forward."

The words feel inadequate, but they're all we have. I blink back tears, refusing to break down in front of the cameras. Summer needs me to be strong. She needs me to fight for her.

A reporter raises her hand, and Georgia nods in her direction. "Mrs. Goodman, how are you holding up during this difficult time?" she asks, her tone gentle but probing.

I take a deep breath. "It's been incredibly hard, but we have to stay hopeful. We have to believe that Summer will come home."

Another reporter jumps in, more aggressive this time. "There have been rumors that the investigation is stalling. Do you feel the police are doing enough?"

The question feels like a punch to the gut, but I force myself to stay calm. "I believe the police are doing everything they can. This isn't an easy process, and they've been very supportive."

It's true. And still not enough.

Georgia steps in, her voice firm. "We are pursuing all leads and working tirelessly to find Summer. This kind of investigation takes time, but we're committed to bringing her home."

Another reporter pipes up. "Greta, what message would you like to send to Summer, if she can hear you right now?"

I stare into the camera. "We will never stop looking for you. Daddy and I love you so very much."

It's all I can get out before I choke on my words.

One of the reporters addresses Georgia this time. "Is there any indication that this could be related to other similar cases in the area or state?"

"We can't comment on other cases at this time."

"Have you received any direct contact or ransom demands from the kidnapper?"

"I'm not going to comment on that."

I see a vein pulse in her neck. She's keeping her cool in the face of increasingly aggressive questions. Yet, I find myself sharing the reporter's frustration. Why aren't there more transparent answers?

"What steps are being taken to ensure the safety of other children in the community?" the reporter asks.

Georgia grips the podium. "This situation is highly unusual. As always, the local community should use general caution as they would in their everyday lives; however, law enforcement does not see any additional threat to children in our area."

"But what about—"

"Thank you," Georgia cuts him off. "That will be all the questions for now." She addresses the camera once more. "If anyone watching has any information regarding the disappearance of Summer Goodman, please contact the Erie police. The Goodman family continues to offer a one hundred thousand dollar—"

I leap toward the microphone. "One hundred and *fifty* thousand," I blurt.

Georgia blinks, looks between Wade and me, then returns

to face the camera. "One hundred-and-fifty-thousand-dollar reward."

With that, Georgia leads us from the room. In the hallway, she meets my gaze, her expression softening. "You did great, Greta."

I nod as she puts an arm around me. This relationship we've formed, this partnership, it's something I never would have wished for, not under these circumstances. And yet, I'm so thankful for her. At times, I feel like she gets me more than my own husband.

"Another fifty thousand?" Wade whispers.

"Is there a price tag on your daughter's life?" I snap back.

"Of course not. It's not the money, I just think we should have talked about it first. The FBI said they'd help with all these decisions—they're the experts."

"Oh, yeah? Well then why haven't they found our daughter?" My eyes narrow, my voice lowering to a hiss. "I will sell my soul before I give up on her."

"Greta," Wade says, "that's not what I'm saying."

I start to turn, but he grabs my arm. "Hey." Our eyes connect. "Team, remember?"

"Right," I say. "A team."

THIRTY-TWO

NINETY-FIVE DAYS GONE

My phone wakes me from a dream in which Summer was running through a field of sunflowers. In it, she gathered up an armful, tossed them in the air, and magically the flowers burst into pieces like fireworks, raining petals down onto her smiling face.

The phone shrills again. I rub my eyes. Two forty-five. Time to get the kids. But wait, that's not my alarm beeping. It's a different sound. I squint at the screen. The school is calling.

"Hello?" I answer, voice raspy from lack of use.

"Hi, Mrs. Goodman? This is Brad Applebaum, Merritt's teacher."

Suddenly, I'm awake. "Is she okay?" I spurt. My heart does a leap.

"Yes, yes, she's fine. Relatively speaking, that is."

"I'm sorry?"

"She's physically fine, yes. Sorry, I didn't mean to startle you. But I'd love to chat if you have a few minutes? I have some concerns about Merritt's academics."

"Oh," I say, regulating my heart rate. "Yes, of course."

On the other end of the line, Brad Applebaum takes an

audible breath. "First, let me express my condolences for everything your family has been going through. I was at the vigil, but we didn't get a chance to talk."

"Thank you." It's become an automatic response. People feel required to offer condolences, and I'm required to accept their sympathy.

"It's been a bit of a rough start to the year for Merritt," he says. "We're almost twelve weeks into the term, and I'm afraid things are slipping, as I'm sure you've noticed. Her grades are declining. She's stopped turning in homework."

My cheeks go warm, as though he were speaking to my face instead of over the phone. "I'm... I'm sorry," I say because it feels like how a good parent would respond—apologize for their child's misdeeds.

"No need to be sorry. That's not what this is about. I'm concerned for Merritt. I spoke with teachers who have had her in previous years and they all agree this isn't typical. Merritt, from what I've heard, is a good student, gets good grades. I can only presume that what's happening this year is because of all you guys have on your plates. Stress can do that. And believe me, I fully empathize."

What does he want me to say here? We're all struggling to keep our heads above water. Apparently I didn't realize how quickly Merritt was sinking. I look out the window. November has brought the changing of leaves, turning our neighborhood into a cornucopia of colors. I don't want them to fall. Falling leaves means time is passing.

"Is there something we can do?" I ask. "A tutor? Extra work?"

"I don't think what Merritt needs right now is extra work."

"Okay, but if she's failing her subjects..."

"It's not to that point... yet. But there are other concerns beyond grades."

Other concerns?

"Merritt's awfully quiet," he says. "She asks to go to the nurse a lot. Doesn't want to participate or play when we go out for recess."

"Oh." My shoulders slump. Merritt's always been a social kid. She prides herself on winning the schoolyard games. How did it get this bad? More than that, why did they *let* it get this bad before contacting me? Once again, I'm feeling hypersensitive, as if this is a covert way of placing additional blame on my shoulders.

"I wish I would have known about this earlier," I say.

"I sent a letter a couple weeks back that expressed many of these concerns. Did you not receive it?"

A letter? I never got a letter. "No, I didn't."

"Hmm, that's strange. Sorry about that. Yes, I met with the school counselor and we drafted a letter to let you and your husband know what had been going on."

"I didn't get a letter," I say again, more forceful. I don't know what he's getting at, but I've had it up to here with mom-shaming. I don't need more from people who are supposed to be on my side.

"Okay, it's no problem," he says. "I'm glad I caught you today."

I picture him in his classroom, even though I've never met him face to face. We didn't attend the open house at the start of the year. But if he's calling me, where are the students?

"Where is Merritt now?" I ask.

"They're at art. This is my plan period."

"Oh."

"Mrs. Goodman, I don't want to put more stress on you, and certainly not on Merritt, but I wanted you to be aware. Perhaps you could bring it up gently."

Thank you, sir. I think I know how to talk to my own child.

"I most certainly will."

"Great. Why don't we keep in touch as the weeks go on?

I'm happy to sit down with you and your husband if you ever want to discuss this in person."

"Thank you."

We hang up. I fall back onto the bed. My heart hurts for Merritt, for all of us. The idea of her withdrawing in school, of not being her typically happy self is enough to make me weep. As they say, a parent is only as happy as their unhappiest child. It's human nature to want to protect your children, to want to do everything possible to make their lives better. And yet, there's a threshold. I don't know how I can take on any more grief than my own.

Mr. Applebaum was certain he'd reached out prior to this call. Am I losing my mind? I think back, searching a mental catalog through the million times I've gotten the mail. And then I remember. There had been a letter, though I don't recall opening it. It must have been flushed away with all the other garbage straight into the trash.

In addition to everything else, I've apparently lost my attention to detail.

The clock reads one o'clock. I could go back to sleep for another hour and a half until my pick-up alarm goes off. The thought is tempting. But now my brain is whirring. Merritt is on the verge of failing sixth grade. We've yet to receive a report card for this school year. Is it really going to come home with Fs? Merritt's never gotten less than a B.

I stare at the ceiling. What if she has to repeat sixth grade? Her friends will move on without her, and she'll be stuck behind.

I get up from the bed, my body now restless, and wander the house. Laundry needs doing—Wade will say he's almost out of clean underwear—but I pass by the full basket without so much as a glance. In the kitchen, I force myself to drink a glass of water, feeling dehydrated. Merritt is like an equation I need to solve, though it's hard to do halfheartedly.

I go back upstairs, and my feet take me to Merritt's room. When was the last time I was in here? Now that I think about it, I haven't tucked her into bed for... gosh, over a month? It's quick "goodnights" from the doorway or nothing at all. Sometimes she's already asleep when I make it upstairs.

Her bed is made haphazardly, the covers pulled up but not evenly and certainly not smooth. I'm not a stickler for bed-making—this is good enough. The little white nightstand holds her alarm clock and a lamp. Knick-knacks clutter the surface: candy-flavored ChapStick, several hair ties. A shiny ribbon, like one on the top of a bookmark, is caught in the closed drawer. I open it and press the ribbon back, then tidy up the drawer. Dollar-store junk and Happy Meal toys litter the inside. An old Valentine she's saved. A random photo of Merritt with my parents. All the treasures of childhood.

There's also a small diary with a purple cover. I remember buying it as a gift for her two Christmases ago. She squealed with excitement—such a rite of passage for a young girl. I imagined all the things she'd write in it. Innocent musings. Crushes. All the big feelings packed into a tiny body. But I've never peeked. A girl's diary is a sacred place, and it couldn't be anything but childlike at this age. Frankly, I'd forgotten about the journal altogether until now.

I pull it from the drawer. My thumb slides along the edge of the cover. Would it be a breach of trust to read it? We established a rule when Merritt got her phone: Wade and I would have full access to her messages. We'd have the right to look and search through whatever we wanted. She grumbled a bit but didn't put up a fight. It was for her safety, we explained. It was to teach her how to stay safe in the digital world.

Now, as I stare at her diary and debate whether to read it, the same rule feels applicable. If Merritt is struggling in school, maybe she's written about it in her diary. If I'm unable to connect with her in person, perhaps I can figure out what's going on through what she's written.

I open the cover. The first page is dated the day after Christmas, two years ago.

Dear Diary,

This is the best present ever!

I flip forward. The entries slowed after a few weeks, greater and greater stretches between them. Like all new and shiny things in a child's life, the diary was probably forgotten about in favor of something new.

But then the writing changes. I look at the date and see it's recent—August 25, about two weeks after Summer's disappearance.

Dear Diary,

Summer is gone and it's all my fault. I was supposed to watch her but I didn't. I miss Summer so so so much. I wish I could make her come back.

My stomach churns. I turn a couple pages forward.

Dear Diary,

Things are so messed up. I know Mom blames me for Summer. She barely hugs me anymore. She's sad all the time. I miss her smile. I think she hates me.

Feeling sick, I flip to the last entry. It's from just this past week. Unsure how it can get any worse, I read.

Dear Diary,

I'm never going back to school. Today in gym class, Cora and Lennon called me a bitch for no reason and said I'm a terrible sister. The teacher didn't even do anything. Everyone's always looking at me weird. They whisper right in front of me. Mrs. Fink tells me <u>every day</u> that she's praying for Summer, but it just makes me feel worse. I wish everyone would stop talking about it. I wish I had a different life.

I close the journal. My hands are numb. So are my arms, my legs. My whole body. I sit there on Merritt's bed for what feels like hours, wrestling with emotions. My daughter is struggling, and I completely missed it. What does that say about me? So many of the feelings from those first days of the disappearance return. I know what I *should* do, but I simply... can't.

I should hold Merritt and tell her it's okay, that I love her, that I forgive her. That the blame I'm projecting is really a reflection back on me. I should reinforce that none of this is her fault. Then why is there such a wall blocking me? The anger has built up so high—anger at myself, frustration at her—I can no longer see over, even with these journal entries staring me in the face.

I hold the diary like it's an ancient artifact. Maybe I should tell Wade. He can deal with Merritt; he's always been better at it than me. More patience, more composure. It's a small comfort, knowing she has him. A tiny release of guilt. But not much—there's still plenty of that remaining wherever I go.

After a few minutes, I replace the diary and close the drawer. What I'll do with this information is still unclear. But for now, it gets filed away. It's almost time to get the kids. I should probably brush my hair.

THIRTY-THREE

MERRITT IS QUIET ON THE WAY HOME FROM SCHOOL. I repeatedly peek at her in the rear-view mirror, but she mostly stares out the window. Her long hair frames her face like dark curtains. I try to see myself in her but struggle to find a likeness. Often, I find myself watching her, trying to understand the ins and outs of how she works. *Who are you and how did you come from me?*

"How was school?" I say, shaking the thought away.

"Great!" Gus says with enthusiasm. "We're learning about meta— metaphor— metastasis— Whatever. It's when a caterpillar goes into a cocoon and turns into a butterfly. Mrs. Rice even has two real ones in class. It's so cool! Today, I was looking at them and—"

"That's nice, honey. Merritt, how about you?"

"It was fine," she says without looking at me.

"Just fine?"

"Yep. Just fine."

Mr. Applebaum's call and the diary entries are not far from my mind. "Is there something you want to talk about?"

She's quiet for a second. "No."

We pull into the garage. The kids get out before me. I follow them into the house.

"Oh, Mom, I got an A on my spelling test," Gus says, emptying his daily folder. "It was the one with all the suffixes. Remember the tricky ones?"

"Amazing!" I say in passing as I follow Merritt through the kitchen. She's headed toward the stairs.

"Mer," I say, but she keeps going.

I trail after her, and Gus trails after me. We're like one big train being led by an angsty, possibly depressed preteen.

"Will you help me with my math?" Gus asks.

"Merritt," I repeat. "We need to talk."

Gus is literally on my heels. "Mom? My homework?"

"Talk about what?" Merritt says without stopping.

"School. Your grades. I got a call from Mr. Applebaum."

She pauses for the briefest second then finally turns around, her lips pressed together. She looks surprised to learn her teacher called me. "I don't feel like talking about it."

My blood pressure rises. The defiance! I'm at the bottom of the stairs and she's near the top. We stand with our arms crossed.

"Well, I think it's pretty important," I say.

Gus pulls on my hand. "Mom?"

"Since when do you care?" Merritt says. Her pale cheeks are flushed.

Here we go again. If this is a foreshadow to her teen years, I'm not ready for it. My teeth clench. The pressure in my ears is about to pop. "Don't disrespect me, young lady. I'm only looking out for you."

She rolls her eyes. I go to speak again, to tell her she doesn't have a choice in the matter, but I'm interrupted.

"Mom?"

"WHAT?" I spin and scream in Gus's face.

He falls back a few steps, fear and hurt etched from his wrinkled forehead to trembling chin.

"I just wanted you to help me with my math homework," he says, shakily.

"And I said I would."

"No, you didn't. You didn't answer me." His voice is small.

I exhale hard. "I was in the middle of talking to your sister, okay?" I swing an arm up, gesturing toward the stairs. "This is important. Your homework can wait."

He doesn't say a word. Simply retreats like a wounded puppy. When I look back to where Merritt was standing, she's gone.

"Great," I grumble and trudge up the stairs. She may think she can get out of talking to me, but not this time. A frank conversation with Merritt is long overdue.

Just as I'm reaching for her doorknob, there's a crash down below. The sound of breaking glass brings me to a sudden halt. *What the...?* I pivot and run down the stairs, nearly stepping on a shard of—

Wait, is that what I think it is? I take in the splinters of porcelain. It's several seconds before my brain processes the familiar blue pattern.

"What the hell?" I say, scanning the hardwood floor, where my precious great-grandmother's lamp lies shattered in a million pieces. I'm too shocked at first to understand. Red splotches swirl and come at me fast. Finally, my vision focuses, and I see him. Gus has backed into the corner, fists balled at his sides, lips curled in a snarl. He's breathing so hard I can practically see his ribcage through his shirt. I didn't need to witness it to know what he did. It's written all over his face.

I'm frozen at the bottom of the steps, a weary traveler at a fork in the road. One child upstairs, one child in front of me.

Both of whom need their mom. Motherhood—it's not always pretty, but there it is.

I pinch the bridge of my nose and close my eyes. Is an empty mother better than no mother at all?

THIRTY-FOUR

ONE HUNDRED ONE DAYS GONE

We've had several sessions with Calista now but it's no less awkward, and no less draining. Each time, I feel like maybe we're getting somewhere—there are aha moments and revelations galore—but then we fall two steps back and the hour is over. I'll admit it: Wade is more confident than I am. It's not that I've changed my mind about wanting our marriage to survive, it's just that perhaps I'm not able to give it the attention he can right now. *Let's talk about this in twenty years*, I want to say. Today is hard. Today I don't have the strength.

And yet, we return.

Calista's hair is pulled back today into a poufy bun on the top of her head. It makes her look even younger, but despite all my initial misgivings, I've come to like her. She's surprisingly insightful. I might even be able to call her Callie.

I hold a small, embroidered pillow on my lap and prepare for another fifty minutes of therapy.

"Thanksgiving is coming up," Calista says, as though I need reminding. "This will be the first major holiday without Summer. How are you feeling about that?"

"We survived Halloween," Wade says.

"True, but Thanksgiving feels a little different, no? A lot of family get-togethers."

Calista looks at me for my input, but I'm not debating whether Halloween was a difficult holiday or not. I'm stuck back on what she said, the specific choice of words. In an instant, I don't like her so much anymore.

"I'm sorry," I say, "but how do you know Summer won't be found before then?"

Calista's cordial smile fades. "Oh, I didn't mean—"

"But that's what you said. You said Thanksgiving, which is still a week away, will be the first major holiday without Summer. So you think she's dead. Or gone forever. Same thing, right? You don't think there's any hope of her returning."

"Greta, I..." Calista's face has gone red.

Wade puts a hand on my knee. "I don't think that's what she meant."

"How could you interpret it any other way?" I ask. "Why not pose the question as, 'Thanksgiving is coming up. Wouldn't it be wonderful if Summer were found by then?'"

"Of course that would be wonderful," Calista says. "I'm sorry for phrasing my question that way. You're right. That was thoughtless of me."

I'm breathing hard. Sometimes I swear I'm the only one who still believes there's a chance of finding Summer. It's like I'm on a raft in the middle of the ocean with no one around, only waves that threaten to upend me. It's a scary and lonely place to be.

I glance at the clock. We still have a lot of time, but I no longer want to participate. Calista fumbles with her notepad. She seems frazzled, trying to redirect us to calmer waters.

"How are things with Merritt and Gus?" she asks.

Wade shrugs. "They're... okay, I guess? I think Gus is having a hard time."

"In what way?"

"He broke Greta's favorite lamp. Slammed it on the ground and broke it into pieces."

Calista looks at me. "Sounds like a cry for attention?"

I nod. I thought we were here to talk about our marriage, not the kids. Not my parenting.

"And how about Merritt?" Calista says.

"I don't want to talk about Merritt," I respond without missing a beat.

She looks taken aback. "Oh. Okay. Um, sure."

Somehow this session has gotten off track. I'm just about to call it quits when Calista leans forward, crossing her wrists on her knees.

"Let's skip the small talk, hmm? Focus on you two. We've been dancing around something for a while now. I sense this is a large part of the struggle you're both facing. And that is the process of grief."

Wade and I are quiet. We've taken the same side of the leather couch at each appointment like some sort of unspoken rule. Still, our hands don't touch.

"Greta, tell me how you perceive Wade's grief over the past three months."

My ribs constrict. This is the big daddy question and we all know it. I take a breath, try to refocus on why we're here. "Well, it seems like he's moved on much quicker than me."

"Mmhmm."

"He's able to move forward, get back into his routines. He's said as much himself—that he just wants to have a normal life again."

"And that makes you feel...?"

"Like he's giving up on Summer. Or that he's judging me because I'm not."

I peek at Wade. His jaw is tight. He stares straight ahead.

"Wade?" Calista says, opening the floor for his rebuttal. I already know what he's going to say. We've been here before.

"I have not given up on my daughter," he says, enunciating each word. "Just because I'm not talking about the case every minute and I don't want to rehash every second of that day—"

"It's because you blame me," I interrupt, letting the rage of moments ago return. "You blame me for what happened. Go ahead, say it. You've said it before, Calista might as well hear it too." My voice rises. Heat travels up my neck, and I imagine it's the color of the pillow I clutch in my lap.

Wade doesn't speak. His chest rises and falls with giant breaths.

"Fine," I say. "I'll say it for you. It's my fault Summer is gone. I put the kids in a dangerous situation and was neglectful. I'm responsible. There, are you happy? Is that what you wanted to hear?" I turn to Calista, whose eyes are wide again. "You really think you can fix this level of bitterness? He'll never forgive me. And you know what? Maybe I'll never forgive myself either."

I dissolve into tears. Wade doesn't touch me.

"Greta," Calista begins softly, "mourning is a very personal experience. Everyone grieves in their own way. Wade's approach to navigating all of this might differ from yours, but that doesn't mean he's not experiencing despair. You're both grieving at your own pace, which makes it seem like he's recovering faster. Neither pace is wrong."

My head is down, but through a curtain of tears I see Wade pass me a tissue from the box on the table—a hollow attempt at comforting me. I take it anyway.

"This is hard work," Calista says. "No one said it was going to be easy. But I'm proud you're both here sharing your truths."

My husband's truth is that he blames me for our daughter's kidnapping. I highly doubt we will ever be able to hurdle something so massive.

THIRTY-FIVE
ONE HUNDRED TWELVE DAYS GONE

DECEMBER BRINGS A SWEEP OF COLD. WIND WHIPS ACROSS Lake Erie, dropping temperatures into the thirties, and I'm met with a whole new fear—if Summer is out there somewhere, she's dealing with freezing conditions. The thought of her tiny body frigid and blue is more than I can bear, and so I've begun imagining her warm as could be inside a house with a fireplace and endless hot cocoa. Maybe she has a colorful quilt to wrap around her, and fuzzy socks that bunch at the ankles.

These are the images that get me through.

The alternative is much more grim. I try not to let my mind go to these places, but it's hard to resist them when insomnia strikes. She might *not* be sheltered and safe. She could be in the elements. The lake hasn't frozen over, and although the water searches ceased months ago, I hold onto the comfort that if she's really in there, at least she won't be trapped under ice until spring.

The thought of that horror is enough to make me go to pieces.

Calista was right. Summer didn't come home by Thanksgiving. So, we survived by pretending it wasn't happening—well, at least that's true for me and Wade. As much as I tried to avoid the holiday altogether, it was impossible. Mom insisted on making a turkey, saying my idea of a rotisserie chicken was sacrilegious. After much debate, I gave in. We would participate in Thanksgiving—for the kids—on the condition I didn't have to cook.

"Deal," Mom said.

But it wasn't the same without Summer. We didn't turn on the big Macy's parade. We didn't go around in a circle saying what we were thankful for. Mom didn't even make her blueberry pie since Summer was the only one who liked it anyway. Everything felt wrong. By the end of the day, I wanted nothing more than to slip back into sweatpants and go to bed.

Which is why I'm dreading the onset of another holiday. If I thought Thanksgiving was bad, I can't imagine the pain Christmas will bring. By now, we'd typically have our tree up, fully decorated, and sounds of the season playing from the Alexa. Every time I pass the storage tub that holds our Christmas decorations in the basement, I want to weep. I've been avoiding everything about it, and so far, no one has pushed me on it.

Winter's imminent arrival means the start of another season without Summer. It feels like yesterday when we were in shorts and tank tops frolicking through Wonderie Land. Now autumn has come and nearly gone, leaving the trees bare and the ground hard.

Normally I would have already changed the kids' wardrobes, putting away warm-weather clothes to make room for bulky sweaters and long pants. Summer used to love helping me with this process. She'd exclaim in wonder with the return of pieces she hadn't seen for half a year. A favorite sweatshirt. The coziest fleece-lined leggings with stars on the knees, now too short but still adored. It was as though she were receiving a brand-new wardrobe each season, reminding me that sometimes it's the little things in life that can bring the most delight.

This year, I'll only get out winter clothes for two kids instead of three. Summer's room is stuck in time—little T-shirts and rompers trapping her closet in the past.

It's Saturday morning and I've been lying awake for hours. My phone vibrates next to the bed. I stare at it, not wanting to remove my arm from the warmth of the covers. Wade isn't next to me. He must have spent the night on the couch.

The phone buzzes again. My brain registers the same familiar reactions as always:

It could be something.

It's probably not.

I snake a hand out and tap the screen. A text from Lolly.

Want to go shopping today?

My lungs deflate. I've done zero Christmas shopping. The other day, an email popped into my inbox from the store where I always get the kids matching Christmas pajamas. It's become a tradition that they open them on Christmas Eve and wear them to bed that night. I'd been practically offended to see the email. How could I order only two sets instead of three?

Christmastime, I've decided, is simply too much. The sound of a jingle bell makes my skin crawl. This will be the first year I don't send holiday cards.

In our most recent therapy session, Calista talked with me and Wade about the challenges that this time of year can bring for families in a situation like ours. She gave us suggestions to help us cope, instead of fighting it.

She said we should create new traditions instead of trying to do the things we've always done. She even recommended skipping town, getting away from all the hustle and bustle. I gawked in her face. Was she really suggesting we take a vacation while our child was missing? I couldn't imagine leaving, being somewhere else in the event Summer was found. Impossible!

What I've come to understand is this: Having a missing child is not the same thing as having a dead child. This revelation has led me down far too many thought spirals and into more than one online forum.

Not long ago, I stumbled across a discussion which posed the central question, "Would you rather your child be missing and never found or know for sure that they are dead?"

The morbid premise made me nauseous, and yet I couldn't read fast enough. There were other people out there feeling the same way I was. A community of bereavement. A topic only a select few could understand. For the first time, I felt seen.

One commenter wrote:

A dead child is better than a missing one. Death allows for mourning, whereas having a missing child keeps you in a place of limbo without the ability to move on.

Another disagreed:

When your child is missing, there's still hope of them returning. Dead is dead.

The comments went back and forth. Dozens of them.

There are things worse than death.

I refuse to accept my child is dead. I'll never give up hope.

I read for hours, getting no closer to a definitive conclusion. The argument is a fifty-fifty split, with strong opinions in both camps. I'm not sure which side I fall on.

. . .

I finally respond to Lolly's text an hour later.

Not a good day, sry.

As if I have any good days? I could tell her the truth—I'd rather pay someone to get gifts for Merritt and Gus—but that only piles on another level of guilt for all the ways I'm lacking. In truth, I'll probably hop on Amazon one of these nights when I can't sleep, and finish everything in one swoop.

Lolly replies almost immediately.

Does Merritt want to come?

I'm about to type "No" out of pure instinct but then a new sensation hits me. Maybe Merritt would say yes. Maybe she'd prefer to be with Lolly, a happier, more fun mother figure than me. I'm failing so badly at motherhood. I think back to the day at the playground, Lolly saying I was hovering. Maybe Merritt getting out of the house will help reset whatever mood she's in. Even though the shopping center will be packed with strangers —the idea of which makes my armpits prickle with sweat—I know I can't keep the kids locked away forever.

I type back a response.

Sure.

Great! Will pick her up in twenty.

I roll out of bed and stop at the doorway, listening for sounds that anyone else is awake. There's a faint melody coming from downstairs that I recognize as Gus's video game. I breathe easier. He's here. He's safe. I wonder if Wade removed all traces of his sleeping on the couch before Gus came down. They don't need another thing to worry about.

I walk to Merritt's room to tell her to get dressed before Lolly arrives. Her bed is rumpled from sleep, but she's nowhere to be seen. My brow crinkles and an alarm involuntarily raises in my head. When one of them isn't where I expect them to be, it's like an invitation for panic.

Merritt's usually our latest sleeper, and I figured I'd find her sprawled in starfish pose, all arms and legs going every which way. I back out of the room. Maybe she's already gone downstairs as well. Before turning toward the steps, a glimpse of light at the end of the hall catches my attention. It's coming from Summer's room. I walk toward it and peek in. My shoulders stiffen. Merritt is lying on Summer's bed, reading a book.

"Oh," I say, startled to see her there. Something in me flares, as though she's intruding on my sacred space. *This is where I come to grieve.* The feeling is nuanced, I know, but it's the most immediate reaction I summon.

"I'm just reading," she says to a question I didn't ask. "Sometimes I come in here..." Her voice trails off.

"No, that's fine. I, uh..." I'm flustered. "Lolly's going to pick you up to go Christmas shopping."

Merritt's face brightens. "Are you going?"

"No."

As fast as her face lifted, it now falls. "Oh. Okay."

Please don't guilt trip me.

"I have stuff to do," I lie. "Besides, you'll have fun with Lolly and the girls."

I leave before Merritt has a chance to rebut.

Back in my bathroom, I jump in the shower. After blowing my hair mostly dry, I pull it up. A few new grays have sprouted at my hairline. I've always thought women who age naturally are beautiful, but the stress and grief of the past few months have put my aging into super-drive, and it's anything but natural. Sometimes I feel like I don't even look like the same person I was this time last year.

I go downstairs to join the land of the living. As suspected, Gus is planted in front of the TV, absorbed in a video game. I round the couch and drop a kiss on the top of his head.

"Good morning," I say.

He stares past me to the screen. "Morning, Mom."

I shake my head and grin. He so desperately wants my attention... except for when there's a new level to beat.

A low murmur of voices comes from the kitchen; Wade's deep tone mixed with one higher on the spectrum. Merritt.

I get closer. There's a sniff. My face scrunches. Is she... crying? I stop just outside of view when their conversation becomes clearer.

"It's okay, sweetheart," I hear Wade say.

"I miss her," Merritt whimpers.

"I know, I know. Things will get better, I promise."

I peer around the corner without them noticing. Merritt's face is buried in her father's chest. Her arms wrap around his waist. He's stroking her hair with a gentle hand.

I back away, feeling awkward about interrupting a private moment. Something in my chest stings. The pain of Summer's absence is acute for all of us. I'm so used to Wade and Merritt turning to each other for comfort, but this time more than ever I wish I could join them. Instead, I retreat and busy myself by folding couch blankets, then take a seat next to Gus.

Not five minutes later, there's a knock on the door. Lolly lets herself in.

"Morning!" she says with a bright smile. She gives me a hug. Merritt comes into the room, eyes freshly wiped. Her recent tears will go unnoticed by Lolly—I myself might not have detected the subtle redness if I hadn't witnessed her crying.

"Hey, girlie," Lolly says. "Ready to shop til we drop?"

Merritt manages a smile. She looks to me, but her eyes

quickly dart away.

"Are you sure you don't want to come?" Lolly asks me. "We can pop through Starbucks on the way."

I give my head a little shake, and she replies with a sad smile. I get it—to her I've become a party pooper, a depressing version of my former self. I don't know how to be anything else.

"Have fun," I say.

They leave through the front door, and I close it behind them.

"Greta." Wade's voice behind me makes me jump.

"What?"

"We need to talk."

I search his face. "Talk about what?" *What did I do now?*

He leads the way out of the living room, where Gus is still punching away on his game controller.

Out of earshot, Wade's face goes stern. "You can't keep doing this."

I'm baffled, searching. My hands wave the empty air. "This... what's *this*?"

"How you're treating Merritt. It's not fair. She's just a kid."

My defenses rise and I feel heat climb my neck. A confrontation is not how I wanted to start the day. "God, Wade, would you drop it? I'm not treating her any different than always. I just let her go shopping for crying out loud."

"That's not true and you know it. You barely talk to her. Christ, you barely *look* at her."

I scoff and go to leave.

"Don't dismiss this, Greta," Wade says. "I know you're struggling, but she needs her mother and you haven't been there for her."

"Being here is all I do!" I bark. "I haven't even let the kids out of my sight for nearly four months. Isn't that what a good mother does?"

"That's not the same. That's not what we're talking about."

I cross my arms.

"You have got to get over what happened that day," Wade implores.

My mouth drops open. No, he *didn't*. "Are you kidding me?" I spit. "Get over losing my child?"

"No, not Summer. Of course not. I'm talking about Merritt's involvement. The fact that she was on her phone. You can't keep blaming her for this."

"I don't blame her," I say, looking down.

"You do. She's eleven years old, Greta. Maybe she has moments where we see those teenage years approaching, but she's still just a kid. You can't put so much on her shoulders. You can't hold resentment toward her."

"I've never said anything to her about blame."

"It's not what you say. It's what you *don't* say. Sometimes actions speak louder than words."

"Okay, *Calista*," I mock with heavy sarcasm.

Wade's face hardens. "This is serious. It's not a joke."

The tension in the room is like a raging storm. I take a deep breath and blow it out. After several beats of poisonous silence, I give in.

"Listen," I say, "I know she's struggling. We all are. It has to be horrific for her to lose her little sister. It breaks my heart to see her cry."

"Cry?"

"Just a bit ago, before Lolly got here. I saw her crying. You were comforting her."

Wade pauses. "That wasn't about Summer."

My eyes squint in confusion. "I heard Merritt say she missed her."

Wade stares at me blankly. "She was talking about you, Greta. She misses *you*."

THIRTY-SIX

LATER THAT DAY, AFTER LOLLY HAS BROUGHT MERRITT home with a full belly and a new pair of earrings—*just because* —I stare into the fridge, wondering what to make for dinner. My parents just left after spending a handful of hours marking new potential search areas on the map. Wade and Gus are in the backyard splitting wood—it's the perfect day for our wood-burning stove—and Merritt is... I don't know where. She didn't say much when she returned from shopping.

After Wade's earlier declaration that Merritt had been crying about me, not Summer, I felt like I'd been hit by a stun gun. I've been stewing on it all afternoon, trying to understand how I've managed to come up so short. Motherhood was always something I'd longed for. I thought I would be a natural. That I'd instinctively know my children inside and out, we'd become the best of friends, and life would be ten times brighter than before. Being a mom would change me for the better.

But it didn't quite happen like that. I never imagined the invasion of emotions that would take over, as though completely changing my DNA makeup. I was right in that I'm no longer the same person I was prior to having children, but I was wrong in thinking that becoming a mom would only bring out good qualities.

Merritt was crying over me. Gus broke my cherished lamp. Summer is...

Evidently, I'm not the mother I thought I'd be.

A Facebook notification pings on my phone. It's from Summer's missing child page. A little shock zaps my lungs and I skip a breath. This always happens—I always think maybe this will be the tip we've been waiting for.

I open the app and click to the post.

Sending peace and love your way during this holiday season.

It's from a woman I don't know but who I've seen comment on our posts before. If I recall correctly, she's an acquaintance of Lolly's or someone from one of the kids' activities—I can't keep everyone straight.

Her post already has two dozen likes.

I try to swallow but it's difficult to hold back the emotion. While I appreciate everyone's sympathy, it's not enough to make a difference. Summer isn't going to be found just because a thousand people wish it to be so.

I should reply to the post, thank this woman for the kind words. But instead I'm staring at the tiny Christmas tree emoji she tacked onto the end, and finding myself growing hotter. Really? Was that happy little icon necessary? Thank you, *Miranda*, but there's nothing jolly happening in this house.

I close out of the app and slam the fridge closed at the same time a craving comes on swift and strong. I need a cigarette. I go to my coat hanging on the hook by the front door, the last place I tucked away the pack. Reaching in, my fingers feel nothing. I dig deeper, as though it's hiding. Nothing. The pocket is empty.

"Dammit," I mutter. Wade must have finally had enough. I grumble under my breath. It's one thing to tell me to stop, but it's another to throw away cigarettes I spent money on. He could have at least let me finish the pack.

I clomp through the house toward the back door. So what if I'm smoking again—how is it any of his business how I cope?

On the back porch, I look out over the yard toward the tree line twenty yards away. We'd been thankful to find a house in this subdivision that butts up against a small, wooded area instead of another property. The kids love playing in the trees, collecting acorns and building forts.

This time of year, the trees are bare. From the deck, I can see Wade and Gus bundled in Carhart gear. Gus stands back as Wade swings the ax down, splitting a log in half.

I'm just about to make my way across the lawn, hands balled, jaw tight, when something catches my eye to the left. The shed that houses our outdoor necessities—lawnmower in the summer, snowblower in the winter—sits against the fence that separates our property from the neighbor's. Overgrown bushes thick with evergreen limbs flank both sides of the shed. Yet somehow through the tangle of weeds I detect a small plume of smoke, followed by a cough. The smell reaches my nose next. I stop in my tracks. I immediately know who took my cigarettes. And it wasn't Wade.

I pivot toward the bushes, abandoning my original plan. The smell strengthens as I approach. Through the brush, I spot a flash of purple. Merritt's coat.

I come around the corner faster than she's able to hide any evidence. It's a surprise ambush. Merritt gives a little yelp.

"What do you think you're doing?" I snap.

Guilt is written all over her face. Her eyes are huge. "I... I..."

"Where did you get those?"

She doesn't respond. We both know the truth.

"This is not okay, Merritt." My volume has reached a higher decibel than I usually employ when outside. I want to shake her. *You know better!* But instinct tells me she wouldn't be behaving this way if our family wasn't going through a shit-storm. My hands shake. I'm sad, but I'm also mad.

"Don't you know how bad smoking is?" I say.

"You do it!" Merritt throws back at me.

I was ready for a comeback, an answer to whatever she would say in her defense. There is no excuse for her stealing cigarettes from my coat and secretly smoking. But her response bushwhacks me. My open mouth clamps shut. I have no rebuttal, except to say, *Oh, Merritt, don't be like me.*

She watches me, waiting for my retort. I could toss out the antiquated adults-can-do-things-kids-can't, but that sounds silly in a situation where we both know the harmful effects of these little cancer sticks.

"Give me those," I say, snatching the pack and lighter from her hand. *How does she even know how to smoke one of these?* "You're grounded. This is unacceptable, Merritt. I don't know what on Earth you were thinking. Now, get in the house."

She crosses her arms and scowls, then stomps off.

I stand there, entire body shaking, for another several seconds. I cannot believe I just caught my eleven-year-old daughter smoking. This behavior isn't supposed to happen for at least another few years. She still watches Disney movies for goodness' sake!

When I finally will my feet to move, I come out from behind the bushes. Wade stares at me from across the yard.

"Everything okay?" he calls. We're far enough apart that he definitely heard some sort of squabble, but not word for word.

"Yes. Fine," I say. The last thing I need is another reason for him to pile on more resentment. Merritt smoking my cigarettes? Failing in school? Wade would lose his mind. I won't tell him. This discovery, Merritt's moment of curiosity or rebellion or whatever it was, will stay between me and her.

The cigarettes throb in my hand as I go back inside. My craving hasn't subsided. In fact, it's intensified. Smoking is a nasty habit, I know, but one I've come to rely on. I'm not proud of it. I'm even less proud of the fact that my daughter just followed in my footsteps. In fact, I'm utterly ashamed.

A battle of will plays out in my brain. I want to smoke. The nicotine would take the edge off immediately. But it would also brand me a hypocrite.

I picture Merritt's face when I caught her and after my tongue-lashing. She looked so young—far too young to be smoking. Something has to give here. If my job were graded like a student, I'd get an F. I don't want Merritt to fall off the straight path we've set for her. But maybe getting her back on track starts with me.

I brace my hands against the kitchen sink and let my head drop. Ten long breaths, in and out. Then, in perhaps the first act of selflessness I've been able to summon since Summer's disappearance, I open the garbage drawer and toss the pack in. Merritt wins this battle. I stare at the pack for another second before closing the drawer.

Goodbye, old friends. Our time is finished.

THIRTY-SEVEN

ONE HUNDRED NINETEEN DAYS GONE

I'VE OFFICIALLY BECOME NOCTURNAL. SLEEP ELUDES ME from the hours of one to five a.m. Lolly says my daytime sleeping is messing with my circadian rhythm, but what does she know? She still has both of her children safely at home.

I wander the halls of the house, searching for solace in the familiar but finding none. The shadows dance mockingly at me. I wonder if I'll ever sleep through the night again. Most nights, I lose myself in thoughts of Summer. Sometimes a surge of mania takes over and I spend hours working on the investigation, going back through notes and leads that we've already checked and double-checked. Other times, I hear her little voice saying things like she wants "bah-sghetti" for dinner, or asking how she came out of my tummy through my belly button. She says "You Nork" instead of New York and calls her big toe her thumb toe. I could never correct her. I secretly hoped she'd always call it her thumb toe.

Georgia claims she hasn't given up on the case, but I'm unsure. The news cycle has moved on from featuring Summer. Most of the online chatter I read is by people who believe Summer is dead. I've taken it upon myself to call the news stations and ask them to please run another story, keep her picture out there, show that grainy screenshot of the woman who took her. Someone has to know.

The uncertainty ravages me.

Tonight, I'm particularly desperate. My skin itches as though tiny bugs were crawling on the surface. Even being in Summer's room among her things isn't helping. I roam through the house barefoot despite the cold floors. Christmas lights glow from the neighbors' homes and I resent the cheerfulness they symbolize.

I clamp the curtains shut even tighter. A winter wind howls outside, making these dark hours even more sinister, like I'm in the middle of a ghost story. A supernatural realm somewhere between life and death. I wonder if Summer would send us a sign if she were on the other side. A mirthless laugh escapes my lips. *Greta, you're delusional.*

But something about it holds. The thought sparks a memory in my brain. The psychic. The letter.

I hurry to the kitchen and pull open the junk drawer. There, mixed in with takeout menus and loose stationery, is the piece of mail I shoved in there weeks ago. I don't know why I kept it. Maybe for a night like this.

I reread the cursive scrawl.

I would love the chance to talk with you about your daughter and visions I have had.

There's a phone number below her signature. I consider it, and then scoff at the absurdity. These people—psychics—are nothing more than scam artists. Talking to the dead, seeing the future—it's ridiculous. I've always felt sorry for people whose anguish has driven them to such hopeless measures. And for the so-called psychics to prey on their vulnerability... it's heartless.

And yet, I saved this letter. I didn't throw it away with all the other garbage and hate mail.

I run a finger over the words. *Visions I have had.*

What if this woman really does have information that could help? What if she knows whether Summer is alive, where she is? Possibility bubbles in my gut. The thought of having answers nearly makes me cry. I'm wrecked. We're running out of time. I can't go on like this. I need to know.

But then the devil swoops in. What if she tells me Summer is dead? What if she says Summer will never come home again? As much as this psychic woman might deliver good news, she could also hand me a devastating blow.

I think back to the online forum in which strangers debated the worst-case scenario, a missing child or a dead child. Knowing or not knowing. I hadn't been able to decide where I fell in the debate. But now, in my kitchen in the dark of night and going on little sleep, my mind is made.

I dial the number on the letter and pray. The clock on the stove says three thirty. I have no idea where this woman... *What's her name again?* Nadine, the letter says. I have no idea where Nadine lives or what time it is there. If she is the same woman from the search party, I'd assume she lives around here, and it'd be the middle of the night for her too. She probably won't answer. My hopes will be dashed once more, and in the light of day I won't have the guts to call again. It's now or never.

The line rings once, twice, three times. I remove the phone from my ear as a surge of doubt comes over me. This is insane. And then...

"Hello?" A groggy voice comes just as I'm about to hang up.

I hastily bring the phone back. "Hi... um, is this Nadine Starr?"

"It is."

I have no idea what this woman looks like—I can't recall her image from that night in the rain—but now I picture her with a celestial scarf wrapped around her neck and dangly earrings that move like wind chimes when she sways. It's a complete stereotype. A movie characterization. The image is laughable, but then again, it's three a.m. and I've officially gone mad.

"I'm, uh... I'm Greta Goodman," I say. "I'm so sorry to bother you at this hour, but I got a letter from you in October. About my daughter. She's mis—"

"Summer," Nadine says. She clears her throat, and I picture her sitting up in bed, wiping sleep from her eyes.

"Yes. Summer." Emotion hitches in my chest. "I know it's super late. Er, early. I don't know, one of the two. Either way, your letter said you'd had visions, and I just hoped... I mean, I wondered if..." My voice cracks. What comes out next is no more than a whisper. "I'm desperate."

"Thank you for calling, Greta. Most people don't. Give me one minute, okay?"

While I wait, I'm struck with the thought that this Nadine woman probably scours the news and reaches out to people all the time with these *visions*. I'm a fool. I should hang up. Is she going to charge me for this? Wade will *kill* me if I give her my credit card number.

But if it meant I could hold my little girl again...

After a few seconds, skepticism gets the best of me. I can't wait any longer. "Do you really have information about Summer?"

"I don't have information, I have—"

"I knew this was bogus," I say, slapping a palm to my forehead.

"No, wait," she says. "I'm not a fraud. What I was going to say is that I don't have *information*, per se. I can't give you an exact coordinate of her location. That's not how this works. I'm an intuitive. Do you know what that means?"

"You're a psychic."

"Yes, but there are many types of psychic abilities. People

like me receive perceptive information through colors, visions, auras, that sort of thing. We can see things that happened in the past and will happen in the future."

"Okaaay," I say, dragging the word out. I can't believe I'm having this conversation. This is insane.

Nadine continues. "I had a vision shortly after I saw your story on the news."

"Were you part of the search party? Did I see you that night at Frontier Park?"

"Yes. I tried talking to you then, but—"

"I'm sorry, I was... It was a very hard time. I barely remember anything of those first days."

"No need to apologize. I'd wanted to tell you my feelings, but you weren't ready. That's why I sent the letter."

I break out into a cold sweat. Do I really want to hear this? The phone shakes against my ear. "What... what did you see? I mean, in your vision."

"Summer is alive."

My sight goes white. I can't catch my breath. Nadine's voice becomes muffled, like I've gone under water. I fumble for an island stool and sit—my legs are no longer legs.

Summer is alive.

The tunnel vision slowly fades. Nadine's voice returns.

"I can sense her presence. She's not far. I believe she's still in the state."

Not far. Still in Pennsylvania. My brain repeats Nadine's words like staccato musical notes. "Is she... is she hurt?" I say through rapid breaths.

"No. She's safe. I feel her spirit as a warm and comforting presence, which makes me think she's being looked after by benevolent forces."

Summer is okay. She's alive and safe and not far. My heart is bursting, and tears spring from my eyes, leaving cold trails along my temples. I clamp a hand over my mouth to keep from crying out and waking the rest of the house.

"What about the woman who took her? Who is she?"

"I can't answer that, I'm afraid. That's beyond the scope of my abilities."

"But you said she's not harming Summer?"

"Her aura is still very bright, very positive. Nothing tells me that Summer is in danger."

Of course she's in danger, she was kidnapped! I want to say, but that's not what Nadine means. I desperately want her to identify the woman who abducted my daughter. A name. A better physical description. *Something.* If she can't tell me a location, at least we'd have some small detail to go on.

"Greta? Are you still there?"

"I'm here," I squeak.

"I feel that this journey will come to a close soon."

I clutch the phone to my ear, absorbing Nadine's words like a lifeline. Any doubt I had before about this woman is gone. I know I shouldn't let her, but she's saved me. She's confirmed what I've always felt. Maybe I can hold onto this to survive.

"Thank you, thank you so much," I manage to choke out.

Nadine's voice remains steady, a beacon of calm amid the hurricane of my emotions. "I'm glad I could bring you some comfort, Greta," she says softly. "Remember to trust in the universe and keep the faith. Summer will find her way back to you."

Tears stream down my cheeks, unchecked now as I struggle to comprehend the enormity of what Nadine has just told me. "I will," I promise. "I'll do whatever it takes to bring her home."

With a whispered thank you and a final assurance from a perfect stranger, I hang up the phone. A colossal weight has been lifted from my shoulders. The room spins around me, but this time it's with the odds on our side.

THIRTY-EIGHT

I FORCE MYSELF NOT TO WAKE WADE UP AFTER MY CALL with Nadine. The clock ticks to four a.m. There's no chance of any sleep for me. Instead, I sit on the couch and daydream about Summer, where she is, when we'll find her. I imagine us all together again and just know deep in my bones that things will be better. We'll be happy. I'll never have those suffocating thoughts of motherhood again.

Wade's alarm normally goes off at five so he can hit the gym before work—at least that's what he says he's doing. I can't imagine why he cares about muscles or cardio during this chapter of our lives, but he says exercise helps him burn frustration. It's like a drug. It helps him through. And who am I to argue—I chose cigarettes for all those months.

Today, however, there's no alarm. Another weekend has arrived, which means the house remains quiet and still a little longer than normal. No frenzied morning rush, no dash to make it to school on time. I'm fairly certain the school has given us leeway in this regard—Merritt and Gus have been tardy more times than I can count, but all the secretary does is give us an understanding smile.

I'm dying for Wade to wake up so I can tell him what Nadine said. We need this, this dose of optimism. *See*, I'll say. *She's coming home to us. We can be a family again.*

I won't add, *I was right.* Calista wouldn't like that, and I want to be a good patient.

When seven rolls around and still no one is up, I go to the kitchen and put a kettle of hot water on the stove for tea. I certainly don't need caffeine from coffee—I'm already wired enough. A few minutes later, the pot whistles and I let it go for several seconds. It is perhaps an annoying wake-up call, but so be it. I'm bursting at the seams.

My tactic works. Within minutes, Wade pads down the stairs, hand ruffling his bed head. His plaid pajama pants are old as dirt, but they're his favorite, and so I continue to launder them. They remind me of the worn-in leather couch at therapy —unsightly but comfortable.

"Morning," I say, handing him a steaming mug before his foot even hits the last step. What I can only presume is a shit-eating grin spreads across my face. I'm high on energy and renewed hope.

Wade takes me in curiously. "Did you sleep?"

"A little," I lie. I don't need him talking to my parents about my insomnia. One intervention is enough.

Wade sips the tea. He'll likely make coffee too, but for now it's nice to share a moment and a drink together. His eyes study my face. "Are you... okay?"

"Yes. Yes, I'm fine. Why do you ask?" *Because you're twitchy and giddy and acting like a weirdo.*

"You just seem... I dunno... happy?"

I pounce then. "Wade, you're never going to believe what happened. Okay, don't think I'm crazy, but a while ago I got a letter in the mail from a psychic. I know, just hear me out. I didn't think anything of it at first. Simply shoved the letter in the junk drawer because that's what it was—junk, right? But for some reason I remembered it this morning, and I couldn't sleep and—"

"Wait," he interrupts. "I thought you said you did sleep?"

"Sort of. Okay, not really. But that's not the point. The point is that I called her."

"Called who?"

"The psychic."

"You called a psychic?"

"Yes. She left her number in the letter. She said she'd had visions of Summer she wanted to tell us about."

Wade's head lolls and he's giving me a look that says, *You didn't really fall for this, did you?*

"I know what you're thinking," I continue. "But something told me to call. I mean, what the hell, right? I never really believed in that stuff before, but one time Lolly—this was, gosh, years ago—she got a reading from a medium and some of the stuff turned out to be true. They predicted that something medical would come up, and wouldn't you know Lolly had to get that emergency root canal. Wade, don't look at me like that. It was the middle of the night and I was miserable!"

"You called a psychic in the middle of the night," he repeats.

"Yes."

He crosses his arms. "So, what did she say?" Skepticism oozes from his words, but I brush it away.

"She said Summer is alive. Not only that, but she's okay. She's not hurt." My eyes are big and eager. I clasp my hands at my heart. It pounds so hard I think it might combust. Wade goes to speak, but I cut him off, afraid he'll kill my moment. "She said she foresees Summer coming home. Did you hear me, Wade? Summer is alive!"

He's stoic, indifferent, not mirroring any of my excitement.

His mouth opens, then shuts again before saying a word. He walks past me toward the kitchen.

I spin, dumbfounded, then follow. "Aren't you going to say anything? Aren't you thrilled with this news?" I want to shake him.

He stops, turns. I'd been nearly nipping his heels, and the sudden halt forces me to take a step back.

"This isn't *news*," Wade says, irritation in his voice.

"What do you mean? Of course it is. This woman—"

"This woman doesn't know anything. She can't *see the future*. She took advantage of you, Greta."

I shake my head. "No. That's not true. I heard it in her voice. She was genuine. It was real."

Wade's expression changes now, and I recognize it instantly —pity. He feels sorry for me, the way one pardons an idiot for not knowing better.

I huff. "I can't believe you're not accepting this gift," I say, defensiveness rising.

"What gift?"

"She's telling us our daughter is alive and safe! That we're going to find her!"

He brings a hand to his brow, as though exhaustion is taking over even though he just woke up. "The police have been searching for four months. Four months! That's—"

"Seventeen weeks. A hundred and nineteen days. Don't patronize me, Wade. I know exactly how long she's been missing. And yes, I know the police haven't found anything. But you know what? Maybe that's why I'm choosing to believe this. We have no proof to the contrary, so why not?"

"Because it's bullshit!" The tips of his ears are red, like when he's pissed at the TV when his team is losing. "Psychics aren't real. No one knows where Summer is."

I wince. My daughter disappeared without a trace, and here I am leaning on a psychic. "Someone knows," I say, my voice suddenly small. It's true—someone knows. The woman who has her, maybe others too.

Wade groans and slams his mug on the counter. The floor above us creaks, and I know that means one or both of the kids is getting up. They've probably heard us arguing—again.

I cross my arms tight across my chest. "I won't let you bring me down. You might have given up, but I haven't. Summer is going to come home."

THIRTY-NINE

ONE HUNDRED TWENTY-FIVE DAYS GONE

Another week has come and gone. It's Friday morning. I should be in the kitchen packing school lunches while Wade gets ready for work, but instead, I dawdle around the bedroom, unable to stop myself from watching him. I've known his morning routine for nearly two decades—the exact order in which he brushes his teeth, shaves, and combs his hair. It's nothing I've ever put much thought into. Only now, I'm monitoring every small movement. The way he checks himself in the mirror. The way he gives his neck a single spritz of cologne. He looks handsome, and I wonder if it's for someone else besides me.

The accusation dangles on the tip of my tongue, begging to be released. Until now, I've kept my thoughts to myself, seesawing between being certain he's cheating to convincing myself I'm being paranoid.

Maybe it was the restless night of sleep, but this morning has me extra jittery. When Wade comes out of the bathroom looking at his phone, the tension in my chest magnifies.

"I'm going out with Rob after work tonight," he says. "Shouldn't be too late."

"You two are quite chummy lately." My mouth is dry.

"What are you talking about? We've always been friends."

"Not the kind that grabs drinks every week."

Wade's gaze drops. He sits on the bench at the end of our bed and pulls on navy blue socks. I thought I knew all there was to know about this man, but now I'm questioning everything. I need to know the truth, no matter how much it will hurt.

"Are you having an affair?" I blurt.

Wade stops mid-pull, the sock dangling off the front of his foot, heel exposed.

He spins on the bench to face me. "What?" His face screws up, forehead a set of deep grooves. "What are you talking about?"

"You're never home when you used to be after work. You're on your phone a lot more. These drinks with Rob... I don't know, it just seems like things are off, and—"

"Things *are* off. We have a missing child." A zing pierces my lungs. "But that doesn't mean I'm having an affair. Why would you even go there?"

"It seemed like a logical guess." I think of the Y name in his texts.

Wade's shoulders drop. He finishes pulling up the sock. "Gee, thanks."

"Is it Brynn?"

"Brynn? From work?"

"Do you know another Brynn?"

"What are you even talking about? Brynn is married."

"That doesn't stop people from sleeping around."

Wade rattles his head like he's seeing spots. "What the hell even made you think that?"

"You're texting a lot. I thought I saw a Y come up in the name."

"You were looking at my phone?"

"No, just in passing, when you would answer it." I'm quiet

for a second. "You didn't answer my question. Are you sleeping with Brynn?"

"God, Greta. No."

Lolly? I almost ask, but the idea is so outrageous. Still, even if it's not Brynn, even if there never was a Y in the name, it doesn't mean there isn't someone.

"You really think I'd do that?" Wade says.

"Well, you know the statistics about couples and trauma. So many marriages fail. It's not like we've exactly been on the same page all the time. And I just assumed—"

"Assumed I'd cheat on you? Jesus, Greta."

"So you're not?"

His eyes fill with intensity. "No, I'm not having an affair. I would never."

I'm dying to pry further, to ask about the late nights, for him to make it all make sense. But Wade seems wired with a new mix of pain, and I don't want to make it any worse. I want to believe him.

He stands, looking less poised than he did just moments ago. There's so much anger in his face, resentment for my accusation, it momentarily makes me feel bad.

"I know we're going through it," he says. "But I love you."

It's the saddest *I love you* I've ever heard.

All I can do is nod. I'd been expecting one answer and got another. With nothing left to say, and yet a million things we should discuss, Wade goes to the door.

"I'll see you later," he says and leaves the room.

I wish I could say that was it. I confronted him, he told the truth, and I let it go. But that's not what happens.

Instead, I fixate on the conversation for most of the day, long after I drop the kids at school and well into the afternoon as I wait to pick them up. The uncertainty has even prevented me from sleeping—as if the thought of betrayal wasn't bad enough, now it's robbing me of my one comfort.

I wish I could prove what Wade says is true. Maybe if Rob confirmed it, my mind could finally rest. Surely Wade's boss wouldn't lie for him, knowing what I'm going through.

I spend the next ten minutes coming up with reasons I can call the office and talk to Rob. Nothing works quite right, but I settle on something that's good enough to pass. I dial the office number and ask the receptionist for Rob's extension.

"Rob Pakowski," he answers.

"Rob, hi. This is Greta Goodman." I keep my voice cheerful.

"Greta, hi." He sounds surprised.

"I'm sorry to bother you, but I was just curious if you were still meeting Wade for drinks after work tonight? I have a—"

"Drinks?" He cuts me off, and I don't even have to finish the made-up story I was going to use. "Uh, no, I don't think so? I mean, unless I missed something on my calendar." I hear clicking, like he's checking his computer. "No, I wasn't aware of that. I can pop in to check with him, but—"

"Did you guys have drinks last week? Or the week before that?" My body is overtaken by a hot flash.

"Uh... no?"

I'm quiet, unable to speak for a solid few seconds. My brain runs a million miles per hour, flashing with images and scenarios. Wade wasn't where he said he was. He lied.

"Uh, listen, Greta," Rob says, voice strained with unease. "I don't want to get in the middle of anything. Wade's a good guy. I don't know what's going on, but I'm sure—"

"Thanks, Rob." I hang up. The phone shakes in my hand.

There it is. My suspicions confirmed. Wade is having an affair. He's cheating on me at the worst possible moment of my life. The whiplash of emotion hits like a one-two punch. Anger. Despair. *Slap, slap.*

Then the guilt comes barreling in. I've been so emotionally detached, it's no wonder Wade went elsewhere for comfort. This is all my fault.

I sit in a daze for what feels like hours, wrestling with layers of torment. No matter how much I blame myself, I keep coming back to our therapy sessions. Wade's seeming desire to make us work. Why would he spend all the time and energy if his heart was elsewhere?

Something still doesn't add up. And there's only one way for me to find out.

I call Lolly and ask if she minds picking up the kids and keeping them through dinner.

"Is everything okay?" she asks.

"Yes, yes. Wade's working late and I... have some stuff to do."

"Okay, sure. No problem." She doesn't pry despite the silliness of the excuse. I never have stuff to do. She knows I sleep all day and stress all night.

With that settled, I wait another two hours, sitting on the couch wrapped in a blanket like a nest. Just before five, I get in the car and drive the ten minutes to Wade's office. The parking lot is still full of cars, including Wade's. I park on the street a block down. With so much passing traffic, he'll never notice.

Ten minutes pass. Then twenty. At five thirty, Wade exits the building. My heartbeat trips in my throat. I watch him stroll to his car, get in, and back out of his spot. At the parking lot exit, he pauses, looks both ways, then turns.

A shudder courses through me, but I hold back the emotion. I let him get a streetlight ahead, then pull out and follow, keeping enough distance for him not to see me.

Wade travels two miles down 26th Street going through light after light, past endless shopping plazas and gas stations and fast-food restaurants. I'm waiting for him to turn onto a side street and wind his way into a neighborhood, where he'll stop at a strange house with a woman waiting at the door. That, or he'll pull into a hotel parking lot, where they always meet. I can't decide which one's worse.

I keep following. A few minutes later, his blinker goes on and he moves into the turning lane. I stay five cars behind and do the same.

Now we're headed north toward the lake. We pass a shabby-looking motel and I'm momentarily relieved. But where is he going? There's not much more ahead of us in this direction. In fact, the last time I was in this area was...

The Wonderie Land sign appears through the trees. The next thing I know, Wade is turning into the park. I slam on the brakes and pull to the side of the road. His is the only car that turned. I can't follow him or I'll be discovered. The lot is completely empty, abandoned from September to May.

From where I sit, I watch him pull into a spot and turn off the engine. He doesn't get out. What is he doing here? If this is the place he meets his mistress, this has taken on a whole new level of alarm.

I wait and watch. Nothing happens. I want to get closer. Maybe I can see something more. Putting the car in gear, I creep back onto the road then make a quick turn onto a smaller street that runs parallel to the parking lot and should afford me a clear but discreet view of Wade.

I slow my speed to as much of a crawl as possible, then stop. There's no one behind me. The sky is dark now, and I have to really squint to see. I peer through the window. Wade is in the driver's seat. He doesn't appear to be doing anything, just sitting. Staring. Then he lifts a hand and wipes his eyes. I freeze. He's crying.

It all suddenly makes sense. There were no drinks with Rob. He hasn't been hard and unfeeling all these months. Wade comes to Wonderie Land, sits in his car, and cries, then comes home with a clean face. He grieves alone because I'm already carrying too much to add the weight of his suffering on top.

I look away, overcome with something I can't quite name. It's sorrow, yes, but it's also unease, dismay. A flood of emotions rains down like the sky opening up on a gray day. Sadness, for the pain he is clearly wrestling with. Regret, for the harsh words I've hurled at him in anger. And shame, for the distance that has grown between us, a gaping chasm that seems impossible to bridge. These sensations swoop in at once, layering on top of each other and pressing me further into my seat, my body as heavy as iron.

I stay there for a moment, watching him from afar, my heart heavy with the weight of our shared pain. And as the tears continue to fall unchecked down his cheeks, I want nothing more than to wrap my arms around him, to bridge the divide between us with the simple act of forgiveness. But something holds me back, a lingering fear that our wounds run too deep, that the damage has been done.

Wade wipes his face with a tissue. Like me, he must keep a box in his car now. I watch as he fills his cheeks with air and then blows the breath out. His mouth moves, and I imagine it's a small pep talk. *Keep it together, Wade. One day at a time.*

He sits straighter in his car, arms locked and stiff on the wheel. It looks like he's about to leave, and so I escape first, having seen enough. The rest of my drive home, I fight a guilty conscience and a searing pain in my heart. My chest ached at the sight of him so vulnerable and alone. People aren't meant to grieve like this. What I just witnessed makes me want to shrivel into nothing. Instead of leaning on each other, we're doing the opposite. We're falling further and further apart.

FORTY

I can't sleep. I replay the image of Wade crying in his car only hours ago. Grieving our daughter, then coming home and putting on a brave face. I watch him sleep—both of us in bed tonight—envious of his escape from reality for a stretch of hours.

In the morning, I'm fully drained. The mental exhaustion has caught up to me, making it a struggle to function normally around my own family. It's like I no longer know how to act, how to think. Maybe I need some air. I sneak to the garage before anyone is awake. Saturdays are for sleeping in—for everyone but me, it seems.

In the car, I open the center console and reach for the pack of cigarettes I keep there. "Shit," I say, remembering I threw those ones out too. Now there's nothing to comfort me besides my own unstable mind.

I reverse from the driveway, my pulse thumping in my ears. I don't know where I'm going, but I need to get away from the house and all the pressure it holds.

I drive around for an hour on country roads lacing between Albion and Waterford. These open spaces are a reprieve from the hubbub of Erie. Every time I accidentally take Peach Street on a weekend, with its nightmarish traffic, I want to move to the country. Here in the rural part just outside the city, I'm met with rolling farmland for miles. My breathing calms.

I'm comforted to know Wade isn't having an affair, that he was telling the truth—sort of. But it doesn't alleviate the doubt about how we're going to fix the mess that is our current situation. If he's not able to talk to me, and I'm not able to let him in, how is this going to work?

The last road leads me north again, and coming back into town, I swing through Dunkin' for a coffee. The insomnia is making my eyes heavy. I've got to get my sleep cycles back on track.

The girl at the window hands me my drink. The cup is printed with a seasonal design of berries and holly. I hate it but think I'd be labeled a Scrooge if I asked for a plain cup instead. Not everyone is wishing this holiday would pass in a blink.

I pull into the driveway at eight forty-five. It's still early and the neighborhood is largely quiet. Next door, Alice Campbell drags her garbage can back from the curb in her bathrobe. She no longer gives me the stink eye but she doesn't exactly exude friendliness either. I wonder if there will be a time when I'm not branded with a dark mark. I take the high road and give her a wave, which she pretends not to see.

The second I get out of the car inside the garage, the faint sound of music hits my ears. A neck vein pulses. It's not just any music—it's most definitely Christmas music. My jaw sets. I'm instantly filled with the same loathing I've been trying to avoid this entire holiday season.

It's just music, I tell myself. I can put in my earbuds to tune it out if I really feel like it. I proceed inside, ready to get on with the day. Wade and I know how to be civil even when apologies aren't given. We walk on eggshells around each other. A weekend should be no different. But there's no sense ruining it for the kids. Maybe I'll even suggest a movie marathon—something to keep them happy, and a chance for me to zone out.

I drop my purse on the bench and hang up my coat. I'm still wearing the yoga pants and sweatshirt I had on all night. "The Little Drummer Boy" blares from Alexa on the counter, but the kitchen is empty. Where is everyone?

The sound of voices filters in from the living room. Rounding the corner, I freeze. Large plastic tubs fill the middle of the room, lids off, contents strewn on the floor and couch. The Christmas decorations. Wade, Merritt, and Gus stand around our faux tree, now erected in its usual spot, hanging cheerful red and silver bulbs on its branches. Gus wears a Santa hat and an enormous grin.

"What are you doing?" I say, revulsion in my voice, as though I've just caught them painting graffiti on the walls.

"Mom!" Gus says. "Dad said we could put up the tree!"

My gaze whips to Wade, who meets my eye before continuing with his ornament placement. His expression is one of quiet confidence, not smug but not scared either.

"Wade," I say with slow caution, trying not to blow up in front of the kids, "I thought we agreed—"

"We didn't agree to anything," he says. "It's almost Christmas. The kids wanted to decorate, and today is the perfect day." He lifts Gus so he can hang a silver ball near the top. "Nice job, buddy," he says, lowering our son to the floor.

Heat simmers under my skin. How dare Wade take it upon himself to do something that has always been a family tradition? I'd said we weren't doing decorations this year. No tree, no snow globes, no wreath on the front door. It's not like I was *canceling* Christmas—I'm not that coldhearted—I just didn't want the daily reminder everywhere I looked. It's too much. It's not right without Summer. The decision was final. Him doing this behind my back is a complete betrayal.

"Wade, can I speak with you in the other room?" I say.

He doesn't skip a beat, reaching into the tub for another sleeve of bulbs. "Not right now, I'm helping the kids decorate. Do you want to join us? We still have to string the beads."

I grind my teeth. I need to put a halt to this, stat. "I'd like to speak with you in private."

"Whatever you need to say, I'm sure you can say in front of the kids."

He's challenging me. He knows damn well I'm about to blow my top. I want to curse at him for going against my wishes —the one thing I requested that would help me get through this awful time. Was that so much to ask?

We're a broken record, the same argument over and over. Wade wanting to move on, me stuck in the past. My nails tear into the stretchy fabric at my thighs. Fine, if he wants to play this game, so be it.

The song changes to "Rockin' Around the Christmas Tree." I want to rip Alexa's cord from the wall.

"I wasn't planning on decorating this year," I say, keeping my tone in check and my eyes locked on his.

Merritt and Gus stop what they're doing and look to their father with fear and confusion. "It's okay, guys," he says. "Keep going." Then to me, "Why shouldn't we? They want to see their stockings hung. They want to have a tree like every other year. Don't you think it's only fair for the kids? Christmas is all about them."

Breathe.

Don't say it.

I can't help myself.

"Not all the kids are here." I say each word with slow purpose.

Merritt lowers her arm and looks at me. I watch her eyes turn to water.

"Greta," Wade says, voice taking a serious turn, "we have to keep living. You know what Calista said. Routine is important for the kids."

Actually, Calista suggested we skip town for Christmas, but at this point I don't feel like getting in another fight over semantics.

"Christmas is not a routine," I say instead. "Christmas is a celebration, and frankly, I don't think we have anything to celebrate."

"We have two children here who could use a reason to smile." His voice elevates. I've touched a nerve. But so has he. A small kernel of guilt wedges itself in my brain. It's teensy, and I know it should be bigger. And then it comes flooding over me. Why am I feeling this way? Why can't I be a better mother? Maybe it's too late—the walls are built around my heart and not even Christmas can bring them down.

I grunt and turn to retreat from them, away from the happiness they bleed. It feels like torture, and yet I can't stop acting this way. I don't want to be this person. The too-cheerful chorus of the song sounds amplified to the point of absurdity. But just as I'm about to leave the room, Merritt's voice cuts through the noise.

"Mom!"

It's loud and with an assertiveness I've never heard come from her petite body. A demand that stops me in my tracks. I spin around. Merritt's fuzzy-socked feet are planted on the floor, arms rigid at her sides. Even from across the room I can see she's breathing hard. Her face is flushed, like someone who's finally been pushed to a breaking point. The image is so unexpected, I'm momentarily lost for words.

"When are you going to forgive me?" she hurls, face

screwed up and pain leaking out from her eyes. "I've said I'm sorry. It was my fault, okay? Are you going to hate me forever?"

My legs wobble and my face burns like it's been splashed with acid. No one makes a peep. Gus's eyes match his father's— wide as the bulbs hanging on the Fraser fir behind them.

Merritt lets out a sob. "I'm sorry!" she cries, collapsing to her knees. She's a mess, a child trampled by a burden beyond her years. It's as though the life has been sucked from her, leaving behind a shell aching for one thing—her mother.

It's in this moment I see it. Something in me snaps, waking me from a trance. A light bulb flicks on in my brain, all circuits rewiring in the span of a second. I've been horrid to Merritt. Wade accused me of this on more than one occasion, but I didn't want to believe him. Didn't want my shortcomings thrust in my face. But now, everything is clear. Everything I should have done, all the feelings I should have felt, come rushing to the surface.

A tsunami of emotion hurls over me and I swoop to the ground in front of Merritt, gathering her in my arms. Her face is wet, her neck damp with sweat.

"Merritt. Oh, Merritt," I cry. My loud, ugly tears mix with hers. We grip each other with everything we have, like two people finally reunited after being separated against their will. "I'm so sorry," I blubber. "This has all been my fault, not yours. Mine."

We're grasping and squeezing, making up for all these months of little touch. She meets my face, and I wipe tears from her cheeks before pulling her close again. Our heartbeats align, chest to chest. This girl who came from me. The one who made me a mother. How could I ever have treated her so terribly?

"I've needed you," Merritt cries into my neck.

"I know, sweetheart, and I'm sorry I haven't been here for you. Please, please forgive me. I love you so much." I keep repeating it. *I love you, I love you, I love you.*

I look up to Wade standing nearby. He's biting a knuckle between his teeth to keep from coming undone.

"Come here," I say to Gus, pulling him down into a sandwich hug with Merritt. Wade joins too, and the four of us kneel in the center of the living room while the soft melody of "Silent Night" plays in the background.

"You are the most important people in my life," I say, voice shaking. "And I've not treated you very well recently. I'm sorry. I promise I will be better."

Gus buries his head in my chest. My forehead meets Wade's over the top of the children. Our noses touch and we breathe each other in. "I love you," I whisper to him. "I'm sorry."

"I love you too," he says back, chin wobbling.

"Forgive me?"

"Already forgiven."

I don't know what the future holds, but I do know that I can't live without my family. And up until now, I didn't realize how close I was to losing them.

We stay in that position for a long time. No one is in a rush to let go—least of all me. My arms enfold my children, and I'm taken back to another time. I remember feeling panicked at the arrival of Summer—Wade and I were officially outnumbered. I had more kids than I did arms. How would it be possible to split my heart three ways? And yet, Summer fit right in as though I'd grown a third invisible arm.

Now though, I feel that limb fading. No longer needed. Perhaps the rest of my life will be just like this—two arms, two kids. I let the thought truly settle in my mind for the first time without fighting it.

This could be it. This could be my life. And if it is, it has to be enough. I don't know if I can do it, but I'll be more of a failure if I don't try.

FORTY-ONE

By eleven o'clock the tree has been trimmed, mantle garlanded, and windows candled. I manage to swallow the lump in my throat and smile, mostly because my smile makes the kids happy, and that makes it worth it. We hit a bump, however, when Gus pulls out our matching embroidered stockings from one of the tubs.

"I can't do it," I whisper to Wade. "I can't look at just four, and I can't bear to hang hers either."

He wraps an arm around my shoulder, and with a soft nod, he addresses the kids. "Guys, Mom and I think we're going to skip stockings this year."

"Skip stockings?" Gus says. "But what will Santa fill?"

Merritt, who's been watching our faces carefully, gives her brother a pat on the back. "It's okay, Gus," she says. "Maybe Santa will leave our stuff on the chair instead. Santa always knows what to do."

Gus pauses, considering, then shrugs. If Merritt says it's okay, it must be okay. She looks to Wade and me and gives us a wink. My heart swells. Our girl, wise beyond her years.

Wade tucks the stockings back in the tub, and we move on.

. . .

"Can we make gingerbread cookies?" Merritt says, clearly eager to keep the festivities rolling.

Gus jumps in place. "Yeah, cookies! I want to put candy buttons on mine!"

My body is heavy with exhaustion. For them, Mom is back. But for me, it's more complicated. It's not as simple as the flick of a light switch. *Forget the past four months! Everything back to normal!* I recognize the hurt my distance has caused and I'm determined to repair any damage I've created, but there's still a large hole in my heart that will never heal. If I'm going to move forward in this new reality, I have to learn how to cope with an insurmountable absence.

It feels close to impossible.

"In health class we learned that ginger helps when you have an upset belly," Gus is still rambling. "Is that true about ginger-bread cookies too?"

I chuckle. "I don't think so." I rustle his hair, and even though his comment is cute, it reminds me of a conversation that's long overdue with Merritt. I turn to her. "Speaking of school..." I say with raised eyebrows.

She looks down, then back up again. "Yeah?"

"What's going on, Mer? We never talked about that call from Mr. Applebaum."

She picks at a hangnail, then finally gives in. "I haven't been turning in assignments."

"But why?" I say. "You're a good student. You know better than that."

"It just didn't seem like it mattered anymore. Summer is missing. You and Dad are focused on finding her. It seemed stupid to worry about dividing fractions..." Her voice trails off. "School isn't as fun as it used to be."

"Well, sure, sixth grade isn't like kindergarten. Classes get harder. There's more homework. That's normal."

"No," she says, shaking her head. "Not just the work. I mean the people. They look at me weird. They whisper. I just want to hide, so I make up an excuse to go to the nurse or something."

My heart breaks for her. I wish I could slap myself for not noticing how much she's been hurting.

"I'm sorry, sweetheart. I should have been more helpful."

"Am I going to fail?"

"Mr. Applebaum seemed willing to help so it doesn't come to that. I'll give him a call to set up a meeting. We'll figure it out, okay?" A new epiphany lands in my brain. I can't give up on Summer, but I won't give up on my other two either. This balance... it feels right.

Gus, who's been quiet this whole time, spots an opening. "So," he says, testing the waters, "about those cookies..."

Merritt laughs. Their adorable faces look to me with pleading eyes and I can't say no.

"Okay," I say, and they both cheer.

While Wade tasks himself with stringing lights on the front porch, I gather the brown sugar, flour, and molasses from the pantry.

"Not too much!" I say when Gus gets a little eager with the ginger. I swipe my finger into the flour and dab white powder on the tip of his nose. He giggles.

There's a heaviness in my chest that I try to breathe through. None of this is normal. None of it is easy. But I have to try. *Just try*, I will myself.

Just as we're about to drop dollops of brown cookie batter onto the baking sheet, my phone rings. I peer at the screen a few feet away on the counter.

It's Georgia. She doesn't usually call on the weekend. My

senses stand on high alert. I quickly wipe my hands on the dish towel and answer the phone.

"Hello?"

"Greta." There's a sharpness to her tone, an urgency that instantly makes my chest tingle. "We've had another tip."

Another tip? But we've had lots of tips and they've all fallen through. Why should this one be any different?

"Okay," I say, guarding myself. The last few hours have been spent trying to come to terms with the possibility of being a family of four. And now this?

"It seems credible," Georgia says. "Someone near State College reported seeing a little girl that matched Summer's description in the back of a car at a gas station. We got a plate number. The vehicle is registered to a woman from Erie."

The room spins. "Are... are you sure?"

"Listen," Georgia says, "I know we've had false alarms, and I almost didn't call you, but I promised I'd always keep you in the loop. We're waiting for a follow-up from the local precinct. Don't get any ideas, Greta. You can't hightail it to State College."

She knows me well. I'd already started calculating the distance.

I attempt to steady my breathing. *Wade, where is Wade?* I stumble from the kitchen. I can see him through the windows that frame the front door. When I get there, I knock to get his attention then point to the phone against my cheek. I mouth, *It's Georgia*, with a look that I hope reads as important. He drops the lights, climbs down from the step stool, and opens the door.

"They got another sighting," I say, rotating the phone away from my mouth.

"Where?"

"State College."

State College. Less than four hours away. State College, also known as Happy Valley. How could such a horrible person be in such a cheerful place?

Through the line, Georgia's voice rises in pitch. "Greta, we've got another call coming in. It's them. Hold tight. I'll call you right back."

She hangs up before I have a chance to respond.

Wade and I exchange anxious looks. We've been here before. This yo-yo of emotions has taken us on more than one rollercoaster over the last seventeen weeks. Frankly, I'd love to never ride another one again.

"What if it's—" I start, but Wade grabs my hand and I know what he's thinking. *Don't get your hopes up.*

We don't have to wait long because my phone rings in what feels like seconds.

"Is it her?" I blurt, holding the phone between Wade's ear and mine.

Georgia's voice comes back clear as day. "It's her. It's Summer. They've got her."

FORTY-TWO

THE DRIVE TO THE STATION IS LIKE A FEVER DREAM. ALL the same emotions from the false sighting in Buffalo come screaming back in full force. Georgia said it's Summer, but I won't let myself fully believe it's my daughter until I see her with my own eyes.

They've told us Summer is being transported to Erie under police protection. They left State College thirty minutes ago, and I pray whoever is driving breaks every speed limit law.

We hit a red light, and I squirm in my seat. Questions assault my brain.

Was she in State College the whole time?

Who is the woman who kidnapped her?

Is Summer hurt? Is she okay?

Georgia had none of these answers for us on the phone. She simply told us to get to the station as quickly as possible. And so we grabbed the kids and left, gingerbread dough on the counter and half-strung lights outside. I haven't called a soul—not my parents, not Lolly. Nobody. Not until I know for sure. I don't want to jinx it. We've been here before, and I fight to keep away the doubt that tells me it probably isn't her.

In the back seat, the kids are mute. Despite my attempts at self-preservation, something about this time feels different. I'm shivering so much my teeth nearly rattle.

Georgia meets us at the door of the precinct.

"Is this really happening?" I say, somehow out of breath despite doing nothing but sitting in the car for the last ten minutes.

"Yes, Greta. This is really happening."

"Oh my God," I breathe as she escorts us to a conference room. The kids take a seat, but Wade and I are far too anxious to sit. My mouth unhinges and the tangle of thoughts comes tumbling out. "Who is it? The woman. Who is she?"

"We're still learning," Georgia says. "But it appears to be a case of psychological distress."

I shake my head and my brows knit together. "I'm not following."

"The woman—we're working on an official ID—told police she'd recently suffered her fourth miscarriage. She saw Summer unattended, and something snapped. She took her."

I blink. "She couldn't have a baby, so she thought she'd just steal one instead?"

"People do crazy things under extreme pressure."

"But did she hurt her? Is Summer hurt?"

Easy, Greta. It might not even be her. Don't put the cart before the horse.

"What we were told is that Summer appeared to be unharmed. She was clean, dressed well." Georgia's voice remains level, and I know she's been trained to stay calm in highly emotional settings.

Tears spring from my eyes, and I grab Wade's hand for support. My baby. She wasn't hurt.

"It's going to take time to get the answers to all of our questions," Georgia continues, "but what's most important is that Summer is on her way home. I know it's an impossible request, but I'm going to have to ask you all to stay here and be patient. They'll be here as soon as possible. Now, if you'll excuse me for just a minute..."

I give a little nod, and Georgia leaves.

"Is it really Summer?" Merritt asks.

Wade and I exchange a look. What if this is another bust? I can't bear letting the kids down again.

"They think so," I say. "We need to wait and see."

I take a seat and fidget with my purse strap. I have so many more questions. Waiting is impossible. After another minute, an urge pulls me from my chair. "I'll be right back."

A thirst for information draws me from the conference room out into the brightly lit hallway. I turn right, headed for a couple doors down. Georgia's office. I've passed it before but have never been inside. All the times we've met to talk have always been in another room.

The door is open, and when I get there, I discover Georgia sitting on a thin armchair, elbows on her knees and head in her hands. She looks up quickly when I step inside. Our eyes meet. Hers are filled with tears.

"Georgia," I say, shocked to find her in such a state. "What is going on?"

"I'm just so relieved," she says, her typically solid demeanor broken. "I told myself I wouldn't give up and... I'm just so relieved."

Overcome, I extend my arms, her words getting me all choked up again. She stands and we embrace.

"Thank you," I whisper.

My gaze travels over her shoulder to her desk, where a gold name plate reads DETECTIVE GEORGIA SMART. Next to it sits a tri-fold picture frame with three photos. Two handsome teenage boys, who I assume are her sons. But there's also a younger girl with a missing front tooth and deep dimples. She looks just like the boys.

Georgia lets go from our hug and follows my line of vision.

"I thought you said you only had two kids," I say.

She looks down. "Now I do. But I used to have three. My daughter... she died a couple years ago. Car accident."

A chill travels to my toes. I'm momentarily dumbfounded. "I'm so sorry," I finally say, still processing. "I had no idea."

"I don't talk about her much. I like to keep her memory private."

"Of course."

"Everyone grieves in their own way. And given the nature of—I mean, given what you all were going through..."

I shake my head. "Sure, I understand."

This whole time, Georgia has been searching for my daughter, knowing her own child would never be coming back. How did she do it? I'm struck with a sharp stab of second-hand survivor's guilt. Georgia stares at the picture of the daughter she lost. A little girl who couldn't have been more than eight. My heart bleeds.

She returns her gaze to me, and with a swift wipe of her eyes, she gives a cleansing exhale. "I'm so glad you're getting your girl back."

We return to the conference room together.

"We can't possibly wait another hour or more," Wade implores the second we enter. "Can't we talk to her? Can't you call whoever she's driving with?"

My eyes fly open. Why hadn't I thought of that? "Yes! Please, I just want to hear her voice. To know it's really her."

Georgia hesitates. "It goes against policy..."

"Georgia, please," I implore.

She pauses for a beat, then types a text on her phone. We wait. Then she nods. "Okay, got the number." She dials from the black desk phone in the center of the table, then puts it on speaker.

My heart is so high in my throat I feel like I might choke on it.

"Skyler," the voice on the other end of the line answers.

"This is Detective Smart. I'm here with the Goodmans, Greta and Wade. They'd like to speak to their daughter."

I bring a hand to my mouth, leaving behind a sweaty imprint on the table from where I'd been pressing. Wade squeezes an arm around my waist. I give him a quick glance. Then Merritt, then Gus. Everyone looks as nervous as I feel. This is it.

"Just a second," the officer says, and then we hear his voice quieter. "Here, honey. Your mommy and daddy are on the phone."

I hold my breath. *Please be true, please be true. I'll know her voice anywhere.*

And that's when I hear the sweetest sound in the whole world.

"Mommy?"

The air releases from my lungs in one giant heave. "Summer! Oh my God, Summer! It's Mommy. I'm here." Hot, rushed sobs erupt from my lips.

"Mommy!" she shrieks this time.

"You're safe now, honey. The police are bringing you home."

It's a rush of relief like nothing I've ever felt. Too much, in fact, because my legs suddenly won't hold me anymore, and I collapse into Wade's arms.

We wait near a large window that looks out over the front parking lot. The one-way glass means we can see out, but those on the other side can't see in. It's a good thing because twenty minutes earlier, a news van came screeching in and promptly set up cameras pointing at different angles.

Someone tipped off the media. Now, Summer's home-coming will be a fanfare. I've developed a love–hate relation-ship with the press—the people who held the power to keep Summer's story visible were the same people who hounded us outside our front door and at the vigil.

The news crew is all hustle and bustle getting ready, but I pay them no attention. I'm watching for the cruiser that carries my daughter.

I bite the nail on my thumb. Wade keeps trying to talk to me, but I can't hold a conversation. Every time I open my mouth to talk, emotion spills out. I keep my lips sealed and sway with wired energy. My parents, who rushed over the second I called, hold their collective breaths. Mom's cuticles might start bleeding if she picks them any more.

Then, finally, they're here.

Two thirty-seven. That's the time the cruiser pulls into the station. I know because I've been watching my phone and seeing each minute change. One minute closer to being reunited with Summer after one hundred twenty-six days, twenty-three hours, and forty-one minutes.

I lunge for the door.

"Wait!" Georgia calls, but I'm already gone. I don't care about privacy. I don't care what the cameras capture. All I want is my daughter in my arms. I'm laser-focused as I sprint to the car. I can see her outline in the back seat, a blurred silhouette as though I'm squinting through murky water.

"Summer!" I cry, ripping the door open.

And there she is. My little package of sunshine. A third of my heart. In that single second when my eyes land on her, I see her entire life flash before my eyes. The first time the nurse placed her in my arms. Summer toddling toward me with outstretched arms as she took her first steps. Bath time with soapy hairdos and bubble beards. Falling asleep in the car, hands folded in her lap like an angel. The million *I love yous* and endless kisses. It's all right here in her wide eyes. This is real, she's really home.

Summer falls into me, wrapping her little arms around my neck. "Mommy!"

Our tears mix together in liquid joy as we both weep and hug and feel each other's faces to make sure each other is real. Her hair smells different—flowery instead of the apple-scented shampoo at home—but I breathe it in like it's the most delicious thing I've ever smelled.

Wade jumps in, enveloping us. Through our cries, I'm vaguely aware of the clicking of cameras. Voices call out, "Summer! Summer, over here! Greta, how does it feel to have your daughter home?" Everything feels like it's moving in slow motion.

There's a hand on my back. "Let's get inside," Georgia yells, and she hustles us behind the protection of the mirrored glass. Merritt and Gus are with us—they must have run out to the car too. Everything's such a blur. They shower their sister with kisses. Gus picks her up by the waist and spins her around.

"I'm so sorry, Summer," Merritt says over and over, and I know none of it registers in Summer's young brain. She doesn't know the fault bombs that have been thrown around in her absence.

"In here," Georgia says, opening the conference room door. Two other officers, including Detective Ocho, follow us in. Even inside the station, a crowd is starting to form. I'm thankful for Georgia's discretion.

"Oh, Summer," I say, unable to stop the tears. "Are you okay? I'm so happy you're home. I love you so much." Now that she's here, I don't want to let go of her. Even when she's hugging Wade or the kids, my fingers grasp her hand, the hem of her shirt, anything.

My mom strokes Summer's hair, repeating, "Thank you,

Lord," and when I look up, I see tears in my dad's eyes. Relief, it turns out, has a face, and we're all wearing it.

Georgia extends a box of tissues and I take one, wiping the salty mess from my face in vain. I do the same to Summer, then pull her back against me. We're both immediately soaked in tears again. Her body trembles, and I hold her tight. Wade wraps us both in an embrace.

There are so many things I want to ask her, but now is not the time. All I can do is close my eyes and hold my daughter in my arms.

FORTY-THREE

SUMMER: THE DAY OF THE KIDNAPPING

Mommy and Daddy get in line for the big rollercoaster. I'm too little to ride it, but that's okay because it looks way too scary. They told us to sit at the table and wait. The bench is hard and leaves red marks on my legs like tic-tac-toe.

"Look at my leg!" I say to Merritt and Gus. It's so funny. I want to show them, but they're not paying attention. Merritt's on her stupid phone. She doesn't play with me as much since she got her phone. Maybe when I'm older I'll get a phone too and we can be twins.

I pick at the paint on the edge of the table. It's blue, Gus's favorite color. Pink is mine.

When are Mommy and Daddy going to be back? This is boooooring. I want to ride the carousel again. Mommy promised.

I swing my feet. A bird flies past and I watch it land on a branch next to the spinny ride Mommy says makes her throw up. It looks fun to me. All the kids are laughing.

I look back to my brother and sister. They don't even know

I'm here. Watching the spinny ride would be way better than sitting here doing nothing. So, I slide off the bench and walk toward it. One step, two steps, three steps. I count as I go. Now I'm fourteen steps away. I hook my fingers onto the fence and look through to the ride. I'm too short to see over the top, but I can still see most of it.

"Doesn't that look fun?"

There's a lady a little bit down the fence. She smiles at me and I smile back.

"Yes," I say.

The lady is pretty, like Miss Nikki at my preschool. She comes closer to me.

"What's your favorite ride?" she asks.

I don't even have to think. "The carousel."

"That's my favorite too!"

My eyes open wide. I thought only kids liked the carousel. "My mommy said we can go on it again before we leave."

"I'll take you now, if you want." She smiles big. Her teeth are very white. "Come on! Standing here is boring, don't you think?"

It is pretty boring. And I really want to ride the carousel.

She puts out her hand. I look back to Merritt and Gus. They're still playing on Merritt's phone.

"I like the tiger," the lady says. "Which one do you want to ride?"

"The white bunny."

"Oh, the bunny is so cute! Great choice! Ready?"

Her hand is still out. I like her pink nail polish. It's almost the same color as mine. I think I hear the sound of the carousel.

She takes another step toward me.

"Okay," I say, taking her hand. I'll ride one time and come back. I'll tell Merritt and Gus all about my adventure riding the carousel by myself!

We walk side by side. The lady swings my arm. "My name's Shelby," she says. "What's yours?" She seems so nice. I smile up at her. "Summer."

FORTY-FOUR
SEVEN DAYS HOME

"Mommyyyyy!"

Summer's voice rips me from my sleep and I spring out of bed like a jack-in-the-box. I dash to her room, probably looking every bit the wild mess that I am.

"It's okay, sweetheart," I say, dropping to her side. I don't know what time it is, but it's pitch black, so it must be the middle of the night. Summer doesn't yet have a clock in her room like the big kids.

"Shhhh... it's okay. I'm here." I stroke her hair, gently rocking her in my lap on the edge of the bed.

Summer's body shakes, and I hold her tight until she starts to relax. The nightmares began a couple days after her return. Most nights, sometimes more than once. She and I rarely get a solid stretch of sleep—one of us is always waking in a panic.

She doesn't say much during these episodes—sometimes I wonder if she's still half asleep. I don't pry, as much as I'd like to pepper her with questions. I want to know every detail about when she was gone, the exact things Shelby Marrow said and did. But the child psychologist warned that pushing for too much information too fast could backfire. Summer will tell us things when she's ready. I have to respect that. So far, we've noticed that Summer eats much faster than she used to—practically shoveling food into her mouth, as if it were the first meal she's had in days. The doctors said physically, she's fine. She didn't lose weight, her teeth are clean. But just because she was well taken care of doesn't mean there's not internal trauma.

Shelby Marrow confessed immediately to taking Summer. She told police she'd watched Wade and I leave the kids at the table, then made her move when Summer wandered toward where she stood. They'd holed up in Shelby's home thirty minutes from Erie. She and her husband had separated after the last miscarriage, and with no family around and few friends in the mix, Shelby had been able to keep Summer hidden. As for why they were found in State College, Shelby remained mum. Maybe I'll never know what her long-term plans were, where she was taking my daughter, but at this point, it doesn't matter.

Whatever Shelby's plans were, they were foiled when a woman named Cynthia, a retired kindergarten teacher from Mount Nittany Elementary School, spotted Shelby and Summer at a gas station.

"I've been around hundreds of kids in my career," Cynthia told us over the phone the day after Summer's return. "I never forget a face. Summer's image was burned in my mind ever since I saw her on the news months ago."

Summer had been in the back of a small white car, but Cynthia recognized her through the window immediately, even with a hat pulled low on her head. She'd quickly pulled her car behind Shelby's at the pump. With another vehicle in front, Shelby had nowhere to go. From there, Cynthia hurried inside the convenience store, alerting the clerk to call 911. The police showed up within minutes.

"Thank you, thank you, thank you," I cried on the phone. "You have no idea how eternally grateful we are."

Cynthia was choked up. She refused the reward money, saying, "I'm just so glad I saw her."

We were told that Shelby Marrow cried when taken into custody, realizing what she'd done was wrong, but saying in the moment—and all those months she had Summer in hiding—she felt like she'd done the right thing. The child was alone. She longed for one. Decision made.

Now, a week later, we're dealing with the fallout of that choice.

When Summer's body goes limp in my arms, I gently lay her back onto the pillow. I slide off the bed quietly and stare for a long minute. She appears the exact same as she did in August. Her hair has grown an inch, and she's lost the sun-kissed color on her skin, but otherwise she looks like the same little girl. How is it possible that so much has happened and no one would know from the outside? I have to remind myself that, like a book, the real stuff is on the inside. Summer might look the same, but she'll never truly be the same kid. Now, my job is to protect as much innocence as I can.

A creak in the hallway makes me jump.

"She okay?" Wade whispers, coming into the doorframe.

I nod.

He flicks his head, gesturing for me to come back to bed.

"I'm going to stay here for a bit," I say. "I'll sleep on the floor."

He leaves and returns a second later with a blanket and pillow. "Here."

"Thanks."

"Do you want me to stay?"

I shake my head. "Get some sleep." At least one of us should.

He pauses for a beat, staring at Summer, a soft smile on his face, the crooked kind. When he returns to bed, I adjust myself against Summer's dresser, where I have a clear view of her sleeping form.

I soak in every ounce of her, from her rhythmic breaths, to the way her eyelashes flutter, and even the curve of her back, curled tight like she was inside me when I carried her for nine months.

I yawn. I won't get any sleep here on the floor, and yet I'd stay awake forever if it meant knowing Summer was safe. Still, my back is cramping. My eyelids beg to close. After another few minutes, when I'm convinced she'll be okay for the rest of the night, I surrender. Making my way to the door, I look back one last time. Summer's deeply asleep, Lucy the Lamb tucked under one arm. I pray her dreams are of the sweetest kind.

Back in our room, I crawl under the covers. Wade's feet touch my legs. They're cold from the hardwood in the hallway. Things aren't magically perfect again, but at least we're sleeping in the same bed consistently. Our family has a lot of healing to do—and that includes my husband and me.

For now, I let his touch linger and don't push him away. Tomorrow is Christmas, but I've already got my gift. I don't need a single thing else.

"Santa came!" Gus shouts as he bounds down the stairs two at a time. Merritt, holding Summer's hand, is not far behind. My heart twinges at the sight of my girls.

Normally, the kids pounce on us in bed, begging us to get up. But this year, Wade and I purposely woke early. I wanted to be fully awake, fully present for every second of their magical morning. After obsessively checking on them like I've been doing morning and night, Wade and I snuck downstairs, put on a pot of coffee, and sat by the wood stove under a blanket until the kids stirred. A silent house puts me on edge. Hearing the noise of

their rousing comes with a release. *They're here. They're alive.*
There are hours that will pass and then panic will strike, only for
me to remind myself, *Oh, yes, she's home. Our nightmare is over.*

Today, I'll do my best to live in the moment. After four
months of hell, we all deserve a respite.

"Merry Christmas!" we say as the kids arrive wide-eyed.
Gus's strawberry bed head makes me chuckle.

"Good morning, sweet girl," I say, giving Summer a kiss.
She doesn't mention anything about last night's nightmare—she
normally doesn't—and so neither do I. Perhaps her counselor
will work on it at this week's session. I pray there will be a day
when the five of us don't need therapy anymore.

"Did Santa eat the cookies?" Summer asks excitedly.

"Looks like it!" Wade says, holding up the plate where only
crumbs remain. Summer giggles.

Her days fluctuate hour to hour. Sometimes she seems like
the same kid from before, not a care in the world, happy to play
and laugh and tell stories. But other times, she's withdrawn, as
though a dark cloud has passed overhead. Sometimes she needs
help doing things she'd previously mastered, like tying her
shoes. Twice, she's had accidents in her underwear. Through it
all, we offer reassurance and a hug.

Today seems to be off to a positive start. It's Christmas, after
all—how could it not? And so I'll take it. I'll savor every moment
of normalcy we can get.

The kids tear into packages, wrapping paper flying through
the air like brilliant fireworks.

"AirPods!" Merritt yells. "Yes! Thanks, Mom!"

"And Dad," I say.

Gus opens a mini basketball hoop for the back of his bedroom
door, complete with scoreboard and LED lights. "Sweet!" he
says, ball in each hand. I can already hear the incessant banging
that gift will cause, but the smile on his face makes it worth it.

"What'd you get, Summer?" Wade says as Summer digs into a gift bag with a cheerful snowman on the front. She rips through the tissue paper and pulls out a light pink baseball hat with metallic embroidery.

"Ohhh," I coo, "how pretty!"

But Summer doesn't say a word. Her face is ghostly pale, her freckles all but disappearing from her cheeks. She holds the hat in her hands and stares at it like it were the scariest thing imaginable. Her hands begin to tremble until finally she drops the hat and scrambles backward away from it.

"No hats!" she cries. "No hats!"

Wade and I look to each other in shock. He quickly grabs the hat and tucks it out of view while I go to Summer.

"Okay, honey. It's okay." I pull her close to me.

"No hats," she repeats.

"No hats," I say. "Okay, no more hats. It's gone. No more hats."

Merritt and Gus watch with eyes the size of pancakes. *It's okay*, I mouth to them over Summer's head. They nod with my reassurance, but I know this new version of their sister is something they're adjusting to. I worry this experience will somehow have forced them all to leapfrog over childhood.

After another minute, Summer relaxes. I stroke her hair. "Better?" I say. She gives a quiet "Mmhmm," and I kiss her forehead. "How about another present?" I offer, hoping to return the mood in the room to one of cheer instead of fear. I pray there's nothing else hidden away behind wrapping paper and boxes that will trigger another memory. There's so much I still don't know. I'd never have expected a hat to scare her the way it did—then again, I'm still learning. We all are.

When the kids are occupied with their new gifts and we've had a moment to relax after the whirlwind of the morning, I get on Facebook and type out a post.

> No gift could come close to the one we received a week ago. Thank you for all the love and support. We are so incredibly grateful to have our family back together.

My phone immediately dings with likes and comments, but I turn the volume to silent. I click over to Summer's page. I considered deleting it after she'd been found, but thanks to a suggestion from Georgia, we've decided to leave it up and repurpose its mission. Summer may be home, but there are thousands of children who aren't. Now, instead of posting updates on our own investigation, I share stories of other missing kids in hopes of helping bring awareness to their families' plights.

I type a new post on the page.

> Wishing you all a peaceful Christmas. We are counting our blessings and thinking of those families who are still hurting. Never give up!

FORTY-FIVE

TEN DAYS HOME

The rate at which the world keeps spinning blows my mind. Sometimes I want to shout, *My missing daughter was just found and returned to us!* as if somehow that will make things stop, or at least slow down and give us a minute to catch up.

But alas, refrigerators run out of milk and pantries run out of mac 'n' cheese. And so here we are—the kids and I—visiting the grocery store.

"Up you go," I say, lifting Summer to put her in the cart's seat.

"No, Mommy, that's for babies," she says, wriggling to get free from my hands.

"It's easier and safer. Come on." I go to lift her again.

She protests with a swift swat at the cart. "Noooo!"

I sigh and pause in the store's entryway. A woman walks past, grabs the weekly coupon flyer, and enters.

"Okay, fine," I relent. "But you have to hold onto the cart right here." I take her hand and wrap her fingers through the metal bars. "Merritt, Gus, you two on the other side."

"*Mom*," Merritt says, giving me a look that says she'd rather die than be tethered to a shopping cart like a daycare leash.

I suck in a breath. An overwhelming need to keep them close makes my nerve ends tingle. I have to shield them from the world and its myriad dangers. Every time they wander out of sight, my heart clenches with fear, my mind racing with all the worst-case scenarios that threaten to unravel the fragile threads of our newfound happiness. That's just on the surface. Beneath it all lies a deeper, more primal fear—that history will repeat itself, that I will once again find myself standing helplessly on the sidelines as my child is torn from my grasp. It's a fear that claws at the edges of my consciousness, threatening to consume me with its insatiable hunger for security.

But amid the turmoil of my overprotective instincts, there's a whisper of reason—a nagging voice that reminds me that Merritt is no longer a small child. I swallow every ounce of pride. "Alright. But stay close, okay?"

It's a truce, an understanding. I won't make her hold onto the cart like a toddler, but that doesn't mean she can dawdle too far behind. I'll give her some independence, as long as she gives me a little grace, too.

We make our way through the automatic doors. Straight ahead is the produce. We stop at a long display of berries.

"They're free!" Summer says, excitedly. "I can read the sign. *Fr-ee.*"

An older couple turns to look, giving smiles and warm-hearted sounds, a cluck of the tongue.

"You have to buy one to get the second free," I explain, putting two containers of strawberries in the cart.

We stock up on all the fresh stuff, including a head of cabbage to make sauerkraut for New Year's Day, before mean-dering the center aisles. Summer keeps hold of the cart like I instructed. Everything is fine. We're just regular people doing a regular thing, and yet the heightened sensation of being in public again remains strong. When my attention is diverted to the shelves of cereal, or the meat case, or a cooler of vegetables for what feels like a second too long, I whip around and count their heads. *One, two, three. They're all here.*

In the bread aisle a woman in a thick puffer coat and toggle hat stops us. I brace myself for a hushed insult or some other piece of judgment like I've been used to.

"I just wanted to say how happy I am for you all," she says. Her eyes practically go misty, and I'm struck by the fervor with which strangers have followed our story. At least this time, the sentiments are kind.

"Thank you so much," I say and keep moving.

The next aisle over, it happens again.

"Welcome home, Summer," a man says.

"Beautiful little girl," a gray-haired woman says. "I prayed for her every night."

Each time, I give the same response.

Thank you.

Yes, we're so grateful.

Our prayers have been answered.

Wherever we go—which hasn't been much or far—people say her name. *Summer, Summer, Summer.* Everyone is interested in the kidnapped girl who made it home. The stories have shifted from Wade's and my fault to our euphoria at her recovery. Just like that, a new narrative. It's as though people forgot how brutal they were to us all those months.

The public might forget, but I won't.

We stop at the deli counter, and the woman offers the kids a slice of cheese. Summer reaches on her tiptoes to grab the thin, orange square.

"I like your tattoo," the woman says, pointing to the temporary princess tattoo on Summer's hand. "Is Cinderella your favorite?"

Summer smiles and nods.

"I have a tattoo too!" Gus inserts. He lifts his hand toward the woman, Spiderman design in full view. She gives him a brief acknowledgment but keeps her attention largely on Summer, cooing over the wonder girl whose return has been considered a holiday miracle.

Gus scowls. I rub his back and lean down to his ear. "I'd pick Spiderman over Cinderella any day."

As the woman hands me the meat over the counter, she lowers her voice. "I hope she gets jail time. Stealing a child because she couldn't have her own. Pssh!"

"Yes... well... thank you," I say uncomfortably, putting the bag of sliced turkey in the cart. We've been told not to talk about the case, and while I certainly have my own feelings, I'm not interested in discussing them with a stranger in a hair net.

Opinions on the case have flown like rapid fire these last two weeks, separating people into two very distinct camps—the ones who empathize with Shelby Marrow and those who want to see her face the maximum penalty.

Here's the thing—if Summer had been mistreated or abused, public opinion might lean more heavily in one direction. But as far as we can tell, Shelby Marrow treated Summer kindly, as though Summer were a replacement for the unborn children she'd lost. She repeatedly told police she'd come to love Summer. There is no evidence that points to any physical harm. And so there is a large portion of people who feel a psychiatric hospital is more appropriate. They say Shelby Marrow needs rehabilitation over punishment. It wasn't a violent crime.

I'd like to see these people live the last four months of our lives, or comfort Summer through one of her nightmares.

Summer doesn't say much, and she's mostly a happy kid, but that doesn't mean there isn't darkness lurking beneath the surface. A crime doesn't have to be violent for it to be harmful. Sometimes I stare at Summer and worry about what's going on inside her head. How will this impact the rest of her life?

So, when it comes to where I stand, the answer is simple—I want Shelby Marrow behind bars. I can't get on board with letting her off easy. Plenty of people experience hardships in life, but that doesn't give them the right to kidnap a child. I hope prison steals the rest of her life, just like she stole those four months from my family. An eye for an eye. I'd consider myself a generally empathetic person, but not this time.

FORTY-SIX

FOURTEEN DAYS HOME

THE KIDS DON THEIR PARTY HATS LONG BEFORE THE countdown begins. The noisemakers are giving me a mild headache, but I don't say anything—if there's ever been a New Year's Eve to celebrate, it's this one.

We're cuddled up in the living room, bowls of popcorn—cheddar, caramel, and butter—on the coffee table. I take a kernel of each and pop them in my mouth—the perfect sweet-and-salty combo. Next to me, Gus blows a fringed whistle in my face.

"Aren't all those people going to get hurt if the ball falls on them?" Summer says, watching the TV. Metallic beaded necklaces hang around her neck—no party hats this year.

"It's attached to the pole," I say with a chuckle. "And anyway, it's not a fast drop. It's more of a slow decline. You almost can't tell it's moving."

She yawns. Ten o'clock is past her bedtime, but the kids begged to stay up until midnight, and like with the noisemakers, I didn't put up a fight. They'll never make it that late, but it's fun to watch them savor the specialness of such a rare occasion.

I look over at Wade on the far side of the couch. The kids

squeeze in the middle even though there's a loveseat and chair that are empty. Wade gives me a smile—the genuine, lopsided kind again. I return it. I am so ready to kiss this year goodbye. Tomorrow feels like the beginning of a new chapter, and while we still have lots of work to do, things are on the mend in more ways than one. Healing, it turns out, is a messy process, but I'm yearning for it. For myself, for Summer, for our family.

I reach for my glass of sparkling grape juice on the end table. My eyes land on the white and blue lamp. I run a finger over the cracks where I tried to glue it back together. It was a mediocre feat, some pieces shattering so finely it was impossible to mend it perfectly. Uneven parts and grooves now exist where a smooth surface once was. I can't help but feel a tingling pull of irony. The lamp will never be the same, but neither will our family. It's a new version of itself. Beautiful in its own way.

Summer is the first to pass out, mouth open, head cocked on a pillow at an awkward angle. The top hat bends and folds near her ear. Gus isn't far behind. It's almost eleven now. Merritt's eyes are red-rimmed in the way they get when she's overtired, but she fights on to stay awake.

"I'm gonna make it," she says.

She's asleep twenty minutes later.

With all three happily sleeping, Wade scoots off the couch and wedges in next to me. I can't remember the last time we sat this close outside of the forced proximity of Calista's office. There, our hands barely touched. Now, I curl into him, his body bringing a warm sense of contentment.

We watch the countdown show, laugh at the bad lip-syncing stars, and wonder just how much the hosts had to drink before going live. We both take turns yawning, but an unspoken goal of seeing the calendar flip keeps us awake.

On the cusp of midnight, Wade pours us each a small glass of champagne.

"To a fresh start," he says.

I raise my eyebrows. "If only it were that easy."

"What, you mean we can't just clink glasses and make everything better?" He winks, and I appreciate the levity.

"This isn't Oz, and I'm not wearing ruby slippers." I lift a foot wrapped in thick wool socks and wiggle my toes.

"I've never been into red heels anyway."

We tap glasses and each take a long swig. So much of our days now revolve around serious conversations—therapy and charges against Shelby Marrow and whether our kids are going to be alright. It's nice to enjoy a moment of lightness. It reminds me that through it all, Wade and I have each other. We're a team.

The ball begins its slow slide downward. I rest my head on Wade's shoulder. Closing out this year feels like closing the cover of a bad book. We've been through hell and are climbing out. I'm just hoping we make it all the way.

Ten, nine, eight...

A surprise wave of emotion lodges in my throat. My eyes fill. Next to us are our three sleeping babes. All here, all safe. The same can't be said for thousands of other families out there. I think of Georgia and the little girl in the picture on her desk.

We are so very lucky.

Five, four, three...

With seconds to spare, I search my heart for a single word to carry into the new year. Something to define my intentions. It comes as the ball reaches the ground. Forgiveness. Not for Wade, not for Merritt. Those slates have already been cleaned. I finally forgive myself.

One.

.   .   .

I wake with a giant heave and lurch up in bed. My heart jackhammers in my chest. Another nightmare—but this time it's me, not Summer. Wade is asleep, snoring gently like he does after a drink or two. He doesn't rouse, but that's okay. I'd rather he slept. All I need is to soothe my anxiety by checking on the kids. It's become a frequent impulse—count them in the grocery store, check their rooms in the middle of the night. I never was the new mom who'd constantly put an ear to their newborn's mouth to feel the air or watch to make sure their little chests rose and fell with breath. But now, paranoia has changed all that. I won't be able to fall asleep unless I take a peek into their rooms. They're always there, of course, and that's enough to send me back to bed. My children are secure. All is well.

I walk softly down the hall toward Summer's room—given everything that's happened, hers is always first on my list. When Wade and I carried the kids to bed after the ball dropped, Summer briefly woke and mumbled, "Is it a new year?"

"Yes," I whispered. "It's a new year. Now go back to sleep." She rolled over and hugged Lucy the Lamb to her chest.

The floor creaks under my feet. I make it to Summer's door and inch it open just a crack. There's a swell of blankets, but I can't see her. My blood pressure involuntarily kicks up a notch. I push the door further, squint through the darkness. Is she simply jumbled among the covers? Still, I don't see her. That's when I fling the door wide and step into the room. I freeze. Her bed is empty, the covers flung. Like someone has—

No. Oh my God, no.

I hurry back into the hallway, panic seizing with each step. It's happening again. The others, I need to check the others. This time, I don't pad lightly. I'm not conscious of my volume. At Merritt's door, I barge in, fully prepared to see another empty bed. We're cursed. I'm the mother in *Peter Pan* discovering her children missing.

I stop in my tracks.

There's not one person in the bed. There are three.

Merritt, Gus, and Summer cuddle together under the lavender bedding. The two older flank the youngest, their little strawberry-haired sidekick. All three are sound asleep. Gus's arm is up by his face. Summer's cheek squishes into the pillow. She's brought Lucy the Lamb with her, and the lovey rests under her chin. Merritt's body curves against Summer's.

An invisible band tightens around my heart. *Ouch*—but in a good way.

My shoulders release all tension as the panic recedes. Tears well in my eyes at the sight of them all together, safe and happy in dreamland where danger can't reach them.

I stay for another minute, wishing I could crawl in with them, hold each of their small, fragile bodies and breathe their hair. But this is their place as one. Mine is in another room next door. And so, I back from the room with a wistful smile on my face and a heart so full I could cry.

EPILOGUE

SIX MONTHS LATER: ONE HUNDRED NINETY-THREE DAYS HOME

THE LAST DAY OF SCHOOL IS NOTHING BUT A CELEBRATION. The kids don't even take their backpacks, and they eat enough junk to rival a birthday party.

I'm waiting at the bus stop ten minutes before their scheduled arrival. In my hands are two cans of Silly String, one pink the other blue. Lolly and another mom from the neighborhood are here too, equally stocked and ready to spray their kids with showers of foam. A dad appears with a cooler packed with popsicles. Our neighborhood is like that—fun and celebratory. It is, after all, Pleasant Drive.

"Oh, oh! Here they come," Lolly says with a grin. I hide the cans behind my back and out of view. The bus pulls to a stop at the curb. The sound of elated woots and excited chatter pours from the open windows. Classic song lyrics roll through my mind: *School's out for summer!* Merritt, of all people, must be relieved, particularly after a heavy load during the spring semester to make up for the work she'd missed.

The bus driver opens the door and a gaggle of kids comes tumbling out, arms raised, toothy smiles stretching from ear to ear.

"No more school!" they shout. "Yay, it's summer!"

They're so unsuspecting, I almost feel bad.

Almost.

Just as Gus gets within a few feet of me, I whip my arm from behind my back and press the spray button, sending blue foam shooting out.

Summer's next, only she gets the pink can. I aim and fire.

"Ahhhh!" they scream, trying to block the foam. All around, the rest of the kids are doing the same. Parents yell, "Gotcha!" Laughter echoes off the houses and thick maple tree trunks. By the time the carnage is complete, the bus is long gone, the ten kids—and the ground—are covered in Silly String, and my cheeks officially hurt from smiling so hard.

"Ew," Merritt says, peeling pink foam from her hair. She'd been saving a good outfit for the last day of school. Even through her disgust, I can see the grin underneath. She may not want to admit it, but she still loves being a kid. She'll be first in line to get a popsicle from Kevin's dad.

I'm holding onto these summer months as long as I can, not only to savor Merritt's youth, but also because I took a part-time job at the college starting fall semester. There will be a lot of changes in a few months, both bitter and sweet.

We all stand there on the street corner coming down from the high of the parents' onslaught. Two boys conjure a football out of nowhere and start tossing it back and forth, wasting no time getting in the summer break spirit. Lolly's twins chase each other across a neighbor's yard with empty cans of spray.

I look to Summer, who is squishing a handful of foam, her hands now a soapy, pink mess. The wonder on her face is unmatched. There's a sticker on her shirt that reads, "First grade, here I come!"

I'm so grateful she was able to attend the second half of her kindergarten year. With a little catch-up this summer, she'll be right on track with her peers. And thanks to an incredible support team, she's functioning like any other little girl.

Lolly wanders over to me. "Margaritas on the porch? Let the kids burn off some steam?"

I link my arm through hers as we all turn to walk up the street to our respective homes. "That sounds amazing, but..." I take a deep breath. "We have plans."

Gus falls into step with me. "We're still going, right, Mom?" he says excitedly.

I tousle his hair. "Yes, we're still going."

It's been ten months and twelve days since I last stepped foot in Wonderie Land. To be honest, I never thought we'd come back here. The idea was preposterous. Wonderie Land was a bad place. A forbidden place. A place we never wanted to think of and yet couldn't forget.

To our surprise, it was Summer who brought up the idea of returning.

A few weeks before the park opened for the new season, we saw a commercial during an evening show one night before bed. It had been promoting a new ride, one where people sat around a wheel and spun it to make the buggy go round. Another spinny ride. My belly hurt just watching the screen.

"Ooh!" Summer said. "I want to go on that one!"

Wade and I stole a quick glance at each other. Didn't she remember what happened last year? Didn't she know that Wonderie Land was the place where she was taken from us?

Even Gus and Merritt seemed to pick up on the awkwardness of the question. Their faces crooked with unease. But not Summer. She watched the commercial in amazement, then asked again, "Can we go soon?"

I can't remember exactly what we said—my brain was spinning faster than the ride on the TV—but somehow, we deflected. *Sure, maybe.* It wasn't until days later, when Summer's request still nagged at me, that I brought it up to Calista in an individual therapy session.

"Why not?" Calista said.

I balked. "Well... because!" *Is she serious?*

"Greta, Shelby isn't going to be there."

"I know that."

Shelby Marrow is currently serving a ten-year sentence, reduced from the twenty years she would have faced without the mental health component. We weren't in the courtroom during sentencing, but Georgia told us Shelby left in handcuffs without a word. The conviction was generally received as fair by the public. Me? I don't know. I suspect her eventual release will bring a certain level of anxiety back into my life. Then again, Summer will be fifteen when that happens, no longer the little girl in the yellow tank top.

I fiddled with the hem of my shorts. "But Shelby Marrow isn't the only predator out there."

"True," Calista said.

"I mean, how could we take her back there?"

"But Summer is the one who proposed it, right?"

"She clearly doesn't remember."

"Maybe that's a sign."

"A sign for what?"

Calista leaned forward. "That she's ready to move on. Are you?"

I was unable to respond. Yes, of course we were moving on. Slowly but surely, things were falling into place, familiar routines were being reestablished. I knew what Calista was getting at, and it made me squirm in my seat.

Don't say it, don't say it.

"I think you should consider it," she said. "Talk to Wade. See what he thinks. Wonderie Land doesn't have to be a scary place if you don't let it."

It took me a while to gain the courage, and I only did because the idea wouldn't leave me alone. I was tired of living in fear. We all were. A week later, the commercial aired again, and I knew it was my sign to speak to Wade.

"What do you think?" I said as we brushed our teeth at the double sinks in our bathroom.

He hesitated. "I don't know."

"I know what you mean. It feels... wrong. Like the last place we'd ever want to go. Can you imagine seeing that blue table?" A chill snaked down my back. I wiped my face with a makeup remover pad. "But I've been thinking. Why should we—the kids —have to miss out on fun just because of what happened? It was Shelby Marrow's fault, not Wonderie Land's. Summer keeps asking to go."

Wade mulled it over. "If you're okay with it."

"I don't know if I'll ever be okay with it. But I think we should try."

Try. My new mantra.

From there, it had been decided. The last day of school. A special treat for the kids.

I didn't sleep for three nights beforehand.

The parking lot is packed. I guess we weren't the only ones with the idea for a celebratory trip to the amusement park. Wade drives up and down the lanes looking for a spot. We pass the exact place where we parked last time. I'll never forget, just like I'll never forget a million small details from That Horrible Day.

"Finally," Wade says, finding a spot and pulling in. The kids chomp at the bit to get out. They've made an official plan of attack, which rides to do first and in exactly which order.

"Now, remember," I say for at least the sixth time.

"Stay with you," they sing in chorus.

"Right." I exhale. "Okay, let's go."

We cover the parking lot toward the entrance, the kids a few steps ahead. Summer holds Merritt's hand. Just as we're about to cross under the towering gate that holds the Wonderie Land sign, Merritt looks over her shoulder at me. Her big brown eyes search my face. It's a look that says, *Are we okay, Mom? Is this okay?*

I smile and give her an encouraging nod. Everything is okay.

My heart has left my chest and floats forward to meet its three counterparts. *We're going to make it*, I think. I squeeze Wade's hand and he squeezes back. His pulse beats against my wrist.

The sights and sounds of Wonderie Land hit us, and it's enough to take my breath away. I look around. In every direction are smiles and laughter, kids skipping, parents snapping photos. This is not an evil place. It's a family place. A spot we've loved for years.

All at once, a sense of certainty comes over me. Maybe it's bravery, maybe it's determination. Maybe it's my husband's hand in mine. Whatever it is, it tells me that today we're reclaiming Wonderie Land as a site of joy.

Ahead, Summer calls back to us. "Mom, are you coming?"

I walk with purpose. "I'm coming."

A LETTER FROM JEN

Dear Reader,

Thank you so much for reading *The Day She Vanished*. I hope you enjoyed it! If so, and if you want to keep up to date with all my latest releases, just sign up at the following link. Your email address will never be shared, and you can unsubscribe at any time.

www.bookouture.com/jen-craven

I would also be very grateful if you could leave a brief review of your thoughts—reviews are so helpful for increasing a book's visibility and also make a difference in helping new readers discover one of my books. Hearing from readers makes my job all the more enjoyable—you can get in touch with me on Instagram, Facebook, or through my website. Again, thank you for your support. You had endless book choices, and I'm very appreciative you chose to read mine.

Jen Craven

www.jencraven.com

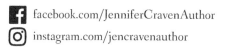

facebook.com/JenniferCravenAuthor

instagram.com/jencravenauthor

BOOK CLUB DISCUSSION QUESTIONS

The Day She Vanished, among Jen Craven's other novels, lends itself well to book clubs, as it's rife with meaty discussion points, juicy plot twists, and plenty of room for insightful conversation. If you're interested in selecting Jen's books for your book club, please reach out at www.jencraven.com. Jen regularly meets with book club groups and would love to join yours!

Here are some discussion questions to consider.

1. Greta faces harsh criticism both online and from her local community. Do you think this treatment is justified?
2. Greta and Wade grieve differently and at different paces. Did you relate more to one character than the other?
3. How does the psychic's involvement in the story affect Greta's hopes and actions? Do you believe in the possibility of such influences in real-life cases?
4. Greta and Merritt's relationship has its ups and downs. Do you feel Greta was too harsh on her

daughter? Could you relate to her inner turmoil and guilt?

5. How does the novel portray the strain on Greta and Wade's marriage? Discuss the turning points that highlight their conflicts and attempts at reconciliation.

6. Which character did you feel the most sympathy for, and why? Were there any characters whose actions you found difficult to understand or justify?

7. Discuss Greta's relentless pursuit of finding Summer. Do you think her persistence was portrayed realistically? How would you have reacted in her situation?

ACKNOWLEDGMENTS

I have a confession: The idea for this book came from a moment in my real life. My husband, three children, and I were at our local amusement park, and after spending hours in kiddie land, I suggested to my husband that the two of us ride the big roller-coaster once before leaving. The kids waited at a table, only our oldest did not have a phone like Merritt, but a smartwatch in case of emergency. Like Greta, I trusted my children would be safe—they were responsible, and we would be right back. Unlike Greta, all three of my kids were waiting when we returned a few minutes later. We went about our day. And yet, the thought later struck me that things could have played out very differently. What would I have done if my somewhat impulsive decision resulted in a life-changing tragedy? It was this idea that stayed with me and grew into a story in my mind.

My thanks go out to the editorial team at Bookouture, particularly my editor, Billi-Dee Jones, for seeing the vision of this book and allowing me to stay true to the story. Thank you to the fabulous copy editors and proofreaders for catching all those pesky typos and making a beautiful finished product.

Thank you to my loyal, trusted author friends, Caitlin Moss and Kerry Chaput, who read early versions of this book and provided invaluable feedback. To my beloved Eleventh Chapter members, your endless support in all aspects of the writing life makes the experience that much better. They say you're only as good as the people you surround yourself with, and I can honestly say you all inspire me daily.

Thank you to Cynthia Hess, who spoke to me about her work as an intuitive guide, and gave me insight into the psychic world.

To Gram, who reads my books in single sittings and then patiently waits for the next one, thank you for being my reading buddy and my biggest fan.

I am so lucky to have such supportive family and friends who enthusiastically champion my books. My local community, including booksellers, has been behind me from the beginning. I'm so thankful for all the love.

Finally, thank you to DJ, Josephine, Elizabeth, and Michael, who make all of this worth it. I wouldn't be able to do what I do without your support, understanding, and encouragement, and for that I am eternally grateful.

PUBLISHING TEAM

Turning a manuscript into a book requires the efforts of many people. The publishing team at Bookouture would like to acknowledge everyone who contributed to this publication.

Audio
Alba Proko
Sinead O'Connor
Melissa Tran

Commercial
Lauren Morrissette
Hannah Richmond
Imogen Allport

Cover design
Emma Graves

Data and analysis
Mark Alder
Mohamed Bussuri

Editorial
Billi-Dee Jones
Ria Clare

Copyeditor
DeAndra Lupu

Proofreader
Deborah Blake

Marketing
Alex Crow
Melanie Price
Occy Carr
Cíara Rosney
Martyna Młynarska

Operations and distribution
Marina Valles
Stephanie Straub

Production
Hannah Snetsinger
Mandy Kullar
Jen Shannon
Ria Clare

Publicity
Kim Nash
Noelle Holten
Jess Readett
Sarah Hardy

Rights and contracts
Peta Nightingale
Richard King
Saidah Graham

Made in United States
Orlando, FL
19 October 2024

52865344R00178